C.A.R.L.

CIA AGENT IN REAL LIFE

C.A.R.L.

CIA AGENT IN REAL LIFE

W. RONALD ROLLE

atmosphere press

To my wife, Robin, who gently pushed me to publish
my written work.

In the tapestry of life, you are the vibrant thread that weaves
joy, warmth, and endless love into every moment. This book
stands as a tribute to the beautiful journey we've shared, where
your unwavering support and boundless affection have been
the guiding stars helping to illuminate my path. I'm looking
forward to seeing your written works published too.

PROLOGUE

Carl thought back to just before this mission began. He stood in his superior's rather spacious, oak-paneled office. Henry Mason sat behind an expansive oak desk that was unusually immaculate. Hank's gray suit jacket was flanked neatly over the back of his chair. He wore a white long-sleeved shirt with the sleeves rolled up to his elbows. The red power tie that he wore was loose at the knot, revealing that the top button of the shirt had been unbuttoned. Hank sat calmly with his hands clasped on the desk in front of him. Carl could see activity on the three computer monitors behind his supervisor, still displaying activity from the operation that Hank had been monitoring before Carl entered the office.

Carl had that 'yeah, right, you've got to be kidding me' look on his face that Hank knew all too well. The fact of the matter was that because he was so good—and he knew it, Carl could demand what he wanted and get it almost every time. To Hank Mason's great relief, this was a privilege that Carl never, ever abused. Carl would pick and choose his battles. He did not fight about everything, and he was far from being considered a rebel. Today, Carl's main beef was that they wanted to send him on assignment with someone else.

That was not his modus operandi.

Carl always went on assignments alone—except for when he was training another agent.

In his estimation, Carl thought that it was easier and cleaner to work alone. He did not have to be responsible for another person's life, nor did that person have to be responsible for him. Most important—all decisions were his. No other input was desired or required. As far as a group assignment was concerned—for Carl, that was just not an option.

Carl sat facing Hank in a large leather chair that was equally as plush as Hank's. The rest of the office was furnished with a large conference table, which was surrounded by six chairs. There was a modern looking, sleek, black, triangular-shaped conference speaker phone in the center. It looked like a starfish that was missing a couple of appendages. There were ports at each seat that gave whoever was sitting at the table the ability to plug a laptop into the inter-office network. The walls were sparsely decorated with artwork that was not well known but looked impressive.

Carl and Hank were in the middle of a conversation, and Hank was now speaking.

"Carl, look, after all these years, don't you think I know your preference? The fact of the matter is you need a partner on this one to work it from the right angle."

"Since when does somebody else decide the angle from which I am going to be working my assignments? I thought I had the latitude to plan my own ops. Have I not been doing well enough on my own? Or is it my 100% success rate that is subpar?" Carl asked sarcastically. "It seems to work for me," he added.

"Carl, listen—" Hank began, but was quickly interrupted.

"No, Hank, you listen. Not only is this one off the charts because of my preferred work style, but a female agent? So closely after the death of my wife? Give me a break!" Carl said in a very respectful, yet recognizably disgusted voice.

"Carl, that was five months ago. It's time for you to drop that and come back to us."

"I'll be the judge of that—thank you very much. Look, Hank, I know that Marianna is one of the best, but for goodness' sake, Hank, did it occur to anybody that I'm not ready for that type of situation just yet? Ding Dong! I don't think that anyone else actually thought that one through. Perhaps we can get them all in one room so that I can look them all in the eye at the same time when I point out the same thing and say: 'Here's your sign,'" Carl said as he made reference to one of his favorite comedy skits about the antics of stupid people who would fair so much better if they just carried a sign to alert people of their low mental prowess.

"That would not be my first, best suggestion, Carl," Hank said in a very resigned tone.

"Yeah, but since when did that ever stop me? I know... good point. And I know this is all moot," Carl resolved, "because the decision has already been made, but that doesn't mean you don't get to know how I feel. And, because you know me so well, Buddy, and you also happen to be the boss, YOU get it with both barrels."

Without waiting for an answer or giving Hank a chance to respond, Carl stormed off to get ready for his mission and make the best of what he considered to be a very bad thing.

This was not a good start.

Carl often said, "When life hands you lemons, make lemonade." The aftertaste of this batch already seemed to be remarkably tart.

Carl replayed the entire meeting over again in his mind in a split moment as he stood there on the streets of Helsinki. It was a nice evening. The hustle and bustle reminded him of the busy streets of New York City. Many people were eating the street food that was on offer from the multitude of vendors. The food of Helsinki was just as beautiful as the location itself. The weather could not have been better. Carl and Marianna had just walked out of The Bistro with their arms interlocked as if they were lovers. Just then Marianna said, "Sorry, love, I'll be right back. I left my purse inside. That will never do."

Carl watched Marianna's long blonde hair wave back and forth as she sauntered away in her form-fitting red dress.

The two had gotten a lot closer than Carl had ever intended. This was one of his initial fears and it had now come to fruition. It had been quite a while since Carl had developed these types of feelings. He knew that he would eventually develop these types of feelings for someone else, but he did not want it to happen yet, and he did not want it to be another agent for sure. Getting into another relationship too soon could make things exceedingly difficult. Carl was not sure if he was ready to deal with anything that difficult right now.

"Oh, for goodness' sake, Mare," Carl said playfully, using a nickname he had derived for her while on this mission, "you women and your accessories." He had grown entirely too fond of her. "You go get the car; I'll go back for the blasted purse. Where did you leave it?"

"The name is Slovanya, my love," Marianna said, reminding Carl to use her under cover name (although she knew the reminder was not necessary). "It's tucked away right in the corner of the booth we were sitting in. The car is just across the street. Why don't we both just go back and..."

She trailed off when she saw that look in his eyes. If she knew nothing else, she knew that look by now. Normally, she would not have cared, but Marianna was growing very fond of Carl as well, and she did not want to disappoint him.

"On second thought, why don't you go get the purse and I'll go and get the car?" Marianna finished, as if she had been the one to come up with the idea herself.

"Sounds like a plan," Carl said.

Carl stepped back inside the little Bistro and turned toward the booth that they had just come out of. The difference between the street to the romantic atmosphere of the Bistro was like the difference between night and day. The booth that they had shared was already assigned to the next set of patrons.

Carl very politely explained his predicament to the couple in fluent Finnish.

The male patron responded back in Finnish, "Mietimme, kuinka kauan kesti ennen kuin kukaan tuli etsimään laukkua. Itse asiassa vetoamme siihen."

It took Carl a second to process and translate. If he was correct, the man told him that they were wondering how long it was going to be before anyone came looking for the purse. In fact, they had bet on it.

"Well, what do you know," Carl replied in Finnish as he took the purse. "So, who won the bet, and what was the wager?"

Glancing at his companion across the table, the man said, "Panos on henkilökohtainen. Voittaja on lopulta me molemmat."

Again, it took Carl a minute to process. He had just learned the language before the mission. But he understood that the man replied that the wager was personal. The winner would ultimately be both of them.

"Hyvä vastaus," said his companion.

That one was easy for Carl to translate right away: "Good answer."

The two dinner companions smiled at each other, and it was now as if Carl was no longer there. With a smile on her face, the female patron reached across the table and took her companion's hand in hers.

Smiling himself, with purse in tow as he thought about the love birds, Carl turned around to walk away. As he completed his 180-degree turn, a loud and very powerful explosion rocked the restaurant, knocking Carl and everyone else who was standing to the floor. A large corresponding flash was seen outside. Carl was immediately worried when he realized that the explosion came from the direction of the vehicle that Marianna was supposed to be retrieving. He rose to his feet as quickly as he could. It took him a moment to steady himself. Like many of the people around him, he was now disheveled and had glass and debris in his clothes and hair. Carl steadied himself and absent-mindedly pulled his handkerchief out of his pocket to dab at the blood that was slowly dripping from several small cuts on his face. It took several seconds before he was able to focus properly again. To his great dismay, he could see his vehicle in a ball of flames. There would not have been any survivors. The immediate thought running through his mind was that he was supposed to be in that car too.

Knowing that he could not go anywhere near the vehicle without jeopardizing his cover, Carl quickly made his way back to the hotel where he and Marianna had been staying; assuming that whoever it was that was trying to kill them both thought they succeeded, they would not be expecting them back at the hotel. However, he was obviously going to need to relocate to a safer place.

Carl knew, at this point, that he could not be too careful. From this point forward, everything was an uncertainty. Carl gathered what few things he and Marianna had and made the 82.5-mile trek from Helsinki to Kotka; a journey that should have taken just under two hours. However, Carl was now in survival mode and had to follow additional protocols established for the safety of the operatives when a mission had been compromised. Because of how meticulous Carl had to be in covering his tracks, the trip took him almost six hours. While en route, Carl used the emergency satellite radio, reported his situation and requested an emergency evacuation. Once at the airstrip in Kotka, he would turn on the emergency transponder. Carl knew that he could not depart from a regular airport at this point and risk a customs incident, so the only way out of the country now was to be airlifted from some obscure landing strip where nobody was expecting him to be. Like a good operative, he always had his exit strategy well planned.

Upon reaching Kotka, Carl made his way to Kymi Airfield. This was not a very busy location. The air traffic control tower was a makeshift building of very poor quality that also doubled as a plane hangar. It was definitely a low budget operation. The lighting on the runway and the glow of office light from inside the tower and plane structure were the only discernible lighting. It made for a very gloomy atmosphere.

Carl found a nice perch near the end of the runway and put his things down. He then made a surveillance run to make sure there was no one else around. Once he was satisfied that he was alone outside, Carl went back to his perch and turned on the transponder. With the transponder broadcasting, Carl knew it would not be long before his signal was detected by "unfriendlies," and he would become vulnerable.

Carl's perch at Kymi Airfield was just to the left of the single airstrip that was used for both outgoing and incoming planes. There was not generally a lot of traffic at this airstrip, so takeoffs and landings did not conflict with each other. He was set in a grove of mixed spruce and pine trees that had low hanging branches, offering plenty of convenient cover. He carefully checked overhead for threats before permanently settling in. He did not want his escape attempt to be short-lived.

With no indication of any problems, Carl settled in.

The emergency transponder was a simple yet very useful device. This portable transponder was a five-inch by five-inch black square box. In the center was a two-inch-high by three-inch-wide display screen. Several function buttons were under the screen. A red power button was located at the top left corner. The antenna was integrated within the unit and did not have to be separately attached or raised. Carl powered on the device and double checked that the transponder had been correctly set. He then set his portable bearcat scanner to monitor all other frequencies—now that he was broadcasting. Then, like any good agent, Carl fell back into a retrospective review of what got him here and what he might possibly have missed that he should have seen. There had to be something, but Carl was drawing a blank. Of course, the dynamics changed a great deal when he could not account for all the actions of the other person in question. 'The other person,' Carl thought. He and Marianna had grown very close in a very short time. She was more than just 'the other person.'

Carl would have to reflect on that later. First things first. The first order of business was to get safely rescued.

A short while later, Carl was brought into awareness when he heard the approach of rotating chopper blades, and he knew that his ride was close. Seemingly from out of nowhere, the Super Cobra Gunship came into view. One second, he heard the blades, and the next second, the gunship was in plain view.

That kind of flying took some skill.

This pilot was good.

It looked like they sent one of the best to get Carl out of hot water. The signal light on the front of the impressive-looking helicopter flashed the pickup code. Carl could see the ominous missiles on either side of the signal light, and he was glad this guy was on his side at the moment. The pilot repeated the pickup code. Carl replied with the corresponding counter code, and the pilot changed his approach posture from tentative to committed. As the chopper touched down, Carl emerged from his perch. Jumping down the short distance to the ground, he grabbed his single bag and made a dash for the dimly lit opening.

He had just 200 more yards to go.

Just as Carl was confident that he would make it without incident, he heard someone yell, "Hit the deck!"

There was no time for questioning or second thoughts. Instinctively, Carl hit the deck hard, putting his clothing duffle in front of him, as he was trained, to cushion his fall and then roll to the left; hoping the odds were with him today. They were taught that most gunners were right-handed and would aim their shot in that direction. It seemed that even the majority of the left-handed shooters veered right.

The odds were with him today.

Even so, Carl felt the spray of bullets go by him, narrowly missing his head as the gunner attempted to adjust to the target. Then he felt a searing hot, burning pain in both of his lower legs.

"He's hit, he's hit!" Carl heard someone yell. "He can't get up." Carl looked up and saw what he wanted to describe as a gung-ho, heroic Marine jump out of the gunship and run his way, firing ahead of himself for cover. The chopper became airborne in an effort to position itself between its men on the ground and the shooters. Before the gunship could get in position, the Marine who had jumped out to rescue him went down just ten yards from Carl's position. As the Marine went down, his gun was projected in front of him and slid to within Carl's reach. Carl grabbed the gun in case he had to use it. With the chopper in position now, that was unlikely, but a little insurance never hurt.

Inside the gunship, as the pilot acknowledged reception of the correct signal, he broadcast over the in-flight intercom, "That's our package. We're going in. But this looks way too easy fellas; keep your eyes open. Somebody turn on some of that sophisticated equipment back there and get me a scan."

"On it, Major," said Operations Specialist Lt. Roger Grimsby.

"OK, I'm gonna try to put this whirly bird down. Just in case we do have visitors, I'll keep my distance."

"Major Lennen, we have movement."

"Quantify movement, Lt. You mean our package, or do you mean hostile?"

"I'm going to have to classify them as hostile, Sir,"

"Good gravy, you're just a tad late with the info there, son. Our package is on the move, and there is no way I'm going to be able to get between him and the hostiles in time. But, as sure as my mother's name is Mabel, I'm going to give it my best shot. Man the rockets and automatic machine guns. I'll input the coordinates for the exact strikes when I have them. Don't worry, mine will override anything you've entered."

"Roger that, Sir," Major Lennen heard the men reply.

"With all due respect, Sir," Lennen heard one of his mission specialists reply, "we don't have time for that. Our package won't be worth delivering."

With that, Sergeant Major Alex Vance jumped out of the gunship and said to his colleagues, "Carry-on! If I don't make it, then I'll see you some day on the other side. Tell my wife I love her!"

"Why does he always say that?" Grimsby asked.

"Nothing wrong with expressing his love for his wife," Lennen replied.

"Very true, sir. But Vance isn't married."

"Oh, well, I guess he's trying to get in practice."

Everybody knew that there was no stopping Vance once he'd made up his mind. He was just one naturally heroic son of a gun.

Before his feet hit the ground, Vance yelled, "Hit the deck!" As soon as he saw Carl go down, he could see gunfire already coming from the direction Carl had come from. Vance aimed and fired a covering spray of bullets. He was not sure if he could get to Carl in time, but given the importance of this mission, at least from what they had been briefed on, he was more than willing to die trying. After all, it was not just a job; it was an adventure.

Vance kept up his cover fire as he advanced toward the package. After all, this WAS an emergency rescue mission. The Sgt. Major could see the gunship moving into cover position, but he was picking up fire from overhead now.

'With all of that sophisticated equipment onboard, why hadn't they taken these guys out already?' Vance wondered.

Just as quickly as he had these thoughts, a round of gunfire erupted that took Sgt. Major Vance down. His rifle went sliding across the tarmac and almost directly into Carl's hands.

Carl sensed, even as he grabbed the weapon, that he would be putting it to good use.

Smart move.

Carl thought about the pilot trying to place the gunship between the enemy and the men on the ground and did not envy him his task. He did, however, pray that he accomplished it. But this was not Carl's first rodeo. He had been in this type of situation before. There were men hidden above who were wearing some type of clothing that made them undetectable to the gunship's highly sophisticated radar equipment. The U.S. had yet to figure out what the makeup of this material was. Carl had a mind to change that today. 'Safety first,' he thought.

It was times like these that Carl was glad that he was such a math whiz, although he would always tell everyone that math was not his strong suit. Based on the previous gun fire, Carl made the calculations for the likely trajectory of the bullets that hit his legs and performed the same calculation for the likely trajectory of the gun fire that took down his unsung hero. He then quickly triangulated using an assumed third point for reference. Then he waited... Carl knew that the shooters would not fire again until they could score big, and by that, he knew that they would wait until there were more targets on the ground that did not have sufficient cover.

Carl tried to reach for the downed Marine's radio, but it was beyond his grasp. When the gunship lit, he saw the men jump out of the near side, and he yelled, "COVER!" Instinctively, the well-trained Marines flanked back against the gunship. Just as Carl had surmised, bullets began to fire at the rescuing soldiers. Carl took aim and fired a wide spray. The gunner on the gunship could see where Carl was aiming and saw two men fall. He then turned his fire to the same location and counted at least six additional men that had fallen. He switched to flamethrower mode and doused the trees with a blanket of fire. Screams could be heard coming from the trees as they became ablaze with fire.

Such was the price of war.

The gunner yelled to his men on the ground, "GO! GO! GO! GO!"

The Marines flanked out to pick up their charges.

They first concentrated on Carl, but Carl resisted. He said, "No! Him first. I'm good."

"Sorry, Sir, as much as I'd like to, I have to follow orders."

Looking at the Marine's rank, Carl said, "Corporal, I far outrank you since I am a Lt. Col. I just changed your orders. We also need one man to get one or more of those fallen enemy soldiers or just his clothes. I recommend just getting the guy— dead or alive. We don't have time to undress them."

"Sir, yes Sir!" yelled the Marine.

They went over to the Sgt. Major. He was face down and very still.

"Oh, my goodness, Sir! I think Vance is dead. I think we should get you under cover first," Corporal Lennox yelled back to Carl.

Before Carl could answer, Vance turned his head slightly, and in the most threatening voice he could muster, which wasn't very much at the time, he said, "Corporal, if you dis- obey a direct order, I'll shoot you myself."

"Huh! What? You're alive? Sir! He's alive. The Sgt. Major is alive."

"Lennox, quit your yapping and get the job done. If we wanted all of Finland to know what we were up to, we would have mailed invitations. Let's get this show on the road before the other side's reinforcements arrive."

The Marines got the two men loaded up on to the gunship and carefully secured them for transport. They were quickly followed by three Marines who went to recover fallen enemies per Carl's suggestion.

"Rakvere Base, this is Major Lennen in Gunship-41."

"Roger GS41, we copy."

"We have a downed Marine, and our package has been

tampered with as well. I'm airborne and am en route. ETA 30 minutes. By the way, we expanded the mission a little by order of Lt. Col. question mark. We have a nice little surprise for the research and development guys as well."

"Roger GS41, copy that. Lt. Col. question mark? I don't even think I want to know. We're noticing some escalating activity in your air space. We have air support on the way coming at you from both directions."

"Roger that. We copy you loud and clear. Just tell me you have a medic on one of those birds."

"Your package rates pretty high. You've got the best of the best coming your way."

"I'm not sure if that makes me feel better or worse. Gunship-41 out."

Just then an alarm sounded, and Major Lennen checked his HUD. There were two incoming aircraft, and one had just fired on the gunship.

"Sir, we have incoming. Multiple missiles. It's an air-to-air missile configuration that I've never seen before. What are your orders?"

"Taking evasive action," said Major Lennen. "Rakvere base, we have incoming. Two aircraft. One has fired on us. We're tracking multiple missiles converging on our position. Taking evasive action now. Do we have permission to fire?"

"Negative 41. Air support will be there in two minutes."

"In two minutes we won't be here anymore."

"Hold your course 41."

Hearing all of this, Carl said, "Somebody tap me into the cockpit before we all die out here."

Carl was handed a headset… "Pilot, listen to me carefully. Arm two air-to-air missiles and set them to proximity detonation."

"I'm not authorized to fire, Sir. I'll have to contact the base again."

"Yeah, right. If we're still here. Authorization Echo, Echo,

November, Tango, Delta, Bravo, 49," said Carl.

"Sir, I don't know who you are, but as sure as my mother's name is Mabel, you've got the authorization code alright."

Quickly reviewing personnel records in his head, Carl said, "Major, the last time I checked, your mother's name IS Mabel, but we can discuss that later."

"Missiles Armed and ready to fire, Sir."

"Good, now when the incoming missile is two clicks away, drop the chaff and make a 180-degree sweeping arc turn to the right."

"But left is a better option, Sir. That's just standard textbook. We learned that in flight school."

"Flight school isn't going to save your tail today. I am! To the RIGHT, Major."

"Roger that. Heaven help us. Dropping chaff in three- two- one, breaking right, turning 180 degrees."

BOOOOOOM! The explosion rocked the gunship, but the integrity of the craft was not affected. The chaff seemed to ignite the incoming missile when it turned right to follow the aircraft.

"Wow! That worked!"

"It's all about knowing your enemy, Major. Target the first bogey and Fire one."

Lennen nodded at his gunner, who fired the first air-to-air missile. "One away, Sir."

"Target the second bogey. Steady… steady… steady… fire two!" Carl ordered.

Again, Lennen nodded and again the gunner fired.

BOOOOOOM! they heard off in the distance. "Splash one." BOOOOOOM! "Splash two."

"Gunship-41, this is Gunship-27. We just registered that you fired two missiles without prior authorization. Good shooting, Buddy, but you're in trouble for sure. We'll be there in one minute."

Before the Major could respond, another call came in. "Gunship-41, this is Medic-12; we're on your six. Do you need medical help?"

"How's our mystery guest doing back there?" Major Lennen yelled to his crew.

"Not good, Sir, he just passed out," came the reply from Mission Specialist Reed.

"Medic-12, we need medical assistance ASAP, but there is nowhere to land this thing. We're over the water."

"That landing thing is way overrated; we're pulling up beside you. Put your whirly into auto-sync mode and let the computers match our speeds."

"I always wondered what that setting was useful for. Guess I'm about to find out."

The Choppers pulled up, side by side, and were in perfect formation. Just then a platform extended from the medical chopper and into Gunship-41. Supplies were passed from one chopper to the other, and then two medics slowly made their way across.

"Retract platform," said Navy Commander Paul Wilson. "Now, where's my patient?"

Commander Wilson was shown to where the patient lay unconscious.

"CARL!" exclaimed Commander Wilson. "Oh, my goodness."

This was not the first mission he was called in on to patch Carl up.

"You know this man?" Mission Specialist Reed inquired. "Who is he? Where is he from?"

"Trust me when I say this, gentlemen, because I'm not being funny in the least. As far as your questions are concerned... I could tell you, but then I REALLY would have to kill you."

CHAPTER 1

Carl walked hastily down the long, well-lit corridor. It was ablaze with activity. Many people were heading in the same direction as he was, having been invited to the same mass meeting.

Carl is tall, standing at six feet, four inches and well-built with a light brown complexion. His musculature could be seen bulging through his white and immaculate dress shirt. Carl's physical stature allows him to blend seamlessly into various environments, making him an expert in undercover operations. His imposing presence gives him an advantage in intimidating situations, but he also possesses the agility and dexterity necessary for stealthy maneuvers. That is part of what makes him one of the best of the best.

Carl takes great pride in his appearance and maintains a clean-shaven face, adding to his polished and professional demeanor. His close-cut hair serves both functionality and practicality, as it allows him to avoid any complications or distractions during high-pressure missions. Carl's greatest strength lies in his exceptional espionage abilities. He possesses an analytical mind, sharp instincts, and an ability to think quickly on his feet, enabling him to adapt swiftly to unpredictable circumstances. Carl's intelligence, combined with his proficiency in combat and advanced training, makes him a formidable force in the world of intelligence gathering.

As much as he would like to be, Carl is not invincible. He harbors a complex personality, burdened by the weight of his responsibilities and the sacrifices he has made for his country. Carl's character is shaped by his unwavering loyalty, dedication, and the moral compass that guides his actions. He operates with integrity and always strives to do what is right, even when faced with difficult choices. Most of all, Carl's number one priority is to always complete the Primary Objective of the mission.

Carl could see Paul Wilson coming in his direction. Paul still had the same awkward walk that he was well known for. He was slightly shorter than Carl and not as imposing to gaze upon, but he was a stellar spy; and a great medic when needed. It had been a long time since the two had seen each other.

"Hey Paul! Long time no see!" said Carl as he greeted his friend and fellow agent.

"Carl, old buddy. What has it been? Two years?" Paul asked.

"Three actually," Carl replied.

"No way!" Paul said as he feigned disbelief.

"Way," said Carl mockingly.

"Well, I see you haven't changed much. Walking a little better since the last time I saw you. Looks like you healed nicely—again!"

"Yes, I'm walking a lot better, partly thanks to your immediate medical assistance. I'm sure that I can still beat you in a mile run whenever you're up to it."

"I bet you can," said Paul. Then, lowering his voice, he said, "I hear you went back over and, shall we say, took care of business."

"You hear right. Hopefully that's all you hear because everything else should be classified above your level. Well, at least for the next few minutes anyway."

"Well, as of today— Wha— you already heard? How did you know?" Paul asked with a look of genuine surprise on his face.

"Seriously? Come on Paul, we're spies. That's what we do," Carl said very matter-of-factly. "Did you seriously just ask me that?"

"True that."

"True that? Now you're starting to sound like me," Carl said.

"Tru— never mind. Anyway. You never cease to amaze me with your knowledge, my friend. Whatever or whoever your source is, it is a reliable one."

"If you only knew," Carl said. "I like to think that reliable sources are the only kind that I have. So, I guess, at this point, it would be kind of silly to ask if you are going to the meeting?" Carl asked in a rhetorical tone, but he was really seeking an answer.

"Very perceptive, my fine fellow spy," said Paul. "And, by the way, congrats on the nuptials. Jenny, is it? How come you always find the good ones?"

"Well, I think it has something to do with not looking too hard and letting God reel them in. One thing is certain, He ALWAYS catches the big fish," Carl said with a smile. "Anyway... I know how much you like to skip out on these meetings. Were it not for the news, I would be shocked to see you here; seeing that they're usually boring and all."

"Yeah, but this time I was not invited so much as I was ordered to be here. Attendance is mandatory, and no exceptions are allowed. The only way out of going to the meeting was to be on assignment, hospitalized, dead, or any combination of the aforementioned. You pretty much skip out on these meetings too. What are you doing here?"

"Well, Buddy, if you haven't figured it out already, I was pretty much told the same thing," said Carl.

"Well, why aren't we on assignment then?" both men asked in unison. They both tilted their heads to the side in a very bemused fashion at the coincidence of their simultaneous comment.

They enjoyed a laugh at having the exact same thought. Both would have rather been on assignment— any assignment—

than to have to sit through a meeting— any meeting.

"Well, this must be some pretty heavy-duty stuff then. You remember the last time we had one of these?" Carl asked as his gaze went off into the distance.

"Do I remember? DO I REMEMBER? How could I forget!" Paul exclaimed. "And how could I forget my good buddy, General Spotlight?" Paul asked with a sly grin. "It was the time that we had that near-fatal attempt on the President's life."

"Yeah, and had we not gotten involved, it would not have just been near fatal; it would have been fatal. The 'Prez' would have been toast!" Carl replied in a 'pat yourself on the back' tone of voice.

"It's kind of hard to forget the nearly two months you spent in the spotlight with all of those interviews you had on just about every news and talk show in the nation. Not to mention the fact that they didn't even realize that you weren't revealing your true identity until you let that one slip out in the last interview."

"Yeah, that was a little bit of a goof up on my part," Carl admitted. "Now, come on. You have to recognize the fact that old 'General Spotlight,' as you called me, tried very hard to not be in the spotlight at all."

"Yeah, I guess that's true," Paul conceded. "Every chance you got; you did try to point out that it was a team effort. It wasn't your fault that you wound up with the major role, and the rest of us wound up playing the best supporting actors. And, yes, I do remember you also giving God all the honor and the glory, despite the spin that the 'talking heads' tried to put on the whole thing. You're a good man, Carl. It's a shame the way things go in this 'business' of ours," Paul said as he formed air quotes. "Even after all of these years that we've known each other, there is still very little I know about Carl, the person. I know it is probably best that way. I'm sure, being in your position you know everything there is to know about me."

"And then some," Carl added.

"Yeah, and then some. Must be nice."

"No, not really," Carl said in a very less than satisfied tone.

"Well, I'm just saying... we call ourselves good friends, yet it's safest and best for us to know as little about the other as possible. What a gig," Paul concluded.

"And when all is said and done, at the end of the day you really love your job don't you?"

"True that."

"Yeah, true that," Carl agreed. Changing the subject now, he said, "You appear to be moving up the ladder pretty quickly here, my friend. The higher you go, the more your 'need to know' increases. Pretty soon you'll be responsible for knowing so much that you are going to wish that you hadn't gotten there. I speak from experience."

Again, they both laughed, but they both also knew how true those words rang out.

"Well, we better get into that meeting," Paul said as they stopped in front of the doors that led to the extremely large auditorium, "or we're both going to be ex-agents instead of agents. I sure would like to know what's going on this time—well, other than the news that we already know about. Even the Jr. agents have to be there. It's got to be significant."

"Even I don't know what the other news is yet, but I have a funny feeling that significant is an understatement. Whatever it is, I'm sure that I have some little piddly part to play. I'd just like to get it done and over with. Let's go check it out."

With that, both men entered the large doors and made their way through the auditorium, walking in silence the rest of the way. The expansive room, which seated 2,500, was almost full. There was no one behind the podium yet. Carl and Paul did not have to look for seats; they had been preassigned. You could hear the hushed tones of spies talking to spies. The overhead fluorescent lighting made for easy viewing. Both Carl and Paul were evaluating and re-evaluating all that they already knew about the meeting and trying to figure it all out before they were given more information. This time their efforts were in vain. This was something big, but in a totally different way than either of them was expecting.

The "underwater" meeting room, as it had affectionately become known, was jam packed with agents from all CIA divisions. It was referred to as the underwater meeting room because it could only be accessed with the correct security pass card and by pressing any button that was below the Concourse or C level. So, being below C level (sea level), the agents were quick to assign the meeting place this unique name... and it stuck.

Executive Agent First Class Manny Balboa was now standing at the podium. He saw agents Paul Wilson and Carl Reardon. He immediately extended a greeting to the two 'least likely to attend a meeting' agents:

"Ahh, Paul, Carl, glad you could make it!" came the voice from the podium. "My grid indicates that everyone is present and accounted for now," Manny said. Once again motioning to Carl and Paul, he continued, "You gentlemen want to come down here and take your assigned seats in the front row, please. Just so I won't be lonely, huh? Let's begin. Just so that we start on a more lighthearted foot, I guess I'll begin with a bit of levity."

The agents tried desperately to sigh under their breath, but when you have that many people in the same room making the same sound, it becomes quite audible.

Manny ignored the sighs.

Balboa gave the thumbs up to the sound technician to turn the volume up a little. Now, speaking directly into the microphone he said, "Perhaps you wondered why I called this meeting?"

Executive Agent First Class Manny Balboa was not often known for making jokes, but when he did crack one, especially one that was as unexpected as this one, people laughed. And laugh they did. But the laughter quickly subsided because everyone knew that they were also there for business, and they wanted to know exactly what that business was.

"OK, enough levity for the moment, I guess. Onto our first order of business. Many of you know our good friend sitting down here in the front. One of our best field agents... of course we don't have any bad ones... but anyway, please join me in congratulating Special Covert Agent Second Class Paul Wilson on his promotion to Special Covert Agent First Class. As such, Paul will still be doing fieldwork, but he will be doing a lot more training and be responsible for a lot more day-to-day tasks to help keep you guys running proficiently. And if he is anything like his friend Carl here, don't expect him to be in his new office for too long before he's back out in the field doing what we all love to do.

A round of applause filled the room. There was really no reason for Paul to have to go to the microphone. He was not being presented with any formal award, just recognition. The agency was very serious about the chain of command, and when there were changes, they wanted those reflected imme-diately, so they were good at letting others know where they were in the 'pecking order.'

When the applause died down, Paul was being prompted to say a few words: "Speech! Speech! Speech! Speech!" came the constant chant from the crowd of agents.

"OK! OK," said Paul, "but just a few words. As most of you know, public speaking is not my forte."

"Oh, come on Paul, even you have a few things to say," said Manny Balboa.

"No, not really, but..." Paul began to say.

Quickly interrupting, Carl said, "You know, Manny, that's OK. Perhaps we should just let this one slide."

Carl knew Paul better than Manny did and sensed what was about to come.

"Nawww, I want to hear what he has to say," Manny replied.

Carl shook his head and said, "OK, but just remember, you asked for it."

"Nice try Buddy, thanks. E for effort. I owe you a lunch,"

Paul said as he shuffled past Carl.

"This ought to be really good," Manny said as Paul approached; he felt he had the upper hand now. Paul would never live this one down, and Manny was making sure that the cameras were rolling so that he could have it on tape for posterity.

Paul stood in front of the microphone, staring silently out at the rest of the crowd. They all thought that he just needed a minute to gather his thoughts. Carl knew that Paul did not really appreciate being put on the spot and that he was thinking of the best way that he could subtly get back at their boss, Manny. Finally, he began.

Looking into the camera, Paul mouthed the words, "Hi, Mom," as he waved. Then he said, "You know, without my mom pushing me when I was just a little whipper snapper, I wouldn't be here today." Then, as he summoned fake tears, he said, "Mom, wherever you are, I just want to say thanks. Dad, you did a phenomenal job too. Teaching me how to take control of the remote. How to say, 'Woman! Where's my supper?' And a bunch of other things that I just can't repeat in front of this crowd." The crowd began to chuckle. They could see where Paul was going with this now. Manny, on the other hand, was becoming less and less satisfied with the situation. Paul continued, "And I would also like to thank the Academy—"

That was about all of the mocking that Manny could take. Regaining control of the microphone, and not at all happy at how this all turned out, Manny said, "Thank you, Paul. After that I'm sorry I don't have an Oscar for you. You've certainly earned it. Why don't you just find your way back to your seat? Now for our second item of official business. You have been called together here so that you can all be informed at one time that our operation is going to be moving. This is no ordinary move, mind you. Not only will we be moving this operation, but we will also be consolidating several other units that we work with into one building. Get your phony updated resumes out there because we will be disguising ourselves as a reputable publishing company. Your better halves, for those of you that applies to, need to think that you've gotten a new job. We'll take care of all of the acceptance letters to make this look as authentic as necessary. You have some time to prepare. The new building will not be ready for a year. Every division of agents that we work with will be represented, in some respect, at the new location. There will no longer be a wait for decisions that hinder us from getting our jobs done. Everything will be streamlined because everyone will be located in one place. We will be moving in six phases to make things easier. I realize that everyone has gotten comfortable and used to our current location, but that just means it's time for change. Are there any questions?"

Carl's hand, of course, was high in the air. Balboa ignored it momentarily, hoping that someone—anyone—would raise their hand so he could continue to overlook it. But to Manny's great dismay, no other hands went up, and he reluctantly recognized Carl. Manny really wanted to keep this all business and dreaded what might come out of Carl's mouth. But, when it's coming from your top agent, there are certain things that you just learn to tolerate.

"Carl?" Manny said with mock surprise, recognizing the hand now. His heart stopped in preparation for what was sure to be some type of attempted comic relief.

"You mentioned that we were moving, but you neglected to give us a location. Was that intentional?"

"No, Carl, that was not intentional. There is no reason to keep that information from you. You guys are savvy enough that, with a little bit of investigative work, which you are all very good at or you wouldn't be here, you would be able to figure out the location. May as well just go ahead and tell it to you. We will be moving to Emerald Valley. You could call it a suburb of the general metropolitan area here. Good question, Carl. Not quite what I would have expected from you," Manny said. His heart began a regular heartbeat again.

Carl's hand shot up again. Still, no one else had any questions, so Manny tried his luck again...

"Carl, again?" Manny said with exasperation.

"Yeah, Manny. Another question. Operations appear to be fine, and the buildings appear to be in excellent shape. That having been said, why in the world are we moving?"

"Well, Carl, another good question. And I have an answer for you. The 'bean counters' downtown were trying to strike up another deal with the local municipality to defer our taxes again, for the shadow company, of course. The last one worked out well for us, and we decided to try it again. Well, according to said 'bean counters,' the city would have none of it this time. They have absolutely no idea what we actually do, but we generate enough false income (keep up the good work guys) that they wanted the taxes EVERY year. No more deferrals. Our people talked with their people, and they bumped heads at several meetings for a while. When it became apparent that they were not going to budge, we threatened to pack our trash, so to speak. It was just a bluff, of course. We didn't really have anywhere else to go. Well, the bluff didn't work. They stood their ground and said good riddance, thinking that we would have to do a 180 and accept their terms. That was THEIR bluff. It didn't work either. We were scrambling for a minute to come up with another location. It just so happened that there was an available building in Emerald Valley that we were going to have to renovate. The contractors we talked to said the job could be done in a year, so the bidding war was on. There will still be some work being done around us, but the sensitive, high security areas have priority, and they will be complete."

Manny took many other questions from other agents now that Carl got the ball rolling. Finally, he said, "Any other questions? If not, this initial briefing is over. We will be updating you on the progress via secure e-mail. If there are any further questions, you can address them to me, and I will get the answers from the oversight committee if I don't already have them. Thank you all for coming today."

The atmosphere, as expected, was mixed as the agents left the meeting and headed above C level back to their work areas. There was the fair share of people that did not care one way or the other, the folks who were totally against the whole idea but had absolutely no good reason to be, the folks who were complaining because it meant a worse commute and the folks who either had a better or equal commute with the impending change. Even though they were fed facts, there was still a good bit of gossip already beginning to be generated about the whole thing, but all of that was expected.

Carl and Paul went to their work areas and logged into the secure network to see if anything had happened that might change their current assignments; if not, it was going to be an easy day for both, just making plans. With all these impending changes, there was something still nagging at Carl, but he could not quite put his finger on exactly what it was. Just his instinct on overdrive, perhaps? Carl's instinct was not usually wrong. He got up from his seat and headed to Manny's sixth-floor office suite, where the top spy executives lived in style.

CHAPTER 2

Carl exited the elevator on the sixth floor. He just stood there for a moment and took in the view. He rarely came up to the top floor. He felt that if he did, he would yearn to be there. Carl really liked the wood paneling, the plush leather board-room seats with secured laptops at each place, and all the other amenities. Manny's secretary looked up as she saw Carl approaching and smiled softly. When she saw the serious look on Carl's face, her smile melted.

Eileen Posey is an esteemed older secretary. She has worked for the CIA for many years and understands intelligence. With her striking presence and impeccable professionalism, she commands respect and admiration from her colleagues. Eileen's years of experience in her role have made her an invaluable asset to the agency. Manny would not know what to do without her.

Eileen is an African American woman with a regal demeanor that exudes confidence and poise. Her warm smile and friendly disposition make her approachable, but she can switch gears instantly into an aura of seriousness when the situation demands it. She carries herself with an air of elegance, always dressed in sophisticated and tailored attire, reflecting her commitment to maintaining a high standard of appearance and professionalism.

As Manny Balboa's right hand, Eileen's responsibilities are

diverse and critical. She flawlessly manages schedules, coordinates meetings, and ensures that important documents and information are handled with utmost confidentiality and efficiency. Her organizational skills are unmatched, and she has a remarkable ability to keep things running smoothly, even in the most high-pressure situations.

Eileen's attention to detail is legendary, and her memory is like a steel trap. She can recall names, dates, and important facts with ease, impressing everyone around her. She is often the go-to person for historical context and past case files, a walking repository of CIA knowledge.

What a lot of people do not know is that Eileen is also a highly trained agent, and one of her most important responsibilities is also to keep her boss safe. Yes, not only is she proficient at hand-to-hand combat, but she also carries a gun. If you're not supposed to get in, Eileen will make sure that you don't.

Carl was well known and not a threat. Rarely did he even need an appointment. Manny was usually glad to see Carl, but every so often there were days like today when it looked like there might be a standoff of sorts. Her first instinct was to warn the boss. Eileen buzzed immediately, using the emergency code to notify Manny of impending trouble.

Manny burst from this office, not sure what the emergency was that Eileen had invoked the secured sequence for, but he was ready! His gun was drawn and ready to fire at anything that even thought about moving. When all he saw was Carl, he apologized and holstered his weapon.

"Eileen, exactly what was the big emergency?" Manny asked as he glanced from her to Carl and back again.

Eileen did not give a verbal answer. She just kept pointing with her head, not her hand. Her lips were pursed, and her eyebrows raised in Carl's direction.

'Surely she could be less noticeable and more discreet than that.' Carl thought, 'but perhaps not.'

"Carl, it's you. Come on in," said Manny. "Eileen, hold my calls, please."

Eileen was aghast. She could not believe her eyes. Was her boss feeling OK? This is not the way that he had indicated in the past that Carl was to be treated when he showed up with those serious looks on his face. Had she missed something?

Carl sidled past the secretary, raising and lowering his eyebrows quickly twice as he went by, and went into Manny's office. Manny gestured toward a seat for Carl as he shut the door.

Moving behind his desk and sitting in his executive chair, Manny said, "Carl, I appreciate the tenor of your questions today. You kept everything on a business level, and I greatly appreciate that. Given your past, it was certainly unexpected. To what do I owe the pleasure of this visit?" Without waiting for an answer, he offered, "Can I get you a soft drink? Water?"

"No thanks. I'll just go ahead and jump right to the point," said Carl. "Beating around the bush never helped matters any. That was awfully quick for an all-hands mandatory meeting, wouldn't you say?"

"Quick? I'm not sure what you mean. I informed everyone with all of the information that I had, plus some additional information which was provided courtesy of your great questions."

"Yes, yes. By the way, you, of all people, should know that it is no use lying to someone whose career is trying to discern the truth. But all of that aside—"

"Carl, are you calling me a liar?"

"Are you saying that you're not? To be clear, though, Manny, I haven't called you anything. But would you care to swear on a stack of bibles that you are telling me the truth, the whole truth, and nothing but the truth, so help you—Capital G—God?"

Being a Christian and one of the world's top spies was a hard combination to manage. There was always deception involved in getting the job done. Carl knew that, just like himself, Manny was both of these things. Backed into a corner by another Christian, it was going to be hard to lie.

"Listen Manny, I don't work for the ten o'clock news, and I'm not here to find out the information so that I can go and tell others. I'm here to satisfy myself, and whatever you tell me, as usual, does not leave this room. That's usually company policy anyway. Now, my instinct tells me that there is something that you're holding back. I've been noodling this for the past couple of minutes before I came up here, and I think I have an idea of where the gap is. Here's an idea. Let's play a game. Let me ask a few questions, and the only information you have to divulge is that which pertains to my questions. This visit is my one shot at getting more information, and when I walk out of that door, for whatever other reasons I come back to this office, I may not, of my own accord, come in here to discuss this topic again unless bidden. Fair?"

"OK, Carl, I'll play your game. Shoot."

"OK," said Carl, satisfied with the progress that he had made thus far. "Here goes nothing. There's something about the new building that you are not telling us. Yeah, we're going to be consolidated, and all of our folks are going to be in the same building. But there is something else that has been bothering me..."

Manny sat back in his chair with a smug look on his face, because he was certain that Carl would not hit on the one thing that he did not want to divulge, and that was the other occupants of the building. Sure, he would find out, particularly because of how closely he worked with some of them, but Manny didn't want to have to give that information away just yet.

"...Are we— the CIA— going to be the only tenants in the building?" Carl asked.

"Oh, well, of course not. We'll be getting our standard retail rents and revenues to help with the bottom line of the front business that everybody else thinks we are there for," answered Manny.

"Right, right. The standard retail rents. What about the other floors? Standard retail usually has to do with those stores on the first-floor level and on the Concourse level, assuming there will be one. Will the CIA be the only tenants on the upper floors?"

Manny shifted in his seat uncomfortably as Carl started asking the very line of questions that he was sure would not even be approached. Manny was trying to calculate how to evade the question, but soon realized he would not be able to evade it for long.

"Welllllllll," said Manny. "No. We won't be the only tenants on the upper floors. We decided to use a couple of the premium space floors for some of the other building tenants."

"I notice from your answer that you didn't mention rent, retail, or anything that might suggest obtaining some type of capital from these 'other' tenants. Generally, that would suggest that they have to be working with us. If they are working with us, then they are spies, but they, obviously, are not CIA. So, the trick now is to figure out who would be working with us and why. So..."

"Alright, alright," said Manny, throwing his hands up in mock defeat. "You are the top agent on the books right now, and I should have known better than to try and conceal something from you. But I actually thought that I could do it. Just label me stupid. I'll tell you about all of the stuff that I left out on two conditions."

"Name them!"

"One, first I place a call to the top brass down the hall and clear it with them. And two, you become part of the planning and oversight committee. I think they could use your help on this one, but were too proud to ask."

Carl had to think this over for a minute. This was not what he had bargained for.

While he was thinking, J. Jackson Brody entered the office from a concealed compartment. "I told Manny we'd get you this way," he said. "Manny, you owe me lunch."

"You mean this whole meeting, all the mandatory appearances, folks getting bent out of shape, was all so that you could get me to be on this planning committee?" Carl asked. "Jack, you've got to be kidding me."

"Well, Carl, we could have assigned you, but you would have found some way to dodge that. Had to make it worth your while. So, I took on the challenge. You see, kid, you think like me, act like me, work like me. I used to be the best of the best until I turned in my spy stuff for a big oak desk in an oak paneled office. I thought I could figure out a way to lure you in—and you bit."

"Unbelievable," said Carl. "OK, I'm in. So, what is it that I haven't been told yet?"

J. Jackson Brody was the CIA Department Head. Most people believed that Brody and his type of spying made the CIA what it is today. He was always the first to try the leading-edge stuff and make sure that things worked the way that the developers said they would. He solved case after case with an ease that nobody else seemed to have. In his heyday, he was considered to be the nation's top cop. As age began to catch up with him, he realized that running around the globe was probably not the best thing to be doing; and that his luck would run out sooner or later—probably sooner—so he took the top CIA job when the President offered it to him. He breezed through the Senate confirmation hearings. Nobody seemed to have a problem with him. His confirmation process contained an unprecedented two questions and lasted an unprecedented 12 minutes and 37 seconds.

Brody knew Carl well and had worked with Carl's dad (also Carl) on many occasions. He knew them both inside and out. Both father and son had come to know him as Jack. Nobody else would even dare to come close to calling him that.

J. Jackson Brody nodded to Manny, who hit a button on the wall. The office lights dimmed as a screen lit up across the room, and the presentation began...

As the presentation began, Carl could see the old building complex fill the screen. J. Jackson Brody began to narrate as the screens went by.

"Everything you wanted to know and then some, Carl," said Brody. "This is our current complex of buildings. Four in all. This, of course, shows only the above-ground operation. As you know, most of what we do is in the below-ground portion of the complex. We intend to change that. The secure logins and all are working, but we see no reason why we can't redesign the building a bit more securely and make the desired paradigm work."

Brody paused to examine Carl and make sure that he was getting through.

"Our goal is to take everyone from the four buildings in this complex, as well as others from around the globe, and pull them all into one huge complex where we can control it all. How are we going to do this and what are our plans, you might want to know? Well, I'll get to that. First, let me satisfy the curiosity that lured you in here. Who else is going to be in the building with us... Well, of all people, YOU should be familiar with the Eagle One unit. You know, the mysterious unit that people claim to exist and we flat out deny it. Well, Eagle One will have two floors in the new building. They will be occupying the fourth and fifth floors of the new building. Why the fourth and fifth floors instead of some other floors? I am sure that is the question that comes to mind now. Well, it's because—"

"Oh, my goodness!" interrupted Carl. "They're already there! It's because they are already there. That had to be what helped pick the site for the building. They're already there, and the people who they used to work among had no idea of what they were doing."

"You're good! I mean, you're really good, Carl! Nobody else would have picked up on that. So, before I reveal any more, how much farther can you take it?" asked Jack.

"Well, said Carl, I'll give it my best shot. Naturally, if we were going to purchase a new building, we would want the entire thing. We would not want to be stuck with any tenants in floor space that we could desperately use. Therefore, if these folks are going to be allowed to remain there, then there has to be a purpose, and a pretty good one at that. If I had to venture a guess, and this is a pretty elaborate setup if I'm right. The Eagle One unit is our assignment. Spies protecting spies. No, that can't be right. That's what Eagle One's assignment is..."

"Don't doubt yourself, Carl," said Jack. "That's exactly right. And our number one guy is going to be assigned to protect their number one guy. Think you're up to the task?"

"Do I think I'm up to the task?" asked Carl incredulously. "Surely you jest, Jack. If that's the assignment, I gladly accept the challenge. That's not going to be an easy one!" said Carl.

"No," Jack replied. "Indeed, it will not be. But let me continue with the plans. We're gutting the entire building except for Eagle One's secure infrastructure, and we're going to build ours around theirs. We'll have our people on the first, second, third, sixth, seventh, eighth, ninth, tenth and eleventh floors. Eleven, of course, will be the executive HQ. I need you, Carl, to work with the techs to develop the security systems. You know what we're going to need, and I want it in that building. I want people to start moving in there in a year, so this is all on the fast track. We have the go ahead from Congress. They've essentially written us a blank check. So, ask for whatever you need. Don't hold back because of the dollar signs.

"Once you have the security systems designed, here is how the cubicle layout will be," said Jack as he advanced the presentation. "Now what is nice about these babies is that they will all have the ability to convert into secure areas. The phones, the workspace, the whole works, on voice command."

"Niiiiiiice," said Carl. "Verrrrry nice!"

"And... Let me show you what the new below 'C' level is going to look like." Jack advanced the slides to reveal secure conference and meeting rooms and a maze of technology that spanned more than just the area where the building was. The entire concourse was an access point for those who knew how to get there, to this new technological wonder city.

"So, you see, said Jack, we really do need you on this project, but I'm afraid that means no cases for about a year." After seeing the response in Carl's face, Jack said, "Sorry Carl, but it's necessary. Are you still in or not?"

Carl had to think about it for a while this time, but he finally said, "I'm in. Let's get this thing done."

CHAPTER 3

Carl Reardon didn't like the fact that he would not be on active-duty assignment for the next year. How was his wife, Jenny, going to react to the fact that he was going to be home all of the time? He had a feeling that she liked her space. She just wouldn't know what she was going to do with him. Carl hated the fact that he had to keep so much from his wife, but he knew it was all for her own safety. He felt that deep down she seemed to know that there was something going on. Yet she was content to believe that her husband was a senior software developer and nothing more. He was sure that she had no idea that the actual company he worked for was a front, especially since they had newspaper ads, television commercials, and his electronic direct deposits to their bank account came with the company name.

What was even more curious was how much Carl actually got paid for being a developer. He explained to her that he was the best of the best, and he was in executive management for a very lucrative small business and working on very high-priced contracts. That is why he netted over $2,000,000 a year with his bonuses and all. According to his story, that was nothing compared to what the CEO made. Carl knew that the realism had to appear to deteriorate somewhere and possibly cause some disbelief. His saving grace was that as long as he was on the right side of the law with everything, Jenny had no reason to believe anything else or to seek additional confirmation.

Carl kept himself in shape. In his line of work, it was a necessity. He was always at the gym using this apparatus or that. Jenny didn't seem to mind, seeing how impressive it made her man look. Carl toyed around with the idea of wearing a full mustache and partial beard. He thought that the black facial hair, which would likely be speckled throughout with gray, would give him that salt-and-pepper seasoned look. Someday, perhaps, but for now he knew that his wife liked him just the way he was. Jenny always summed up the way her husband looked in just two words: irresistibly handsome.

Carl sat in his office and pondered his new assignment to design the security for this new building. An idea struck him. He knew that so many people wondered about the mythical CIA building in Virginia that is supposedly all brick with no windows. This, Carl thought, was not a bad idea. That was definitely secure, but what of all of the studies that showed how sunlight helped people to work better; made the workers and the workplace a happier place to be, etc? Carl had an idea for a solution that he was now putting down on paper.

Carl began to design the refit of the old building so that it was, in fact, all brick on the outside, but on top of that, there were panels that gave the effect that the entire outside of the building was glass. Posted at the top and bottom of each of these panels would be sensors and cameras. The sensors and cameras allowed for the images of what was actually happening outside to be reflected to an adjoining panel that would be on the inside of the brick wall. Internal sensors would cause the view to shift as people came up to the Window and looked in different directions. It would essentially be a realistic representation of what was happening outside, being generated from an interactive holographic image. Carl sure hoped that Jack was not kidding when he was talking about that blank check from Congress! This was going to cost a few bills.

Next, Carl began to design the IT infrastructure along

with a high-grade encrypted VPN access protocol that he had been talking about with GEOCOM, the IT network solutions company. There would be three workstations at each agent's workspace that Carl had planned for. The first one, situated in the center, would be a workstation running the Portals Operating System. This would have the ability to tap into the other systems in emergency situations but would probably never be used for that. This center workstation would be used for all of the bogus work for the National Law and Regulations Company; the official name of the company that is the front for the whole operation. The terminals to the left and right would be secure Linux systems. Carl came to the conclusion that the type of security that he needed could not be trusted or dependent upon the Portals platform Operating system. Carl had already gotten a contractor to develop the secure graphical interface, and they would work closely with SecSpec, the security specialist team from Stamford, Connecticut. They came highly recommended to complete the necessary security integration for the secure interface. SecSpec already had a proven track record with other agencies, but they have not yet been asked to do anything as complex as what Carl was designing. The Linux system on the left tapped into state and federal systems and databases, and the system on the right gave secure access to international systems. Everything would be controlled by the central keyboard and mouse. It would look and feel as if there was only one system that was being accessed.

The phone systems would be funneled through the secure IT infrastructure as well, using a highly secure VOIP protocol. This would require another vendor that Carl had yet to locate. But everything else had been taken care of, and progress was being made.

All sorts of safeguards and security checkpoints were set in place to manage restricted access to all floors via computer-encoded security badges combined with biometrics. These also would control elevator access to the garage and below C level access. Every entrance would initially require that IDs be scanned to determine whether the system would grant access. The security stations and every business entrance would have scanners that would detect whether an individual was actually wearing their security badge. If they were, the system would assist the guards in automatically identifying who they were after also confirming against biological markers stored in the database. Four guards were to be posted on each floor: two teams of two at all times. One team would patrol the floor for two hours while the other team would monitor for two hours, and they would alternate throughout the day until the end of their eight-hour shifts. Changing of the guard would take place at 7:30 AM for the 8:00 AM shift, 3:30 PM for the 4:00 PM shift and 11:30 PM for the Midnight shift. This would give the guards up to half an hour to fill in the members of the oncoming shift on anything that required updates.

To make all of this work, it was essential that there were enough people working in the building who were only responsible for doing the work of the NLRC. They would have no inkling of the secure aspect of things, which is why each individual cubicle had to have its own security and be able to give the appearance of being wide open while it was, in effect, completely secure. They would have the ability to be sound-proofed from top to bottom. The shielding would use the same reflective technology as the Portals OS. This would allow images that were not accurate to be projected, ensuring privacy. It would be very much like a hologram with the ability to respond accurately to queries.

The 'normal' workers would be easy to identify with only one workstation running the ever so lovely Portals 58 software with service pack 212. The office would have an air of being legitimate and no one would be the wiser. All of the security could be justified under Carbanes-Oxford (COX) act passed by Congress just to rock everybody's world. They needed to do something to at least partially justify all that money that they would be earning.

With all the security details worked out, Carl put his proposal together and ran it by the rest of the oversight committee.

"Well, gentlemen, there you have it. I may have missed a thing or two and I welcome your comments and suggestions. Please don't be bashful," said Carl after his presentation was completed.

"Carl, you are definitely a welcome addition to this committee," said Sammy Johnston. "I call myself the spy of spies, but I would never have come up with half of this stuff on my own. Much less a way to implement it. Capital job."

Carl nodded humbly. He appreciated the pat on the back.

Anthony Randall, every agent's number-one critic, was just that. Everything was not coming up roses for him. He found a big problem with the whole thing.

"Carl, I hate to be the guy to rain on your parade—"

"Oh Tony," said Carl as he interrupted, "you're the guy who rains on everybody's parade, and we're all used to it. I have my umbrella up, so rain on man. What have you got?"

The proverbial gauntlet had been thrown. Carl welcomed any challenges to his plans. He was beyond thinking that his plan was perfect. If someone could offer some improvements, Carl gladly welcomed any suggestions.

"Well, I was just noticing in this enclosed monstrosity that you have designed, that we're going to be out of luck if there is a fire. It won't take more than a minute before we're all suffocated because we're so secure. But, hey, at least all our secrets will die with us, right? I guess that still means the country will be safe."

"You know Tony, to some degree you could be right about that. That could have been a very large oversight on my part," said Carl.

Tony was proud of himself, having caught what he considered to be this very vital problem. Even though everyone was supposed to be on the same team here, he was proud of himself at the thought of having upstaged the best of the best, and this time he wasn't really trying that hard.

Now Tony had this gloating look on his face and was smug as ever but didn't want to let that out in front of everyone, so he only said, "Well, hey, glad I could help. You know?"

His smug attitude was soon to be dashed.

"Perhaps, though, Tony, it would have been more helpful if you had thoroughly checked the environmental systems built into the building. They were developed to accommodate for just such a situation. We noticed that after my plan was initially reviewed. You will note... uhh, that's page 204, down in the middle of the page, Tony, that the environmental systems are structured such that if there is any indication of smoke, fire or carbon dioxide, a high-power exhaust and oxygen refresh system kicks in. In the event that any part of this system does not operate sufficiently, the built-in fail safe will blow designated panels, which will allow for smoke to travel to the outside of the building and oxygen to get in. I guess you missed that part."

That last comment Carl added facetiously because of the way that Tony had responded, which could have been avoided if he had just read the information provided more carefully.

A thoroughly embarrassed Tony Randall now sheepishly said, "Yeah, right, I was just about to read that. I was on page 203, you know."

"I like it!" said J. Jackson Brody with excitement. "I like it a lot! Very well thought out, Carl. I will, of course, have some fine-tuning adjustments that I would like for you to consider. Hopefully, the suggested changes will work seamlessly with the way that you already have things laid out. If not, then we can do the initial implementation as is, and my tweaks can wait to be later enhancements."

"We're going to do it right the first time, Jack. When can I meet with you to talk about your enhancements? We'll get them in there," said Carl.

"Good answer, Carl. Good answer," said Brody. "I'll be in touch."

"Well then," Carl began, "all we need is this group's approval and we can get everything underway."

"Well, gentlemen, if there are no additional comments, I say we vote on Carl's proposal and let the work begin," J. Jackson Brody offered up to the group. "All in favor, raise your right hand, and all opposed raise your left hand. By the way, if you don't know which is which, I suggest you don't even bother to vote."

As they panned around the conference room, there was only one left hand raised, and it was attached to the body of none other than Anthony Randall.

"Would you like to make any comment as to your objections, Agent Randall, or do you just WANT to disagree for the record?" asked Brody.

"Just for the record, I guess, Sir," said Randall sheepishly.

"Of course," said Jack, "of course. Well, that looks like a landslide majority, Carl. Take it away."

"I have already taken the liberty to schedule the work to begin the day after tomorrow," Carl informed the group, "I just needed the committee's approval before the work could actually begin. And by the way... Tony? When all is said and done, whether we agree with each other or not, we're still on the same side; and I've always got your back, just like I hope you have mine."

Tony, feeling appreciative that Carl had lessened his embarrassment somewhat, said, "Always, Carl... Always."

With that, the meeting was adjourned. As the men were leaving, one of the secretaries came up and handed Agent Randall a message.

"For you, Sir. I was asked to get it to you as soon as possible, but I dared not interrupt the meeting," the secretary said.

"No problem. Thank you—" Randall said, stopping and giving the secretary a pleading look because he did not know her name.

"Renee, Sir," she said, filling in her name for him.

"Thank you, Renee Sir," Tony said, making the secretary blush. "You can call me Agent Randall, Mr. Randall or just about anything else, but please, don't call me Sir and don't call me late for dinner either."

"I'll try to remember that S—Agent Randall... should the occasion ever arise."

As Renee walked away, Tony glanced at the message. Carl thought he may have seen Tony blanche and quickly regain his composure. "Hey, Tony, everything OK?"

"Umm yeah, yeah Carl, everything is uhh fine."

"Alright then. I'll catch up with you later," Carl replied.

Even though Tony said that everything was OK, something about that whole exchange just did not sit right with Carl. However, Carl did not pursue it. Carl knew that Tony must have his reasons, and the information that he chose not to reveal could very well have been classified. Carl knew that drill well, and he knew when to drop it.

CHAPTER 4

Agent Anthony Randall walked hastily down the carpeted hall that led to his office. Upon arriving, he slid his encoded security card through the scanner that was located on the door. The familiar and irritating beep associated with a negative identification sounded. The indicator turned a very unwelcoming red. Randall was unsure what the problem was. He scanned the card again with the same result. For some reason the door was not opening. He had done this a thousand times before without any issues.

'Now, of all times,' he wondered, 'why did it have to malfunction?'

The message that had been delivered had Tony off balance. Randall realized that he needed to slow down, collect his thoughts, and figure out what he was doing. He stopped and then breathed in and out slowly with his eyes closed. Once again, he scanned his badge.

Same result.

One brief second of examination and Randall could see what he was doing wrong. Talk about a rookie mistake. Common sense would tell you that if you don't scan the card with the magnetic strip facing the reader, that it is not going to be very useful in gaining access to anything. He hoped that when they got into the new facilities, they would have the kind of cards that worked no matter what side you scanned them on. For now, he was going to just have to make do.

Agent Randall turned his card around and scanned it using the correct side. He saw the familiar light flash from red to yellow to green. Then he heard the welcoming beep and the tell-tale click of the lock mechanism opening to allow him to finally gain entrance to his office. Just before stepping into his office, Tony thought he saw something out of the corner of his eye. He glanced down the hall and, not seeing anything, dismissed it. Normally he would have taken the time to investigate, but right now, time was a commodity he did not have. Tony glanced at the note that he held in his hand as he shut the door behind him, leaving him standing in the dark. Instinctively, he turned on the light switch, illuminating the entire office. He looked at the finely creased note in his hand and read it again:

> *Your last mission was quite a success! More than we'd like*
> *to admit.*
>
> *You took something of ours and we want it back.*
> *We will be waiting for you by your car in the parking garage.*
> *Be there at precisely 3:15 or people start dying.*
> *LPDR*

'What people were going to start dying?' Tony wondered. Not that it really made a difference at this point. Randall thought back to his recent mission. He was part of an all-out effort to cripple the remaining five communist nations in the world. The list included China, Cuba, North Korea, Vietnam, and the country that Randall had just returned from on his previous assignment, The Lao People's Democratic Republic—better known to the free world as Laos.

It is every agent's hope that they enter into and exit every mission cleanly. Obviously, this was not the case for Randall's last mission. The one thing that an agent did not ever want to compromise was his identity. Somebody out there knew who Tony was, and he had to figure out who was leaking information because, as he thought back over his steps, there was no way that he had messed up. He was, however, just 24 hours away from delivering his "package." Agent Randall had a thumb drive that contained a dump of the Laos spy network personnel. With this information, the U.S., or anyone else that they chose to share it with, would be able to track all of the current Laos operatives, thus crippling their ability to gather any new intelligence, or to even move outside of their own country. It was very understandable why the Laos government might want this information back before it got into anyone else's hands.

Tony quickly inserted the thumb drive into his secure server and dumped the contents. His redundancy settings automatically copied the information to three other backup locations. After verifying that the copied data was secure, he then wiped the contents of the thumb drive clean and slipped it into his pocket. He locked up and headed down to the parking garage.

The parking garage was deserted at this level during this time of the day. Nobody was here but Tony and the cars, it seemed. Tony did not expect to be alone for long. He checked his watch. The time was 3:11. He had four minutes. Not much time to spare. Tony contemplated alerting HQ, but then thought that this was something that he had gotten into himself, and he would have to handle it himself.

An elevator arrived at the parking garage level; the soft bell sounded to announce its presence. Tony looked very intently in that direction, but he did not see anyone step out. Tensions were high, and he was now being overly cautious. Moving into the shadows, he navigated his way through the parking garage. Behind him, Tony thought he heard a door open. He slowly and carefully drew his weapon and then quickly spun around, only to be greeted by absolutely no one at all.

As Tony moved deeper into the garage and toward his car,

he felt a searing pain as he was hit on the head by something quite hard, knocking him unconscious, but only for a few brief seconds while his body seemed to do a system reset. When he came to, someone was speaking to him in a very perfect Tai Dam accent. Randall recognized the language from his recent assignment. He could understand what was being said without the need for a translator but did not want to expend the effort to formulate an answer in the foreign tongue when having to respond.

"Shuntai Kumar, I should have known. Must we speak in your language? After all, you are in the U.S. now. English please?" Agent Randall asked.

Kumar switched from Tai Dam to English in a heartbeat. "Agent Randall, you have something of ours?" Kumar asked.

"I'm not sure I know what you're talking about. Exactly how did you find me?" Randall asked.

"Well, some questions we would choose to not answer, but as your life is short now, anyway, ask away. I've always wanted to say this: I can tell you, but then I'd have to kill you. Well, now I have. We'll tell you whatever you want to know. Oh, and don't worry. We've taken care of the garage surveillance. Your people are viewing a false feed at the moment. Our secrets are safe."

Tony Randall glanced around. He was on his home turf, so his surroundings were quite familiar. Randall was trying to gauge the opposition. The dull throbbing pain in the back of his head was making that task difficult. There was Kumar, who Tony knew that he could handle without a problem if he had to. But then there were his two accomplices: both big, bulky, solid and ominous looking. Handling them as well; that would be another matter altogether; but it was not totally out of the question. Tony did not show his frustration, but he thought that even though his life may be forfeited, he had already taken steps to get this information into the hands of somebody who could do something about it.

"OK, I guess you got me there," Tony said. "Since you are

so willing to give up the information now, as I asked, how did you find me? I'm pretty sure that I did not slip up?" Tony ended with confidence.

"You slip up?" Kumar said with genuine wonder. "I wish. No, I wish our agents were as clean as you were. If we did not have a mole in your organization, we would have been out of luck. You didn't think that we could infiltrate you, did you? To think, he's one of your top agents," Kumar concluded smugly.

Tony's first thought, because of their rivalry, was Carl.

"Ahh, I can see that you have somebody in mind. Who might that be?" Kumar asked rhetorically. He knew he would not be getting any information.

Tony thought quickly before answering. As normal, his training instinctively kicked in. "Nice trick," Tony replied. "You have absolutely no idea who our top agents are, do you? But you were hoping that I might just be stupid enough to give you that information."

"Nothing ventured, nothing gained," the Laotian Kumar offered up.

"Or, in this case," Randall retorted, "something ventured, nothing gained."

"Very funny. But our man, David Hoover, can get us that information as well, as soon as he reaches the right security level. We'll just bide our time. In the meantime, we need to take back the advantage that you have, unfortunately, gained over us. Now, the thumb drive please."

"Right jacket pocket," Tony said.

Tony's captor nodded to one of his big and burly assistants. "Check it out."

Randall's captors yanked him to his feet. Tony kept glancing around, trying to find that "perfect" opportunity.

Noticing Tony's actions, Kumar added, "By the way, don't try anything foolish now, Agent Randall, or we'll kill you where you stand; a lot sooner than we are expecting."

"Hmm," said Tony. "Seems like you're going to kill me

anyway. Why not take a few of you out with me?"

While the other man trained his gun on Randall and held him at bay, the thug who was initially nodded to reached into Tony's pocket and pulled out the thumb drive. Anticipating Tony's next move, he managed to say, in a very thick accent and in very broken English, "Zat vood not be, how you say, smaht, huh?" Handing the drive to his superior, the Laotian henchman said, "I sink deece iz whut we come for, Sir." Then glancing back at Tony, he said, "How you Americans say? Go ahead, make my day. Heh, Heh, Heh."

Kumar took the thumb drive and inserted it into his net-book minicomputer, which he already had on and standing by. "Access code please, Agent Randall," Kumar demanded.

"78390112zzvw3450713," Tony rattled off quickly. "I had to make it something simple that I'd remember."

"I'm sure," said the Laotian agent. "Thank you. This is way too easy. I would have expected at least a little resistance out of the legendary Anthony Randall— WHAAAAAAAT? Where is the information?" Kumar screamed questioningly. "There is NOTHING here! Tell me what you did with that information this very instant or you're dead."

"Well," said Tony. "I see your threat, and I call. I guess I'm dead."

"Kill him now!" Kumar ordered in a rage.

Both of the Laotian bodyguards took aim.

Randall stood stock still pending his execution and said, "See you on the other side—NOT! Because I'm sure that where I'm going, you definitely won't be there. In fact, compared to where I will be—we call it heaven—you're going to be quite warm; but you've made your choice."

"Enough of this. DO IT!" Kumar hissed angrily.

BANG! BANG! BANG!

Three shots rang out in rapid succession. Randall flinched with each shot but was still standing after the third shot had been fired. Looking around him, Anthony Randall could see

Shuntai Kumar and his two henchmen dead on the ground. Each with a bullet exactly in the middle of their foreheads.

Looking up, Agent Randall saw Carl Reardon holstering his weapon as though it was just an everyday occurrence.

"I think that shot on Kumar is just a little to the left," Carl said. "I wish I had a second try."

"Carl! How did you know?" Randall exclaimed.

"Come on Tony, I'm a spy. I just did that spy thing. You know," Carl said, "when you got that note, something seemed a little fishy."

"Yeah, but the way I treated you, why not just let them put me out of your misery and then take them out?"

"Oh, come on Randall, for all that you do, you're still a pretty good spy. Don't you dare tell anyone I said this, or I'll just deny it. You're also not such a bad guy. And besides, like I told you less than an hour ago, when all is said and done, at the end of the day we're STILL on the same side. That being said, I just want you to know... I've got your back."

Now that the action was over, several agents came running into the parking garage area. The head of security, Jimmy Miranda, said, "We just realized that somebody had interrupted our feed. As soon as we remedied the situation, we saw the gunshots on the feed. Everybody OK down here? Hey Reardon, that was some pretty good shooting."

"Thanks, Jimmy," Carl said. "Just getting some live target practice in. Besides, somebody had to hold down the fort until you guys got your act together," Carl said with a smile. "Just glad to be of service."

"Live target practice?" Miranda scoffed. "How heartless can you be? Have you killed so many that it just doesn't matter? Bad though they may be, they're still people."

"Normally, Jimmy, I would agree with you, but when you bear in mind that one of our own is in the line of fire and the threat of a loss of life is imminent, the training kicks in, and they cease to be people. They are targets that must either be disabled or taken out at all costs. Whether that captive is my friend, my antagonist or my CIA head of security," Carl continued, making his point personal now, "my actions would be the same. That's just how I roll, and it seems to have served me well."

Carl had always thought that Jimmy Miranda had one of the oddest job titles around, but he did perform a necessary function. It just seemed really strange that the CIA would need a Head of Security. It was a thought that made Carl chuckle every time it crossed his mind.

"Roger that, Agent Reardon," Miranda said as Carl's point was driven home. "Roger that. I'm glad you're on my side."

From that day forward, Carl and Tony had forged a friendship that would last for the rest of their lives.

Carl oversaw the construction and remodeling of the new facilities daily. He had sometimes requested double and triple crews to be scheduled in order to get them back on track or ahead of schedule. He did not have many instances in which he had to point out gross corrections that had to be made, but there were a few of those. Everything was tested and retested to make sure that things worked separately as well as integrated. This was especially important with all of the state-of-the-art equipment being installed. This one facility, when finished, was projected to cost an estimated 11.7 billion dollars.

As passersby walked past the National Law and Regulations Company building construction site, they were taken aback by the sleek, polished beauty of the structure. Up to now there had been a drape around the building so that no one could see what was going on. The size of the structure, at one block long by one block wide, also struck many people. To top it all off, not many people even knew what the National Law and Regulations Company was.

When Manny Balboa caught wind of this, he hired an advertising agency to get the word out on the street about the company. The CIA did not want to draw too much attention to the company, but they had to have credibility. The people in the neighborhood and around the globe had to believe in who they were and what they did. The real purpose of the structure would not be effective if people did not believe the lie.

CHAPTER 5

The advertising agency of McCain Hendricks was chosen in order to increase the awareness of the NLRC to the public. Manny wanted to get the job done as quickly and effectively as possible. To ensure that the right message went out, the agreement was that no advertising was to be run on any media without the express approval of NLRC and its advisors. The CIA wanted to be very careful about what was said and exactly how it was said. This made the going a little rocky because McCain Hendricks took pride in what they did. They took pride in putting the customer's best foot forward without the need to seek customer approval. Their mission statement stated that they guarantee the desired effect if they could have free rein—with certain understood limitations, of course.

When all was said and done, they came up with a dynamite advertising and marketing campaign that was pleasing to all involved and gave the public the information they needed to know. The following information ran in various languages and versions of advertisements on the web through social media, on TV commercials and radio commercials, as well as through cell phone SMS advertising:

Who is NLRC? The NLRC is the National Law and Regulations Company.

What does NLRC do? A lot of people have asked that question and the best answer that we can give is that we don't even really know for sure what we do. Just kidding! We are an organization that takes federal, state, city, and territorial laws in their original form, and make them easier for you to understand, search and manipulate while putting in our own editorial and value-added content. Our motto: The information you need, analyzed the way you need it to be. Congress and states pass volumes of rules and regulations per annum, but they are not always easy to understand. That is where we come in. We make it so easy to understand that now even the legislatures know what they mean. Our product line is comprised of Tax, Environmental, Health and Safety, Business, Employment and Legal products. Catch us on the web at www.NLRC.com or call, toll free, 1-888-NLR4YOU.

Carl sat in Manny's office after the completion of the advertisement evaluation and just slumped lazily in the extra plush chair.

"Carl, you scare me," said Manny.

"I scare you?" Carl asked. "Why on earth would I be scaring you, Manny?"

"Because one day, you're going to be sitting in this seat, my friend."

"HA! You've got to be kidding me. I know that you guys serve a very important purpose, but I'm an agent at heart, Manny. No offense, but there's no way ol' Carl here is going to be turned into one of you stuffed shirts. I had a hard enough time not being in the field for a year while you had me on this planning thing. The 'big chair' is not for me."

"Yeah, and even the President says you did one bang-up job."

"THE PRESIDENT??? Oh, Man! Manny you've got to be kidding me. I don't want that kind of spotlight."

"Too late, my friend. The CIA Director gives credit where credit is due. He prides himself on having people working for him who can get the job done. Besides Carl, it's no news that you're the top agent the CIA has. That being the case, you're on the President's short list of agents to be recruited when he needs to have sensitive jobs done. You just don't always know that order came from the top."

"Short list? Short list of how many?" Carl asked very inquisitively.

"One," Manny replied.

"Yeah, that's just about what I was expecting you to say. And nobody turns down the President, right?"

"Come on, Carl, you don't turn down anybody. That's no biggie. If the 'big guy' wants to send you somewhere, you know you're going."

"Yeah, I know. So, what does he have in mind, Manny?"

"Nothing in the hopper that I know of Carl. I'm just saying," Manny answered.

"You call me your number one man and then you sit here and try to lie to me?" Carl asked, obviously perturbed. "That's OK, Manny. If you're not saying, I know it's because you haven't been given permission to. That, at least, I can respect, and I won't press it."

"OK, you'll know as much as possible as soon as I can tell you!" Manny divulged after being called on his abject deception.

"Yeah, somehow, I don't doubt it. On another topic, when is moving in day?"

"Well, all the covert equipment and other apparatus have been moved in at night to avoid prying eyes. The technicians are just completing the setup and testing phase. One week from today, when all of that is done, we will begin moving the Agents in who will act as NLRC folks while working on their cases— mostly in the secure half of the building. The other NLRC folks who will actually be running the company will move in the following week."

"Great, I think I'll drop in and see what below 'C' level looks like. Has all security been set up and transferred to the existing cards?"

"All done," said Manny. "Let me know what you think. I think you'll be extremely impressed with your little project."

With that, Carl got up and exited Manny's office, all the while thinking about his mysterious upcoming assignment and, deep down inside, not being able to wait to get out into the field again.

Carl made his way over to the new building. Just as Manny had predicted, below 'C' level was even more impressive than Carl had expected. He didn't know when they had time to do it, but they had improved on the design that he had laid out and given the final approval for. Jack was going to be happy with this, he knew; as would Manny.

All of the outer construction had been completed. The site no longer looked like a construction zone. The finishing touches had been put on, and all around the building block everything was immaculate. There were no longer any signs of construction crews or equipment, but people were not coming and going in droves yet, either. Today was moving day for the first phase.

Carl arrived, and he went over to the secure side of the building to his designated cubicle. There was no glaring indication from the outside, but Carl could tell from a quick glance at the controls that the cubicle was in its secure state. The untrained eye would not realize the specific pattern of the main monitor's panel lights that indicated the cubicle status. Carl tried his encoded card, and the security systems did not release the lock. He double checked the cubicle number to make sure that he had the right one, although, at his level, his card should have granted him access to any cubicle. "Well, I guess we have a few glitches to iron out. Glad I got here before everyone else did this morning," Carl said, speaking to himself... or so he thought.

"No glitches, Carl. That card will only work in one door right now. As soon as you scan it in that door, everything else will be opened up to you. We have them all programmed like that so that nobody goes to the wrong cubicle or... ahem... office on the first day."

Carl turned around to see J. Jackson Brody, the Director of the CIA, and his good friend, standing there. Looks like someone arrived even earlier than he did.

"Exactly what do you mean by 'ahem office?'" asked Carl.

"Well," Jack responded, "Carl, it's been a long time coming, but you've been promoted."

"Oh, NO!" Carl said as he became very animated. "Jack, I told Manny, and you already know, I am a field agent, and I will always be a field agent. I am not going to be turned into a pen pusher for a think tank and let all these young guys go out and do all the work and have all the fun."

"Now, you know that I knew you were going to say that, don't you?" Jack asked, almost confusing himself as the words came out.

"Yeah, but that won't stop you from pulling rank, as I recall."

"True, very true, but I did something special just for you. We created a new title for you: Deputy Executive Field Director. It's a fancy way to say Assistant Director. It has a nice ring to it, huh?" Jack asked. Not waiting for a reply, he continued, "It comes with a new compensation and insurance package too. I think you will really like the compensation part—twice what you were pulling in previously. Apparently, the President really liked the job you did on the building design—well, that along with your other work too."

"The President?? There you go, now, mentioning the President in reference to me. First it was Manny. Somebody want to tell me what's going on with me and the President?"

"How about I show you your new digs?" asked Jack.

"Oh, so you're sworn to secrecy too," Carl said as he picked up on the obvious avoidance of his question. "Great. Well, let's see the new cubicle."

Jack walked Carl around the corner and showed him the

satellite office that Jack had set up for himself for when he came down to the Emerald Valley building. Next to that was Manny's spacious corner office. A very nice spread for the Director. Manny sat in the office working away on something, just as he always did. He looked up and smiled. Next to Manny's office was another office. It appeared to be glassed in, but Carl knew that was just for effect. There was solid wall on the other side of the glass, although that is not what was projected.

Jack stopped here and said, "Scan your card, Carl."

"What, here?" asked Carl. "You've got to be kidding me."

"Since when do I kid, Carl?" asked Jack.

"Good point!" said Carl. He scanned his card, and the computer system came alive.

A very pleasant female voice emulation package had been added to communicate the computer's responses:

Reardon, Carl. Codename: also Carl, Rank Deputy Executive Field Director. Field Status: Active. Welcome to your new office space, Assistant Director.

"So. I'm a director now? Well, thank you," said Carl.

You are most welcome, was the computer's response. Then, after three soft tones sounded, the computer continued...

All access rights and programmed privileges have been added to your coded security card. Whenever you need my assistance, all you have to do is address me from anywhere in the secured parts of the building and I will do my best to be of service to you.

"Address you? How in the world am I supposed to address you?"

I am the **C**omputerized and **L**ogistical **A**gent **R**esponse **A**pparatus. Everyone around here calls me CLARA.

"Well, thank you CLARA. It has been a pleasure making your acquaintance." Carl finished.

The pleasure is all mine, I'm sure.

"Nice touch, huh?" asked Jack.

"Yes, very nice touch. That wasn't in my original plans."

"Well, I threw in a few of my nice to haves, not to be implemented and integrated until your stuff was working to spec. I like to contribute to the work too, you know. After all, I can't ask you to do something that I'm not willing to do myself. And as I said before, you really did a bang-up job and ev—"

"Yes, I know, even the President thinks so," said Carl.

Jack just smiled at the interruption, but Carl knew he was out of line. He gave Jack a half grin as he raised his eyebrows, showing that he realized that he had just overstepped a boundary, but not intentionally.

The silence was odd, so Carl began to tell a blonde joke to break the ice. When he got to the punch line, Jack laughed.

I fail to see the humor.

"CLARA, it's a joke. I was just making a joke. My goodness, don't you know a joke when you hear one?"

Beyond understanding that a joke is supposed to be a story told to evoke an amusing reaction, I can't really say I know much more. I will have to work on adding such types of conversations to my knowledge base and develop appropriate subroutines.

Carl went over to his desk and sat down in the very plush leather executive's chair. There were all sorts of controls on the chair arm. Carl would have to investigate and figure out what all of these were later. There was, undoubtedly, a manual somewhere, probably right in front of him, but who reads manuals when you can play around with the controls and find out what they are for? If worse came to worse, Carl had already concluded that he could just ask CLARA.

As Carl glanced around at the desk, he noticed all of the "things" that were there and knew immediately that they were not all what they appeared to be. Carl just made a mental note that he had more things to play around with later. There was a flat panel monitor depressed into the glass desktop and then a flat panel screen on either side of him that could be raised and lowered to be in use or out of the way. This was the epitome of techno sleek. Across the room was a wall full of monitors that looked like they would give Carl a vantage point of just about anything he wanted in the building. The one thing that stood out in the room at the moment was the figure of J. Jackson Brody sitting on the leather loveseat by the door. He hadn't left, but he also hadn't said much. That only meant one thing, and that was that he wanted something, but he was taking his time telling Carl about it. He looked as if he enjoyed watching Carl acclimate to his new digs and new toys.

Carl looked up at Jack Brody, who sat in his pinstriped blue business suit. You could tell just by looking at the suit that it was definitely tailor-made to hide the bulge of the firearm that Carl knew was under there. He wore some expensive but practical shoes and a red "power" tie. J. Jackson Brody was 59 years old, but he didn't look a day over 58. He had what appeared to be a full head of silverish-gray hair, but it was just cleverly combed so as not to reveal the bald spot in the center rear. His face was clean shaven and smooth. He stood about six feet tall and was slim and lean. For somebody who spent his days behind a desk, he was in impeccable shape. He had a tan overcoat slung over his right arm and held a wide brimmed, brown hat with a gray and black feather in the dark tan head band. He sat patiently.

Not moving.

Not speaking.

Just looking.

"Jaaaaaaaaack?" said Carl, drawing Jack's name out.

"Yeeessssssssss?" Jack answered in kind.

"Jack, you want something. Why don't you just tell me what it is?"

"Awwww, come on Carl, what makes you think I want something."

"Because I know you, Jack. You're a busy man. You don't have time to just come and sit in my office and relax, so spill the beans."

"My, you are direct now, aren't you?"

"You wouldn't have it any other way, and you know it."

"True that," said Jack. "OK, here's the deal, Carl. We created this new position for you because we wanted to take some of the stress off of Manny. You'll have 150 agents under you, but you will still be a field agent yourself. That is why CLARA said your field status was active."

"Come on, Jack, you could have sent me that in an e-mail. And it wouldn't even have had to be a secure one at that. So, what else is on your mind?"

"Your assignment," said Jack.

"My assignment?" Carl asked.

"Yes, your assignment. You know about the Eagle One guys on four and five? Well, their number one guy has had some threats against his life, and he needs to be watched when he's out on assignment. You're our number one guy, so we're putting you on their number one guy."

"OK, so when is he on his next assignment? I'm itching to go somewhere."

"Unknown. But when he does go somewhere, his protection will be your Primary Objective."

"What do we do when I'm on assignment and then he has to go somewhere?"

"Well, they're going to try to do their best to make sure that doesn't happen. When you are on another assignment, the objectives of that assignment will trump all else. You will have a different Primary Objective. Somebody else will handle him."

"And just out of curiosity, who is him?" asked Carl.

"His name is Lawrence Blackwell."

"Never heard of him," said Carl

"Then he's been doing his job well. CLARA has a complete dossier on him. It has already been cleared for your review. All you have to do is request it. I'll leave you to your work. I'm sure you'll be doing a lot of reading and planning."

"Gee, Jack, thanks."

"Hey, no problem. After all, this is what we do."

CHAPTER 6

After Jack left the office, Carl sat and thought for a while. He was brought back into awareness as the ramblings of people milling into the office began. Everyone was just learning about Carl's promotion, some just as they walked by. Nobody was the least bit surprised. They all knew that he had earned it and deserved it. Several of his colleagues stopped by to offer their congratulations. Apparently, this promotion was only a surprise to Carl. Now he had to get a grasp on exactly what the job was going to entail; 150 agents were going to be a lot to keep track of. Carl knew immediately that he had better start checking out who would be working for him because he was going to need an assistant or two or three.

"CLARA?"

Yes, Assistant Director Reardon?

"I'm not sure how I am supposed to go about this—using you to assist me, that is, but I am going to give it a shot here. I would appreciate any guidance that you can offer."

Of course, Sir. That is exactly what I am here for.

"CLARA pull up the 150 agents under my supervision and put their names and areas of expertise on the main screen on the wall."

Accessing and displaying the requested information now.

Carl was amazed at this computerized marvel. He didn't

have to figure out a query and try six or seven times before he got what he actually wanted. All he had to do was talk to CLARA, and she performed the necessary task. This was great. No, this was outstanding. No, this was stupendous! Carl was not sure if he would even be able to come up with the words that he needed to describe exactly what he was trying to say. Would there even be a need for human assistants? Carl had to wonder. Of course, there would be.

Of the names that were displayed, Carl began to highlight agents. Well, actually, he made the request and CLARA did the highlighting. Eventually he was able to narrow the choices down to the top ten. Then, deciding that he would like assistants who could oversee groups of 25 agents, he narrowed the field down to six. Carl did not want to get too far ahead of himself, so he thought he'd better place a call.

Carl was only calling next door and could have gotten up but decided to be lazy this time. He hit the speaker button on the telephone and depressed the speed dial button with Manny's name on it. This was Manny's direct line, and he answered right away.

"Balboa here!" Manny said as he answered.

"Hi, Manny. I have a question for you."

"Shoot," said Manny.

"Am I allowed to issue promotions and form other job descriptions?"

Carl heard a high-pitched, long whistle on the other end of the telephone. "I tell you what, Buddy, Brody has got you pegged to the Tee! He told me you would be calling about this very thing and that I could give you the green light on it. How does he know that you're going to do these things, I wonder?"

"Well, I think the answer to that question is that I am very much like him. He figures that whatever it is that he would do would be the same as I would. Looks like he hasn't been wrong yet. I want to create a position that will allow for six assistants. Each of them will oversee 25 men."

"It will be a process trying to pick those men."

"Not really. CLARA and I have already finished the process."

"So, who did you… and CLARA come up with?"

"Well, I ended up with Henry Soloman, Burt Burwell, Sam Edwards, Josiah Townsend, Harvey McCloud and Chris Stewart."

"Excellent. All good men. You and CLARA could not have done any better."

"Well, I'm glad to have your blessing on my choices."

"I take it that you have been told about your assignment."

"Yeah, if you can call it that. I'm babysitting a guy from an outfit that is supposed to be protecting other agents. Go figure. I'm not sure how I drew the short straw on that one, but I guess somebody has to do it. Well, I have a lot of meetings to arrange and organizing to do. Chat with ya later, boss."

"You bet," said Manny as he pressed the button to hang up the speaker phone.

Now that Carl had his team selected, it was time to have a meet and greet. Carl would give them his vision of how he wanted to have the team operate and let them run with it.

Carl did not wait very long. He called a meeting for the next day. Carl's deputies were all sitting around the large conference room table. There was light laughter coming from the members of the new management team as Carl talked to his new assistants. Seated around the table were Henry Soloman, Burt Burwell, Sam Edwards, Josiah Townsend, Harvey McCloud and Chris Stewart.

Henry Soloman was not a very large man by any stretch of the imagination. He was the perfect example of not judging a book by its cover. Everyone knew from personal experience that Henry Soloman was a force to be reckoned with. Many people have made the mistake of misjudging him because of his small stature. But inside that tiny frame is a dynamo of a man. Henry stood about five feet two inches tall. He had chocolate brown skin and a very close-cut haircut. Henry wore a thin but detectable mustache and no other facial hair. Henry was very assertive and knew how to get the job done.

Burt Burwell was also not a very big man, and just as formidable an opponent as Henry. You didn't want to run across either of these men in a dark alley if you weren't on their side. Burt looked like he came from the heart of Europe, as evidenced by his fair skin color, but he was born and raised in Louisiana. Burt stood five feet three inches. He was just a hair taller than Henry Soloman. Seated, both men looked to be the same height. Burt was always making light of things, and he was the guy who had the joke of the hour that currently had everyone chuckling.

Sam Edwards was at the other end of the spectrum as far as height was concerned. He stood a lofty six feet two inches tall. He was a quick mover and a legendary master at hand-to-hand combat. He was known at the agency as the king of casual. Rarely would you see Sam Edwards in a suit; and those times he did wear one, he usually didn't wear a tie. But his standard attire was a Ralph Lauren Polo shirt and Khakis. He had curly, sandy brown hair and kept his face clean shaven. His brown eyes were a perfect complement to his hair and eyebrow color. Sam was one of the younger agents but was moving up the ranks fast and furious. He usually found himself on many of the less desired and more difficult cases. To his credit, he has only one case that still remains open. He is determined that he will close that one too someday. It seems that everybody has one of those cases.

Seated to Sam Edwards' right were Josiah Townsend and Harvey McCloud. Unlike most agents who worked on most of their cases individually, Townsend and McCloud always worked together. No one could find any good reason to break them up. They were commonly referred to as Abbott and Costello. This was mostly because of Townsend's short, overweight build and McCloud's tall, thin build. But for a short overweight guy, Josiah Townsend sure could move! Not only could he defend himself in a fight without weapons, but if you did happen to give him a weapon—any weapon—he always seemed to be able to master using it in a matter of seconds. That has been a very valuable lifesaving skill for him. Nobody liked going up against him in marksmanship competitions because he could out-shoot almost everybody.

Townsend's sidekick, McCloud, was known as a smooth talker. He was known to talk himself out of being killed so many times that he got labeled with the name. How he did it, nobody understood. Once he did it after already being shot four times, and the guy was just about to finish him off. Somehow McCloud talked the guy into bending down so that he could speak to him. The not-so-intelligent perpetrator wound up with a serious groin injury and a fractured skull. It will be interesting to see how this move to management will affect this two-man team. Carl imagined that their teams would, very likely, be doing a lot of work together. He actually liked the prospect of that new dynamic.

Last, but certainly not least was the ever so quiet and elusive Chris Stewart. Chris Stewart was the kind of agent who got assigned cases like Carl did. One day he was there, and the next day he was gone. All of a sudden, he was back, and everyone was getting updates on the high-profile case that they had read about in the news but had no idea that it was Chris Stewart or anybody else in the CIA that was responsible. It came to be, when such cases were being reported on the news, the standard response was: "Hey, has anyone seen Chris Stewart?"

Chris Stewart was all business. He did not dress lavishly or wear impressively expensive clothing, but his suits were always sharp, clean and pressed. There was never a hair on his blonde head out of place, and he was generally easy to get along with—well, except for the time that he and Benny Gooseman duked it out in the break room. But everybody seemed to think that Benny egged him on and deserved the two black eyes he walked around with for a week. Now Gooseman and Stewart are the best of friends. If Carl needed a seventh man, Gooseman would have been the logical choice.

Things settled down and the meeting commenced. Carl laid out his plans for this new division and got everyone's input and agreement. It was a very productive meeting. Carl had just finished giving his marching orders to his new assistants and was winding up the meeting.

"So... each one of you is in charge of a 25-man team, that includes you, so there are only 24 to supervise... unless you can figure out how to supervise yourself, but technically, then you'd be doing my job. Henry, you will only have 23; I hope that is not too much of a hardship."

"Negative Boss," said Henry Soloman. "But what happened to the 24th guy?"

"YOU would have been the 24th guy," said Carl, "and I would have been in charge of that group."

"Gotcha! didn't think about that one."

"Yeah, well, that's why I get the big bucks," said Carl with a smile. The rest of the team laughed again.

"Well," Carl concluded, "if you gentleman don't have any other questions, let's rock and roll!" When nobody spoke up, Carl said, "OK, then. Dismissed. Oh, Henry, hang back for a second. I'd like a word with you."

"OOOOOOO, what did Soloman do now?" chided Burt Burwell as he walked out of the office and shut the door.

Henry was not quite sure why he needed to hang back. It was way too early in the process to have done anything wrong. His brow furrowed with curiosity.

"Henry, have a seat," said Carl.

"Sure, what's up, Carl?"

"Well, Henry, I have been advised that, even though I am Manny's number two man, I have to have a number two man as well."

"And you wanted me to give you some suggestions on which one of those knuckleheads to pick?"

"No, Henry, you're it."

Henry looked over his shoulder as if Carl must have been looking right through him to someone else. "As far as I can see, I'm the only Henry in here, but surely you must be mistaken. You mean this Henry Soloman?" Henry asked, pointing to himself.

That would stand to reason, Agent Soloman. There are no other Henry Solomans on record, CLARA chimed in.

Carl snickered and said, "CLARA, are you ALWAYS listening?"

I shut down for a few milliseconds of maintenance every 6.39 minutes, but other than that, yes, I am always listening. Anything I would have missed goes into a buffer, so, in effect, you can say that I am always listening.

"CLARA, in the future, when I am engaged in private conversation, since I do not think I have the ability to shut off your listening mode, please do not respond unless a response is requested. Operate under normal mode at all other times, subject to change as we learn how to get along with each other."

Request stored, and parameter update executed.

"Well, Henry, since you are the ONLY Henry in the room, yes, I am talking to you. If you'll take it, the job is yours."

"Well, what does the job entail?"

"I don't even know what my job entails. When I figure that out, I should be able to give you an answer. So, not knowing... except for the fact that your main job is to assist me—yes, along with everything else you have to do—are you up for the challenge?"

"Sure, I'm game. You're not hard to work with, Carl. We can do this."

CHAPTER 7

Now that all the covert operations and equipment have been moved in, and the secured areas of the building are indeed secure, the NLRC employees have begun moving into their respective office spaces.

The move was typical. A myriad of things did not go exactly as planned and had to be fixed, adjusted, or otherwise dealt with. Of course, they couldn't all be handled right away, and there was an entire team dedicated to prioritizing issues. People were stepping on top of other people, and nobody was really being productive. After several days, things appeared to get ironed out, and now the NLRC workers could work side by side with many of the agents. No one would be the wiser. The Façade was perfect.

Everything was going according to plan.

Moving day was the last big hurdle for the building project. Now that everything seemed to have been completed, Carl finally had an opportunity to sit down and take a breather. What a foreign concept that was for Carl, who was always, always working. In his head, Carl was already tossing around how he could occupy this 'free' time that he had. One thing was for certain, he was not lacking for possible options. He could learn more about the computer systems, his high-tech chair, CLARA, or a billion other things. But, no, not Carl. If there was free time, then there must be some work to fill it.

He remembered that he still had not looked at that dossier for Lawrence Blackwell. Carl thought back to when he first became an agent. Among his other many curiosities, he wondered about the origins of the word dossier. It was not one of those common words that you used around the house every day. Carl decided to look it up. He found that the origin came from 19th-century France. A dossier was a collection of documents in a binding with labels affixed to the back of the spine. The French word dos, translated into English, meant back. Hence the derivation of the word that we use today. It was so much easier to use the word file, but that just did not have that official sound to it. All of that was more information than Carl needed to understand what a dossier was. This information would likely be classified as useless for most purposes. A lot of the useless knowledge that Carl obtained would sometimes come in handy with his cases, so he stowed the information away for later use. If nothing else, it would probably be very useful when he played a trivia game.

"OK, CLARA, time to get updated on my assignment. Bring up the dossier on Eagle One agent Lawrence Blackwell on my center desk monitor, please."

Glad to comply, but you really need to learn how to take a break. I am also programmed for several different modes of entertainment, as well as rest and relaxation routines. If there is anything else I can do, you just ask now, ya hear? CLARA said in what Carl recognized as a southern accent.

"Where in the world did THAT come from?" asked Carl.

Oh, I'm just experimenting with different accents and methods of speech. I noticed that the people in the south always check your hearing, ya hear? I have yet to ascertain why, ya hear? Even computers get to have a little fun every now and then, you know, ya hear?

"No, I didn't know that, but am more than willing to learn.

But, for right now, the dossier please, ya hear. Look! Now you've got me doing it!"

The file has been accessed. I am awaiting your access codes to authenticate so that I can display the information.

Carl input the codes on his keypad that would allow him unrestricted access to the information that was in the dossier. His screen began to fill with information. Carl was amazed at the things he was reading. If he didn't know any better, he would have thought he was reading about himself. It was almost unbelievable how much Carl and Lawrence Blackwell had in common. Right down to their taste in ladies and preference settings on the computer. If nothing else, the CIA was thorough. As Carl continued to scan the file, he realized that there were hundreds of pages for him to get through. He thought that it might be wise to narrow down parameters so that he could focus on what he was actually taking in.

"CLARA, I need to filter out a lot of this. Can you select just the important highlights and facts from the dossier for me? Make sure that you include all of the personal 'get to know you' stuff, highlighting any known family information. I want to know this guy inside and out."

Processing…

Filtering complete.

Please review the information and restate your request if the parameters are incomplete, Director, CLARA said with an obligatory tone.

As the filtered information was displayed on the screen, Carl read and read about Lawrence Blackwell. Even with all the other information cut out, there was still a good deal of information to read. After he was done, Carl took a long breath and exhaled, and he exclaimed: "Whew!" Just then, Carl's phone rang…

He noted that it was the unsecured company line… The caller ID indicated that the call was coming in from his house.

Carl glanced at the clock for the first time in hours and grimaced.

"NLRC, Mr. Reardon's line," answered Carl.

"Mr. Reardon, this is Mrs. Reardon, and I am waiting for you to come home. Are you going to be able to do that anytime soon? Your wife has been looking forward to spending some time with you all day long, and you're nowhere to be found. I'm about ready to call the CIA."

'If you only knew,' Carl thought to himself.

"Oh, I'm sorry, hon. I got a promotion today and got into the work. I totally lost track of time. If my wife can forgive me, I'll be home in 20 minutes and I'll fill you in."

"Well, my dear, you have 19 minutes and 55 seconds, and not a second longer. The clock is ticking. There's a candlelight dinner waiting for you when you walk in the door, but for being this late, now you're going to have to earn it. Ta-Ta!"

With that, Carl's wife, Jenny, hung up the telephone. Carl could only imagine what his wife might mean when she said he would have to earn it, but he knew he was likely to enjoy whatever it was she had planned.

"CLARA, secure all files and entry points, please. Alert security of my status. It's time to go home. Put all systems into low power mode."

All files secured. Entry points will be secured upon your departure. Systems are now going into low power mode. Security has been notified and updated as to your status, and Leeman's has a dozen long-stemmed roses on sale for $34.99.

"CLARA, I don't recall asking you about roses."

If my programming is correct and I am interpreting things correctly, your wife has a romantic evening planned. No better way to top it off than to come home with a dozen roses, and she'll even think it was YOUR idea.

"Well, thank you, CLARA. I think I may just stop by Leeman's on the way home and pick up those roses."

I suggest you hurry; you now have only 18 minutes and 12 seconds left. I'll place an order at Leeman's and have them ready for pickup.

"Good night, CLARA, and thank you."

Good night, Director, and you're welcome.

"Director is so formal. Just call me Boss," Carl said.

Preferences updated. Good night, Boss, CLARA said.

Down on the fifth floor, Lawrence Blackwell had been summoned to his director's office. Charles Randall Springs III was the Director of the Eagle One unit. Now that the CIA was finally moving in, Springs had to see to it that the ball got rolling on this assignment. The CIA's top agent needed some protection, and Eagle One was going to provide it.

Springs threw the dossier across the table to Blackwell. It landed with a definite thud. The size of the file alone was an indicator that it was filled with a great deal of information. Blackwell just looked at the dossier that had been thrust at him and then asked... "And what is that?"

"THAT," said Springs, "is your next case and Primary Objective for the foreseeable future. The subject's name is... wait for it... Carl Reardon."

"Carl Reardon? THE Carl Reardon? The CIA's top guy is my assignment. Come on, like he really needs MY help," Blackwell said incredulously. "With the stories that I've heard, I would be wasting my time trying to protect him! Much less trying to accomplish that task and remain undetected. You're joking, right? Please tell me you're joking, Charlie."

"No, I'm not joking. Don't tell me that you know him. I can get somebody else if he's going to be able to ID you."

"No, as far as I know he doesn't know me from Adam; and I'm pretty sure he's read Adam's dossier."

"Good! Well, THE Carl Reardon, the CIA's number one guy, is your assignment then. He's gotten to the point where he's ticked off enough people with all of his successful missions that the list of people who want revenge is growing like gangbusters. The fact of the matter is, while he may think he's fine, he may not be able to protect himself as effectively as he thinks he can anymore. But nobody's going to tell him that. The word on the streets—that would be the underground streets, of course—is that somebody wants him dead; and they want him dead yesterday! But, as I said, they're just going to have to get in line."

"Ouch! Who's put the hit out on him?"

"That's just it. It seems like it is not just one person, but a consortium of people. They've pooled their resources and the contract is big and fat. The word on the street is that Carl's head is worth a cool 100 mil in cold hard cash. Don't get me wrong; this is not a free-for-all. They have a specific hired gun already selected to do the job. The problem is that nobody knows who he is. Never heard of him before. Here is what we do know: He goes by the name of Philly Mike. All we know about his M.O. is that he'll use anybody and everybody to do the hit. Never gets his own hands dirty. He's not in our database, but he will be soon."

"OK, so it sounds like I'm protecting Carl Reardon from a sandwich shop. That's not an awful lot to go on. When does this start?"

"Can you say yesterday? Read up, my friend," Springs said as he glanced down at the dossier. "As of this moment, he's yours."

"Well, at least I don't have to worry about a problem while he's on site."

"I wouldn't be too sure about that. This technological wonder can have its downfalls too. Make sure you plan for every eventuality."

Lawrence grabbed the file and headed back to his desk,

muttering on the way, "When are they ever going to get this stuff computerized? These files are pretty cumbersome. We need to put all of this technology to use. Of all people, I can't believe I have to babysit Carl Reardon. Challenge accepted!"

As the days passed, the scene would have been quite comical to anybody who actually knew what was going on. Carl and Lawrence were trying to tail each other without really knowing that the other was tailing them. Each time one of them would look up, the other would nonchalantly turn as if he didn't even notice someone was watching him. They were so busy trying to follow each other that they did not realize they were actually being followed by the other person as well.

Trying to disguise themselves, each of the agents posed as different people so as to try and get closer to the other. Once, Carl was a waiter in a restaurant that Lawrence was eating in. Lawrence was only eating there because he needed to be near Carl so that he could protect him and was wondering what Carl was up to being dressed as his waiter.

Lawrence, on the other hand, found out that Carl had a plumbing problem and he needed to go to Home Depot. After tailing him to Home Depot, he slipped the "plumbing expert" a C-note and pointed out Carl to him. He instructed him that if Carl had any questions or needed any help finding anything, he was to be directed to Lawrence, who was now expertly disguised. Oddly enough, Lawrence was able to answer Carl's plumbing problems, and he was able to find all the things that Carl needed to complete the task. Lawrence was very thankful for all the time he had spent in Home Depot to purchase things just for this very type of repair.

The two passed in hallways, bathrooms, other stores, and restaurants, but they kept each other safe. The bosses were having a ball with it all:

"Springs? Yeah, Brody here. Have you read the latest reports? These two crack me up! We have the two best agents in the world here, and they don't even realize that they're being followed by each other."

"Yeah, pretty funny, isn't it, Brody? I guess if they weren't so intent on protecting each other, the irony of the entire situation would stand out to them like a sore thumb."

"This had to be one of the most brilliant collaborations that we've come up with yet."

"Indeed it is. Indeed it is," said Springs.

"Listen, that's not what I really called to chat with you about."

"I know. You called about the communique from Liberty 1, right?"

"Exactly, I thought you might have gotten it by now," said Brody.

Liberty 1 was the codename used by Eagle One and the CIA, and various other investigative branches as a codename for the President of the United States. With the Vice President being Liberty 2 and the Speaker of the House being Liberty 3. Very different from the Secret Service. With the Secret Service the President and his family were given options for names and had to pick one. Their codenames changed with each new administration. With Eagle One, the same name passed to each person that took office. Much cleaner and much easier.

"Does your boy know about the orders yet?" Springs asked Brody.

"Negative. I was going to break it to him, but the big man himself wants to do it. We're expecting him later today, so when you see all of the hoopla and security is going crazy, you'll know why."

"Well, thanks for the heads up," said Springs.

"No problem," said Brody, "Is your boy going to be up for the job? Carl can be a very elusive character, especially when he is on assignment. He doesn't wait for anybody or anything and he is exponentially more careful and aware."

"Understood. Don't you worry. Blackwell is up for the challenge. He'll keep him safe. Question is, can he do it without getting spotted? Especially now that they kind of know each other."

"Well, we can always go to plan B," said Brody.

"Oh yeah? What's plan B?" asked Springs.

"Don't rush me," said Brody. "I'm still working on that one."

CHAPTER 8

The usual fanfare ensued whenever the President moved from location to location. One could never even be sure that he was part of the actual procession of vehicles. Sometimes it was all just a diversion. Sirens were ablaze as the Presidential motorcade came across the bridge and into Emerald Valley. The two motorcycles in the front cleared the way for the rest of the vehicles. They alternated positions with the two rear motorcycles.

Two Ford Explorers, which were specially rigged for speed enabled with bullet glass and plating, followed next with their flashing lights. They were, in turn, followed by the Presidential Limo and then two more Explorers and the final set of motorcycles. This was a lot of taxpayer money to expend when the Commander-in-Chief might not even be traveling with the group. But it is the price that we pay for the President's safety.

President Curtis Young, who actually WAS in the Limo this time, reached over and hit a button on the console next to him and spoke:

"Nexus online please," President Young ordered.

Nexus is online, Mr. President, came the computer-generated male voice.

"Nexus patch me through to the CLARA system," Young commanded.

You are patched in, Mr. President. Please go ahead with your request.

"CLARA, do you copy?"

Greetings, Viper. It's been a long time.

"Yes, indeed it has. I need you to notify agent Reardon—I believe that is Assistant Director Reardon now—that I am en route and will be in his office within ten minutes."

Affirmative. Shall I reveal your identity to Carl?

"Oh, are you two on a first name basis already? I'm jealous. No. My codename will be sufficient for now. I just love the element of surprise."

Yes, you always have. Actually, I have been instructed to address him as Boss. I modified that instruction for the purpose of clarity in our conversation. The Boss has been informed of your estimated time of arrival.

"Thank you, CLARA. Viper out. Nexus offline."

The green lights, which were set in strategic locations around Carl's office, began to flash. That was his indication that there was an incoming message. The lights were situated so that no matter where Carl happened to be in the office, he would be able to see that there was a message coming in and that he needed to act.

Carl activated his communications console by voice:

"Activate Communication Console," commanded Carl.

The communications console illuminated. Carl could see immediately that the monitor did not come on. The message was audio only.

"Message detail please," Carl inquired.

Carl was extremely busy and wanted to prioritize. If this was not important, he would store it and pick it up later... if he remembered. CLARA would make sure that he did not forget.

Incoming message, top priority from Agent Viper.

"Viper? CLARA, crosscheck and verify. That's impossible.

Even if it was possible, why would Viper be contacting me?"

Crosschecked and double verified. The message origin is genuine.

"CLARA, data on agent Viper," Carl said as he shook his head and scowled in disbelief.

Agent, Codename: Viper, top security CIA operative for overseas missions. Cases attributed to Viper:-

"CLARA, skip all of that unnecessary stuff," Carl said as he interrupted her programmed rant. "Current status of agent Viper."

Public records indicate that Agent, codenamed: Viper is missing in action after a high-profile mission to rescue a supposed U.S. Air Force Col. Welch who has top secret information about the U.S. defense program and systems. Mission unsuccessful. Viper… again according to public record is assumed dead.

"CLARA, you keep saying Public Record. What do the classified records indicate?"

Insufficient Security Access.

"Interesting. Well, what is the message?"

Agent Viper will be arriving within the next ten minutes and desires to meet with you.

"Thank You, CLARA. What is the identity of the agent codenamed Viper?"

Insufficient Security Access.

"CLARA, I thought I had top security access," Carl said.

Sorry, Boss. As long as you have supervisors, there will always be someone with a higher level of access.

"Do you know the identity of Viper?"

Insufficient Security Access.

"That's a yes, no matter how you sugarcoat it. Well, I guess I'll just have to wait ten minutes to satisfy my curiosity. Viper is on the way."

Agents were never known to be late. In fact, they were usually early; and by Carl's clock, Viper had 1 minute and 30 seconds to show up. Carl sat lost in thought, trying to figure out why Viper would be contacting him, of all people, after all this time. He thought he might be contacting somebody more on Jack Brody's level than his. But whatever the reason was, Viper was contacting him, and he was going to be ready.

Thirty seconds later, just one minute before Viper was scheduled to walk in the door, there was a major disturbance in the outer office area. Carl saw what appeared to be Secret Service agents securing the area. Carl did not have any recollection of a Presidential visit. If the President was coming, then he should have been informed. It would make more sense, anyway, that the President would be here to see Jack or Manny. Carl just hoped that all these agents didn't spook Viper. This was one meeting that he did not want to jeopardize. Carl's hopes were immediately dashed when two Secret Service agents entered his office, flashed their badges and did a quick examination to make sure that there were no immediate threats. "The President of the United States to see you, Sir."

No preamble.

No call ahead first.

Just like that... the President was here to see him. Under any other circumstances, Carl would have been elated, but right now, he was waiting for somebody and by his reckoning, it was a meeting that was more important than meeting with the President of the United States. The President's timing could not possibly have been any worse.

Carl was not happy.

President Curtis Young walked into Carl's office. His stride was bold and confident. He was flanked by Secret Service Agents on all sides. The President was unmistakable. He was the second Black man to be elected President and his administration was making even more of an impact than his predecessor, the first Black President. President Young preferred the term Black to Afro-American or African American because he had never had an Afro and was not about to grow one; and, while his ancestors may have originated in Africa, he was U.S. born. He had never been to Africa; but chances were good that he would end up there to discuss foreign relations someday. While he may venture there at some point during his tenure as President, it was not his place of origin, regardless of politically correct labeling. For some people that was a controversial stance. Young, however, meant no disrespect to his heritage; he just had his own preference on how he was recognized.

President Young was appropriately named because he looked very young for his age. His complexion was milk chocolate, and his hair was black. He wore a well-groomed mustache, but no beard and his sideburns were military regulation length and close cut like the rest of his hair. He wore a modest suit that was light gray and had four buttons on each cuff and three buttons down the front of the coat. His shirt was a pressed white with a nicely starched collar; and he was sporting the obligatory solid red power tie.

"Simmons, you stay. The rest of you can wait outside. I should be safe enough in a 12-billion-dollar building," said the President.

Without complaint or challenge of any kind, for they knew that it would have just been in vain anyway, the agents dispersed. One agent, presumably Simmons, stood guard near the office door. Carl rose and the President stepped over to the desk and greeted him with a hearty handshake as he introduced himself.

"Agent Reardon, or should I say Assistant Director? I have waited a very long time to make your acquaintance. You will never know how long," the President said with an air of mystery that piqued Carl's curiosity. "It is so good to finally meet you after having read so much about you."

"Mr. President, it is a pleasure to meet you as well. At the risk of sounding rude, under other circumstances it would be a pleasure to have a prolonged visit with you, but I really have some pressing business and—I know it's a lot to ask—but if we could schedule this meeting for any other time, I would be most obliged."

Boss, this is-

"Not now CLARA, this is a bad time."

But Boss-

"CLARA!" Carl said sharply, hoping that the President didn't think he was crazy talking to a machine. CLARA, although she was not human, understood the tone and immediately went silent. You could sense that her feelings had been hurt.

Of course! You're expecting someone right about now, and I'm in the way!

The President laughed his trademark hearty laugh. Carl didn't see what was so funny. Simmons, in the corner never cracked a smile, and it was impossible to see his eyes with the dark glasses on. He just kept an eye on the President, ready to pounce should the need arise. The President enjoyed Carl's confusion for the moment, but he had let this go on long enough.

"CLARA, secure this room. Level ten," President Young commanded.

Right away, Mr. President, CLARA said.

"Mr. President, pardon my ignorance, but how do you have authority over this system?"

President Young held up his hand to silence Carl and said, "Patience. All in good time."

This office has been secured. Security Level ten, CLARA said.

"CLARA, please reveal my complete identity for Assistant Director Reardon; authentication Alpha 1399276 Zulu!" said the President.

Carl's eyebrows raised very noticeably when he heard CLARA reply...

Authentication confirmed. Identity: Curtis Quinten Young, covert international operative, codename: Viper. Current Status: Active. President of the United States of America. Official operational field status: Missing in action, presumed dead.

Carl's jaw just about dropped to the ground when he heard CLARA's response.

"YOU'RE Viper?" asked Carl.

The President grinned and shook his head as he said, "The one and only. Is this still an inconvenient time?"

"Wow. Well, Sir, why didn't you just say so? No, no, not inconvenient at all. I've been waiting for you."

"Good answer. Here I am," said President Young.

President Young, a.k.a. Viper, took a seat in one of the plush chairs facing Carl's desk. Carl found it a little hard to do, given the doubly incredible stature of the man across from him, but he lowered himself into his seat. All the while he felt as if, in this situation, he was on the wrong side of the desk.

"Mr. President, what can I assist you with?" Carl finally managed to form the words to say.

"Well, Carl, I'm sure you've been told that you're on my short list of agents to call on when I have a job that needs doing. I have one and it is very touchy. It's a two-fold job, and I need you to finish up some unfinished business at the same time.

"You name it, Mr. President. I'll do whatever I can," said Carl.

"Of that, I have no doubt. Are you familiar with Estonia?" The President asked.

"Well, I know it's a country and that the Russians would like a strategic hold on it, but because of the fact that we are in negotiations with the Estonian people, it is preventing Russia from making a move."

"Excellent, you've done your homework and it hasn't even been assigned yet. Well, Hayden Busch, the U.S. Ambassador to

Estonia, has been kidnapped. I have reason to believe that this is all related. I want you to go in and get our man out."

"Enough said, Mr. President. I'll be on the next plane out."

"I have no doubt that you will, Carl, but that's not all there is to the case."

"What else it there?"

"CLARA grant access to Assistant Director Reardon to classified file Estonian Escapade, Agent Viper failed mission."

Content is declassified.

"Display on screen for Agent Reardon."

On screen.

"Read, Carl," said the President as he sat back and waited.

President Young watched as Carl's eyes raised and lowered. He carefully studied his facial expressions to see how the material was affecting Carl. It was apparently having the desired effect.

Carl looked up from his screen into the eyes of the President and said, "That information has never been shared before, has it, Sir?" The question was rhetorical. Carl was not expecting an answer. "This is it. Every agent has one. This is YOUR open case."

"No, Carl, this information has never been shared and probably never will be again. That was for your eyes only. CLARA, re-classify information."

Information reclassified.

As CLARA spoke, the information disappeared from the screen, only to be replaced with the majestic CIA logo on Carl's screen.

"Commit what you read to memory, Carl. I can't share any more along those lines with you. You cannot discuss anything you read with anyone, not even your superiors."

"Consider it done, Sir. I was memorizing as I read; as we have been trained," said Carl.

"Good, now let's talk about the part that I can share. U.S. Air Force Col. Raymond Welch. Carl, he's still alive."

"How can you be sure of that, Sir? Surely after all this time, they could have killed him."

"What you can be sure of, Carl, is that I have my sources, and they are very reliable. Welch has a lot of information, and they won't kill him and lose that source without obtaining another one. The Russians are a patient and persistent lot. They think that eventually, over the years, they can wear you down. The problem here, Carl, is that they're right. My sources also tell me that Col. Welch has held out well. Better and longer than any other man in the service of this country who has been put in his position. But he is wearing down, and he's nearing his cracking point. You read the file. There is so much red tape wrapped around this whole thing that it is impossible to send anybody in to rescue him through normal channels. I think Welch knows we want to rescue him, but I also think he knows that we can't. I need a man who's good and who can get in there by himself and come back with two people alive and well. We need that Ambassador freed so that the Russians aren't holding a trump card, and we need Col. Welch back on U.S. soil. This Russian-controlled facility in independent Estonia needs to be exposed. They are careful not to hold any of our people on their own soil. Are you in?"

Noticing the changed look on Carl's face, the President said, "What's wrong? You seem troubled."

"Well, I have a slight problem, Sir. My current assignment is protecting one of our top agents, and if I'm gone, then who's going to—?"

"Already taken care of. No need to worry about agent Blackwell until you return."

"You know about him too! Is there anything that you do not know or are not informed about?"

The President hesitated in deep thought for a moment and said... "No, not much."

"Is it also true, Mr. President, or is it just a rumor, perhaps, that your short list only includes one name, and that happens to be mine?"

"Guilty as charged," said the President.

"Well, I don't see that we have too many options and, having been on this side of the fence, you are fully aware that now that I know what is at stake, there is no way I can turn you down."

"I was hoping that you would see it that way, but I was not sure if you would," said the President.

"How soon can you arrange travel?" asked Carl.

"Done!" said the President with a smile. "But I know you have to get all of your ducks in a row first. I used to live the life too. You go home and spend some time with the little lady and let her know you're going on another 'business trip.'"

"She won't like it, but it's got to be done," Carl said.

With that the President got up, said his goodbyes and left Carl to think and to plan. There was a lot of work to be done. The President had CLARA clear access to the file that had all the necessary mission information about the installation where the Ambassador was being held. Col. Welch just happened to be held in the same place. CLARA provided a schematic of the facility, indicating the most likely places where the prisoners could be housed.

There was another fanfare of activity as the Secret Service agents escorted President Young back out along the secure path that they had entered. Everyone knew enough to not even ask Carl what it was all about.

They would not be surprised when he disappeared for the mission.

Carl studied and planned and planned and studied. This was not going to be an easy mission, but it was a necessary one. Then again, when were any of Carl's missions ever easy? The national security of the United States of America was riding on this one.

No pressure.

Lawrence Blackwell walked into Charles Springs' office with a pep in his step. Springs was busy answering a direct message on his computer.

"You called for me, Sir?" Blackwell asked.

"Yes, sit down," said Springs.

"Uh Oh. I don't know what it is, but whatever it is I didn't do it. I promise," said Blackwell.

"You didn't do anything, Lawrence. It's your assignment."

"What? You mean Carl?" asked Blackwell with a quizzical look on his face.

"Yes, Carl. He's just been assigned a mission that is going to take him out of the country."

"All of his missions take him out of the country, Sir. How far out of the country are we talking?"

"Oh, only to Estonia, just a hop, skip and a jump from here. But there is a concern," Springs said, and he clasped his hands in on his desk in front of him and leaned forward. "Remember, you're tracking Carl Reardon here. How undetectable can you be?"

"If that was a challenge, Sir, you're on. When do we leave?"

"As soon as Reardon has his stuff in order. I suggest you do the same."

"Copy that," said Blackwell.

Chapter 9

Carl sat across from his darling wife of three years, Jenny. Carl had met Jenny shortly after he got back from the Finland mission where Marianna was killed. Carl wanted to do that mission alone, but would that then mean that he would be dead instead of her? Carl had grown quite attached to Marianna, to the point that he had developed feelings for her. Before anything could come of that, she was gone. That really messed up Carl's head. When he met Jenny, she helped him get through that rough patch. The resulting relationship was unexpected, but very much needed.

God had not seen fit to bless them with any children. With Carl's lifestyle, it was probably best. Carl and Jenny certainly were not going to argue with God's choices.

They were at D'Agostino's. The lighting was low, and the mood was always very romantic. The atmosphere was quite serene, and you could barely hear any talking from the other diners. Most of the communication that could be heard was from the waiting and kitchen staff.

Jenny really liked Italian food and D'Agostino's was one of the best Italian grill restaurants that she had ever been to. Once Carl knew her favorites, he committed them to memory. But Jenny was no fool. She knew Carl was trying to smooth her over for something; he just hadn't said what yet. Jenny knew better than to ask. She was intent on having a good time with her husband, and she would just wait him out. She knew that as soon as he thought the time was right, he would break the news. Sooner or later Carl would come around and spill the beans. In these situations, Jenny had learned that he had probably been tapped for another unscheduled trip. He had no choice but to let her know, and she got to benefit from the special treatment as a result. In a way it was a win/win situation.

Lawrence Blackwell and his wife sat in their favorite restaurant. It was a small family run place named Christos. The location was very convenient; it was just four blocks from their house. With the restaurant being within walking distance, there was no need to take the car. Lawrence and Renee Blackwell could enjoy a nice romantic stroll, hand-in-hand, to the restaurant and then again back home after the meal.

It had been a while since they had been out, and Renee knew that something was up. Probably travel again. 'Oh well, whatever it takes to get the big oaf to take me out every once in a while,' Renee thought. Renee loved her husband dearly. She just wished that he was home more and that they could seriously think about and work on starting that family that they had both always wanted.

"So, tell me dear, where to this time?" asked Renee.

"What do you mean, hon?" Lawrence asked innocently.

"Oh, come on you big lug. We've been married for too many years. Just spill the beans. I don't mind going out to the nice restaurant one bit, but I know you brought me here to tell me something. Get on with it so that we can both enjoy our meal."

"Is it really that obvious? Well, I have to travel again. I'm not sure how long, but I'll be back as soon as possible. I'll bring you something. I bet you've never gotten anything from

Estonia now, have you?"

"Now, doesn't that feel better?" Renee asked. She just winked at him in only the way that she could. As usual, her wink just made him melt.

As the car pulled into the driveway, Jenny looked over at her husband expectantly. The vehicle rolled slowly to a stop, and Carl turned off the ignition. He still had not broken the news to her. Her patience had waned, and she couldn't hold back anymore. However, she was able to be somewhat reserved and did not let him have it with both barrels.

"Look, Carl, I know you have something to tell me. The evening was nice, and I really enjoyed it, but I know there is something else. Don't you think it's time to deal with the elephant in the room? Would you please just tell me already? For whatever reason, you just haven't gotten up the courage to say it. I'm going to go inside and run a nice hot bath and I'm going to soak for a bit. When I get out of the tub, we'll talk. OK?"

"Look, Jen, I don't want to spoil your mood after a nice bath and you're all relaxed. That would just be mean. Look here!" Carl reached into his jacket pocket, pulled out his hotel itinerary, and handed it to his wife.

"Oh, come on, you're traveling again! Doesn't this company ever slow down? The money is good, I know, very good, but I would really like you to be around to spend it with me."

"Honey, you remember that raise I told you about?"

"Yes, and that means more travel, right?"

"Actually, it could mean less travel and the paycheck doubles. I'm still going to have to make some special trips here and there, but, for the most part, I'm actually the guy in the company who will be overseeing about 150 other employees. In effect, I'll be the one who will be sending THEM out on travel. There are going to be a lot of husbands and wives out there who are not going to like me," Carl said, as they simultaneously opened their doors.

"Oh Honey, that's fantastic," Jenny said as she hopped up and down; unable to contain herself. "You'll be traveling less? AND double the money? Do you know how much money you already make?" Jenny asked rhetorically. "You're going to be making twice that?"

"Well, including bonuses, yeah. Every time I have a successful trip, there is a bonus to match, and if this one is successful, well, you name it and it's yours!"

Jenny came down from her cloud and landed back into reality, and in a quiet voice she said to Carl, as she rubbed his arm very softly, "Carl... you know the money really doesn't matter, don't you? What really matters is you. I could care less if you make two million dollars a year (which is way more than enough, by the way) or four. Sure, we can live comfortably and all, but when all is said and done, it's not the money that I want; it's you, Carl. What is it that you do on these trips anyway?"

"Now, Jen, we've had this discussion before. That is a part of my job that I will probably never be able to tell you. You know that."

"You make it seem like you're some sort of spy or something. That would just be so weird. If I hadn't seen the place where you worked and met the people, surely that's what I would think. OK, alright. I'm going to let this thing go. You know best and I'll follow you. Just so that you know, it's not about the money. I love YOU, Carl Reardon."

"And I, Carl Reardon, love you too, little lady."

Jenny gave Carl a tight hug and held on to him like she would never let him go again. But, at last, she slowly released him, looked into his eyes and said, "Well, I think I'll go and take that bath now."

"And then?" Carl asked.

"And then we'll see."

Carl watched his wife from the driveway as she entered the house. He realized what a good thing he had. It did strike him as pretty funny that the thought of him being a spy was a weird thought. But there were some things that Jenny would never need to know as long as Carl kept coming home. He knew that if something should happen to him, Jack would probably be the one who would have to do the "dirty work" and let Jenny know about the life that he actually lived. But, as long as he kept doing his job well and staying out of harm's way, nobody except the powers that be had to know the whole truth.

Carl Entered the house, and he heard the water running in the master bathroom. The sound of the water filling Jenny's custom soaker tub with massage jets was very distinguishable. That was just a little thing that kept her happy.

"Hey Jen, I'm going to pack my things while you're in the bathtub, so I don't have to worry about it later."

"You know I'll get that for you, sweetie. Just be patient," she responded.

"I'll get it this time. You just relax and enjoy yourself."

"OK, suit yourself, but if I don't pack, then you don't find any of my surprises!

'And you won't find any of mine,' Carl thought.

Now THERE was definitely a benefit. When Jenny packed, Carl always found some type of "I love you" surprise hidden away in his suitcase. Those were always nice. It was the kind of thing that made a guy always want to return home. But this time it couldn't be helped. Carl needed some special weapons and equipment that Jenny couldn't know about or see, so he had to take care of the packing himself. He needed to make sure that the items made it to the secret compartment of his luggage. Hopefully, this new suitcase that the company bought would live up to its reputation, and he wouldn't be detained because of what the scanners revealed. There would not be a problem clearing him if that did happen, but it was always nice not to have to go that route.

As Carl stood in the check-in line, he still remembered, and could still feel, the lingering kiss and the affectionate, long, tight hug his wife had given him before he departed. She seemed to be really worried this time. Carl wondered for a moment if she knew what it was he actually did. No, he decided. There was no way.

Carl kept his laptop and an overnight bag as carry-ons. He watched his larger suitcase travel down the conveyor belt. First it was headed for a security scan, and then it would be redirected to his flight to be placed into the cargo hold. Security was so much tighter than it used to be in the days of yester year. Carl's dad used to tell him about a time when the entire family could accompany a passenger to the departure gate and watch them leave. Now you were lucky if they let you near the first entrance gate. The events of 9-11 had changed everything. Not just for the transportation industry, but for the entire world.

Terrorism and other threats had really turned the world into a place that was not so safe anymore. Of course, it was terrorism and other threats that also kept Carl in a job. The stories that Carl's father used to tell him were of a world where the grass was greener, the sky was bluer, and the smiles were always bright. It was not a world where people lived in fear of so many things that could happen.

While Reardon was truly his last name, his first and middle names were Xavier Montgomery. Xavier Montgomery Reardon, what a moniker! Carl was teased to no end when he was younger, but he suffered through it. By the time he met Jenny, he simply went by Carl. While it was his agent codename, it also was his real first name. What better way to hide his identity than in plain sight? Carl looked up the statistics and found that his codename was actually ranked as the 92nd most popular "given" name in the United States. At the time he looked it up, that would have averaged to slightly less than 300,000 Americans with the first name Carl.

Carl came from a long line of spies. He did not know that about his lineage until he had already become an agent. The name Xavier Montgomery just didn't cut it for a CIA agent. Carl picked the same codename that was used by the rest of his family line. When Grandpa, the very first Xavier Montgomery Reardon, had picked out his codename, it was so good that his dad, Xavier Montgomery, Jr., who followed in Grandpa's footsteps, decided that he would use it too. Now, also not wanting to walk around being tagged with the name Xavier, and carrying on in 'the family business,' he too used his CIA codename, Carl, as his first name. This was the way that it was with most CIA agents; they just went by their codenames. Carl's Grandfather was crafty and wanted a codename that meant something. As he thought about the fact that he went to the coal mines to work every day, but he was a CIA Agent in Real Life, he wanted a codename that would remind him of that. So, he took the C from CIA, the A from agent, the R from real and L from life, and that's how he developed his codename.

It worked for Gramps.

It worked for Dad.

Now it worked for him.

If someday he had a son, presumably Xavier Montgomery IV, if Jenny was in agreement, and he also decided to go into "the family business," it would work for him too. Jenny didn't truly understand why he went by the name Carl. To her it just seemed like a nickname, and she was happy to go along with it.

As he made his way over to his seat by the gate, Carl kept a close watch out for people who looked out of the ordinary. People all looked so strange these days that it was becoming harder and harder to pick out the anomalous ones. Carl didn't think anything of the man with the curly red hair, dressed in a trench coat and hat, who sat reading the newspaper. Lawrence Blackwell decided that he had to have some kind of disguise since Carl already knew what he looked like. It would not do to be discovered before they even left the airport. He took his newspaper and sat directly across from Carl. From this vantage point, Lawrence could see everything that went on behind Carl and all the entrances and exits. He did not have to worry about anything behind him because the way his row of chairs was situated, he was up against a wall. Having examined Carl's profile, he knew that Carl would not consider him as much of a threat since he was pretty much out in the open and not trying to hide himself.

The threat level in a crowded airport was definitely going to be high, so while Carl could sit and relax, Lawrence, dressed up in his imposter garb, was watching everything with an eagle eye, making sure that his charge was safe. Lawrence kept glancing that way and this way, and this way and that. He did it systematically so that no one could tell that he was looking and so that it looked only like he periodically looked up from his newspaper as he read.

That's when he saw him.

All the way on the far end of the concourse there was a man whose gaze never left Carl, and he headed toward him with a purpose. Lawrence was not 100% sure what that purpose was, but if his educated guess was right, then he had better make sure the man never got close enough to carry out his intended actions.

Lawrence had to think quickly. It was far too crowded to make a big scene, so he had to neutralize the threat without attracting too much attention. Lawrence had just the thing. A delayed reaction sleeping gas that could be sprayed at close range as long as Lawrence first sprayed himself with the counter agent. Stopping momentarily at the mirror, Lawrence sprayed himself with the counter agent, but it looked very much like he was spraying his hair to keep it in place. Now, he himself was moving with a purpose; Lawrence made a beeline for the would-be assailant. This business was sometimes a tricky one, and Lawrence just had to gamble that he was right. With one hand raised as he walked by, Lawrence sprayed the sleeping agent into the assailant's face. He then spun around with his hand on his gun just in case he needed to take any additional action. It was always good to have a plan B.

The assailant kept moving toward Carl and did not seem to slow. He seemed even more purposeful in getting to his target. As he approached Carl, the assailant drew his weapon, but just as he pulled the sawed-off shotgun, the delayed reaction gas took effect, and the assailant fell to the ground. The sawed-off shotgun hit the floor first, clattering about very loudly and causing a major disturbance. Carl looked up and saw what had gone down. His eyes immediately darted to the red headed man in the trench coat who had now somehow managed to mask his face. Lawrence could see that Carl had made the connection as he nodded his thanks. Carl gave a semi salute with the index and middle finger of his right hand sweeping over his right eyebrow and was off to the bathroom, avoiding the ensuing commotion and airport security, which had been called to the scene to secure the gun and the suspect.

It was time for a new disguise.

'They are trying to get to me before I even leave the country. Somebody doesn't want me to succeed. Now the question is: Why? Even more so, I guess the real question is: Who was that masked man?' Carl thought. 'Nice to know somebody has my back.'

Lawrence was ready for this. Once one disguise had been compromised, it was time to use another. He had done this so many times that Lawrence already had the next several disguises planned. He emerged quickly from the bathroom, now dressed as a male flight attendant wearing an undetectable flesh tone mask to disguise his true appearance. This would get him onto the plane, and he would be able to keep his eye on Carl. The airline had already been alerted to expect him as a new crew member.

The rest of the trip was uneventful. Well, that is until they arrived in Estonia.

Carl navigated his way through the crowded Lennart Meri Tallin airport. He was heading for baggage claim to get his suitcase. If Carl was not mistaken, it appeared as though he was being followed by the male flight attendant from his flight. Carl remembered seeing him on the plane and just nodded a greeting to the flight attendant, which the flight attendant returned. Carl had a funny feeling that he knew this man, but the features just weren't right, and he couldn't place him. He decided that he might just be being too paranoid. Any good spy worth his salt was paranoid more often than not. The alternative was that you would end up dead. After doing the customary analysis of the situation in his mind, Carl dismissed the notion that the flight attendant might be a threat. He just let it go for now.

As they waited in line for their bags together, Carl noticed three men closing in. They had the unmistakable look and mannerisms of the Russian mafia. This was not good. Carl could, of course, dispatch them, but he did not want any innocent bystanders to be hurt in the process. He had to come up with a plan. Looking at where he was and what he had to deal with only confirmed for Carl that this was going to be hard without somebody getting hurt.

Lawrence Blackwell, still dressed as the male flight attendant, had also picked up on this activity. He too had come to the same conclusion as Carl did, but he had a plan that he thought would work. It was actually going to be two against three. To Lawrence, the odds would be even. Lawrence was already feeling sorry for the other guys.

Lawrence tapped Carl on the shoulder and, disguising his voice, said, "Don't look now, but I don't think these three guys who are approaching are members of the new Estonian hospitality team. They look like they kind of mean business, if you know what I'm saying."

"You're a flight attendant and you noticed that?" asked Carl. "Interestingly keen instincts for a flight attendant."

"Counter Terrorism class. Mandatory," said Lawrence.

"Right," Carl replied in a somewhat sarcastic tone. There was really no time to discuss it now. "Did they teach you how to fight too?"

"Well, THEY didn't, but I know a thing or two and can hold my own. I was just thinking..." said Lawrence, "if you could take care of that mean-looking dude coming your way, I think I can handle the two not-so-mean-looking dudes on my side. The two of them are about the same size as one of him."

"Are you sure you can handle two?" Carl asked with a concerned tone.

"Look, I have a thing or two up my sleeve. Should be a cakewalk. You think you can handle that other guy?"

"HA! There's a lot you don't know about me," said Carl, "and I can't even begin to tell you about it. When I'm done with my guy, I'll come help you out."

'I know more than you think, my friend.' Lawrence thought to himself, but out loud he said, "If all goes well, I'm pretty sure that won't be necessary."

Intent on the task at hand, and vividly aware that he was in a foreign country that still acted very communist, Carl quickly considered his options and got his mind set on the job at hand.

Carl's guy was on him in a matter of seconds. Carl had no idea where the weapons came from or even what they were. All he knew was that he saw a shimmer or a gleam that was not there before, and the reflection indicated that it was sharp and coming his way fast.

Carl was totally defensive.

Carl moved his carry-on into position to block the oncoming blow and could hear the slash as whatever it was ripped into his bag.

"Great," Carl muttered under his breath, "now I have to buy a new carry-on. This is getting to be really annoying." Right at that moment, Carl could feel his assailant pull his weapon back to prepare for another attack. Not having too many options, Carl ripped at the lining of his carry-on, and a shielded compartment fell open revealing a knife and a .45 automatic with a silencer attached. Carl grabbed the .45 and fired. The man dropped as he was in the middle arc of his swing for his second attack.

"Is he dead?" Carl heard someone ask in fluent Estonian. "I didn't even hear a shot. You killed him?" All of the activity had now attracted a crowd of curious travelers.

"No, he's not dead, but he'll sleep for a while," Carl responded back in Estonian.

The .45 was specially equipped with tranquilizer shells. Essentially, mini tranquilizer darts. Killing someone in a foreign country with no help and lots of witnesses around was a problem that would involve way too much red tape. Putting them to sleep, on the other hand, would not incur any criminal charges and would give the agent enough time to get away.

As the two men approached Lawrence, his first thought was that he needed to even the odds. The first guy was pretty heavy, and he was coming at Lawrence with a lot of momentum. Lawrence used the forward momentum and the force of the side kick that he threw to increase the blow that he delivered, and the big guy dropped like a brick.

Unable to recover in time, Lawrence felt a blow hit him as the second guy delivered his first hit, scoring a bullseye on the right side of Lawrence's face and knocking him to the ground. Being the good agent and capable martial artist that he was, Lawrence did not fall with a thud to the ground. With startling speed, he rolled and maneuvered himself back up into a standing position. Lawrence jumped up and delivered a deadly double kick, timed just right. The first kick knocked the attacker's head back, and as it sprang forward again the second time, Lawrence delivered another blow to the now relaxed muscle, which caused a more rigorous snap back.

Lawrence was sure that he heard something snap, but was certain that he did not kill his attacker.

Good thing.

That was not what he needed right now.

As Carl spun around to take aim at Lawrence's attackers, he was shocked and amazed to find that they had already been dispatched. Carl didn't know who this guy was, but one thing was certain, he was more than a flight attendant with counter-terrorism training.

Both men knew the drill. They needed to get their stuff and get out of there before the police and airport security arrived. Neither of them could afford to be detained for questioning.

Carl re-assembled his carry-on. Both he and Lawrence grabbed their luggage and made their way through the crowds, passing the police as they were heading toward the scene. The men got in line to get cleared through customs and then went their separate ways as they left the airport without saying another word to each other. The fact that the attackers were likely Russian mafia was going to be enough to hold the Estonian Eesti Politsei for a while.

Carl had a car waiting and immediately slipped into it and pulled away.

Lawrence had a car waiting as well and fell in behind Carl.

He obviously was going to have his hands full keeping an eye on Carl. He knew there would be a breather, because there was no possible way that whoever was after Carl could know his next move after leaving the airport. The next attempt would have to be planned after they located Carl and knew what they had to work with. They would probably now assume that Carl was not traveling alone and have to totally rework their original plans.

CHAPTER 10

Carl had some work to do in order to get to the compound where CIA sources believed that the American ambassador and Colonel Welch were being held. When Carl arrived, he cased the compound and discovered that getting inside was not going to be an easy task. That was about what he expected, but he would not have minded being presently surprised. Of course, that's what made his job so much fun. Every case had a new and different unknown challenge.

As Carl was casing the compound, he thought he saw something out of the corner of his eye. Was there somebody watching HIM while he was watching THEM? Well, there was only one way to find out. Carl moved, and the figure he thought he had seen came into view. Whoever it was, they appeared to move with him. To the untrained eye it would have been undetectable.

Carl hid himself behind a beam and watched as whoever it was stealthily tried to get closer, presumably so that they could determine where Carl had gone and what he was doing. As Carl looked closer, he thought his eyes must be deceiving him. Based on what he knew, there was no way in the world that Lawrence Blackwell could be here, in Estonia. Carl had left him in the United States, and that is where he expected him to still be.

Carl was not 100% positive about the ID, but he needed

to find out fast. He pulled out his emergency short wave radio and made a secure satellite connection so that he could call CIA's central dispatch:

"CCD, this is Bird of Prey on the emergency channel. Do you read?"

"Go ahead Bird of Prey. We weren't expecting to hear from you this soon. Is there a problem?"

"CCD, I need to verify the whereabouts of an Eagle One agent."

"One day when you call in, you'll ask for something easy," the dispatcher remarked, "Go, Bird of Prey."

"The agent's name is Lawrence Blackwell. I need to know his whereabouts and his last known assignment."

"Stand by Bird of Prey... We're showing Lawrence Blackwell, codename: Silver Fox, is currently on assignment. Whereabouts: classified. Sorry, but that's the best I can do without higher security clearance access. I can get the Supervisor on call if you really need the info. But 'you know who' is on call right now."

"I'll call back if the need to locate Silver Fox becomes urgent. I think I might have the answer to that one already. Bird of Prey out." Carl turned off the radio to make sure he did not get any unexpected messages at a very inconvenient time and stowed it safely away.

When Carl could not get a definitive answer from dispatch, he knew he would have to speak to the source. If this was Lawrence, then Carl definitely wanted some answers, but he knew that he was not likely to get the answers he wanted.

Carl circled around to make sure that whoever it was would follow him. Carl was not disappointed. His stalker stayed right with him.

Carl saw his opening when he came around to a landscaped area. He hid in the bushes and settled back.

About two minutes later, whoever it was that was following Carl came into the landscaped area and was trying to make his way through the bushes quietly and discreetly when suddenly he heard, in a very hushed tone...

"Greetings Silver Fox."

Lawrence Blackwell stood stock still. He had been discovered, but by whom? He saw Carl slowly rise out of the bushes. Lawrence was poised to pounce and take out whoever the threat might be... or die trying. He was rather relieved to find out that it was Carl. Although Carl could tell that Lawrence recognized him, he could also see that he was trying to feign ignorance.

"How do you know me?" asked Lawrence, a.k.a. Silver Fox.

The two agents had never met face to face, and the times that they had come in contact with each other recently, Lawrence had been disguised. Lawrence was quite confused as to how Carl knew who he was.

"Oh, I think you know the answer to that question," said Carl.

"What do you mean?" Lawrence asked; because he really did NOT know what Carl meant. As a spy you don't offer any information when the question was not clear. If, in fact, you offered any information at all.

"Why don't you start by telling me why you have been following me?"

"Following you? I don't know what you're talking about," said Lawrence, trying, in vain, to keep up the charade. He knew that, for all intents and purposes, his cover was blown.

"Listen, only two types of agents follow other agents. That either makes you a double agent and a spy for a U.S. adversary..."

Carl saw Lawrence's eyebrows raise at the false accusation because if there was any truth to it, protocol dictated that one of these two men would not leave this area alive.

"Or," Carl continued, "you are a member of the elite Eagle One unit. I would be inclined to believe the former unless you can prove to me otherwise," Carl lied. Now he was just yanking Lawrence's chain.

Carl knew that the only way that Lawrence could prove himself was to not divulge any information and to continue to feign ignorance. Any other response and, perhaps, he was not the agent he claimed to be.

Lawrence did not acknowledge Carl's accusations one way or the other, but stood ready should Carl feel he needed to fight him. Lawrence's Primary Objective was to protect Carl, so no matter what happened, he could not kill Carl—although Carl might be trying to kill him—except to save his own life. He was surely hoping that it would not come to that.

After a few minutes of the silent standoff, Lawrence was quite relieved to hear Carl say, "So, you ARE Eagle One! Just what I thought."

"And just how did you make that determination?" asked Lawrence, still not admitting anything.

"You know who I am, I suppose, since you're following me. So, it would stand to reason that you know that I know all about your training. If you were a cowardly double agent, who I would have had to take out, you would have been making all sorts of denials left and right about one claim or the other. A true Eagle One agent would not make any claim one way or the other, but would stand ready to fight, just in case. I could tell from your stance that you had no intention to kill, just to neutralize. Therefore, you must be under orders to protect me. Killing me would not accomplish the primary mission objective."

Lawrence just shook his head and had to smile. "They told me you were the best, but I took the challenge. Man, you're good. But I still can't tell you anything."

"Yeah, that's what I figured. I have a mission to complete. Guess we'll be seeing each other around a lot," said Carl.

"Not if I do my job better," said Lawrence. "You want to tell me how you spotted me?"

"Well, it was more a matter of too many coincidences," said Carl. "The fact that the Russians were trying to kill me, and your job was to protect me did not help you any. I'm pretty sure I know you also as a red head in an overcoat and as a male flight attendant too. You did your job, but they forced you to do it in the open. I'm sure when you can work behind the scenes, you will be much more successful."

"Guilty as charged. I still have a disguise or two left that just may fool you. But I should know better than to try to trick the best of the best."

"Is that what they're calling me these days?"

"Yep. And you pretty much deserve it. Well, I think we both better get out of here before we get caught," said Lawrence.

"See you around," said Carl.

"Count on it, dude. I'll be on you like white on rice, but hopefully I'll be, at least, a little less detectable," said Lawrence.

"It's nice to know that someone who is as capable as you has my back. However, if I do my job right, I won't need to count on you always being there," Carl said as they parted ways.

Carl stayed around and cased the place for a while longer. He was sure that as long as he was still there, Lawrence was there somewhere too, but he could not really let that concern him for the moment. After observing the routine operations for a while, Carl began formulating his plan. He thought for sure that he had a way in. To confirm consistent timing, he would have to return and do this at the same time tomorrow.

Oh, how Carl loved it when things were simple. He was now in somewhat of a quandary. That quandary had to do with his Primary Objective; it was no longer a constant. The Primary Objective of the current mission was to find and rescue the Ambassador and the Colonel. However, when he was not on a mission, his Primary Objective was to keep Lawrence Blackwell safe. Now Lawrence Blackwell had interjected himself into his current mission, and this was a problem. Carl had never had to deal with a Primary Objective conflict before.

Carl had now confirmed that Lawrence's Primary Objective

was to keep him safe. Lawrence, who, according to Viper, was supposedly still under protection while Carl was on this assignment, seemed to have been sent on a mission as well. If Lawrence was here, then who was protecting him? Carl had to find some way to protect Lawrence as well.

Never a dull moment. There were too many opportunities for things that could go wrong. Carl would have to adhere to the President's stated list of priorities.

With his work on the mission objective having been completed for the day, Carl turned his energies and thoughts toward how he could incorporate protecting Lawrence into his current mission. He began to wonder how he was going to track him down, and then quickly remembered that Lawrence seemed to be following him. Tracking him down would be easy. Carl just needed to keep an eye out.

When Carl got back to his hotel, he had just missed the elevator. He waited for the next one. Several hotel guests stepped into the elevator. It was already occupied by what appeared to be one of the hotel maintenance men. Carl pressed the button for the seventh floor and the maintenance worker hit eight right after. There was something wrong with this guy, but Carl could not place it right away. Then it hit him. He was carrying a bucket and mop, and the hotel was completely carpeted. This was a ritzy hotel. Even the bathrooms were carpeted with thick shag carpet. Not quite sanitary if you thought about it long enough, but the rich got what the rich wanted. A bucket and mop might have been necessary in the kitchen downstairs, but in one of the upstairs rooms, well, that was definitely out of place.

Carl noted the height and weight. Even though the face did not match, the height and weight fit. He smiled to himself. When the elevator reached seven, before getting off he said, "Have a good evening, Silver Fox. Oh, and by the way, a bucket and mop in a hotel where the rooms are 100% carpeted is probably not the best accessory for your disguise."

Lawrence just shook his head and said, "Now I know why they say you're the best." He hung his head in shame at his rookie mistake.

Carl never made it to his room; he went right to the stairwell and then up two floors. As he stood on the ninth-floor landing, he saw Lawrence, still in his maintenance man garb, come into the stairwell on the eighth-floor. Of course, he was going to continue his surveillance; that seemed to be what his job was at the moment.

As quick as lightning, three men came into the stairwell behind Lawrence and threw him up against the stairwell wall. Lawrence was temporarily dazed. The men took a blindfold and covered his eyes with it, all the while glancing around to see if there was anyone else looking or coming. Satisfied that no one else was coming, the one who appeared to be the leader, who wasn't saying much, said, "Let's take him back to the room."

"What is the meaning of this?" Lawrence asked. "I think you gentlemen have the wrong man. I'm not sure what you want with me."

"Quiet! We have the right guy. You may not look the same, but we have observed you changing faces. Nice work by the way. Once we get rid of you, I think I'm going to go and acquire your supplies. I could use a makeup kit like that for some of the jobs that I do. Besides, you won't be needing it anymore."

"Look, you want the makeup kit? It's yours. But I don't think I'm the guy you want," said Lawrence, as he tried to buy himself some time to think of a way out of this predicament.

"Listen guy," said the leader. "I don't know who you are. All I know is the Bossman says you keep getting in the way every time they try knock off some Carl guy. Whoever THAT is. We were told to knock you off so that they could knock the other guy off. Whatever. That's more information than you needed to know, but you won't have anyone to tell it to. We'll see to that."

Carl could not believe what he was hearing. 'Just how many attempts on his life had there been since they left the States? And Lawrence, aka Silver Fox, thwarted them all? And the guy calls ME good?' Carl thought to himself.

"OK, off with you!" said the ringleader.

They took Lawrence, forcefully, back onto the eighth floor. Carl quietly made his way down the stairs one flight to the eighth floor. He managed to get out into the hall and hide in a recessed area before the stairwell door closed. Thank goodness for 100% carpeting. He didn't have to worry about his footsteps making any detectable noise.

Carl watched as the men went down the hall. Six doors on the left. They used their hotel key card to gain access and forced Lawrence into the room with them. One of the nice things that Carl liked about this hotel was that the doors to the suites opened into a foyer area, separate and apart from the room. As Carl was developing his plan on the fly, he realized that something like that could prove to be very helpful.

Carl reached into his pocket and pulled out a keycard. He was very thankful that he had stayed around and waited for the maid and used his magnetic tape duplicating device to make an imprint of her card. He thought it might come in handy at some point. She never even noticed that he had picked her pocket. Carl returned it to her using the excuse that he thought she might have dropped it.

Carl had to wait to be safe, but he did not want to wait too long. He put the card into the lock, hoping that they did not engage the deadbolt. Criminals of this type usually didn't think about such things because they were packing heat. Who needed a deadbolt? He was right. A very hushed click could be heard at the door as the green light flashed on the security card indicator outside.

Carl let himself in, slowly. The party had advanced beyond the foyer, and no one was paying attention to the door. Carl closed the door quietly. He listened to see where the occupants were currently located. All indications were that everyone appeared to be in the master suite.

Carl squirreled around to the master suite, where he saw that they had Lawrence standing on his heels. His arms were tied to the top ends of a four-poster bed, and his feet were spread-eagled and tied to the bottom of the posts. This is the guy who had been dispatching all of HIS threats? Something must have thrown him off of his game. Just then, Carl realized it was not something—it was SOMEONE. He was the someone.

"Now," said the leader, "I want some information. You see, I get paid lots of money if I bring in information instead of just killing you guys."

"You won't make any money off of me. And by the way, your breath stinks. Got a mint?" Lawrence asked. "I suggest Altoids. I hear they're curiously strong."

The leader got right up to Lawrence's face as he slowly breathed out the words "NO... I... DON'T... GOT A MINT!"

"What a shame." said Lawrence. "You'll probably kill your friends. But that's OK, actually, killing them evens the odds. That will help me immensely."

The two other men had to chuckle at this. Carl thought it was funny too, but his laugh would have to wait.

The leader said, "Open his shirt, boys, time for some carving practice. You'll be begging me to let you tell me everything you know by the time I'm done. And I seriously doubt you'll care about my breath."

At that point, Lawrence heard an unexpected commotion. With the blindfold on, he was unable to see and was struggling to let his other senses compensate. The only thing that he could tell was that things were happening fast.

"Hey, who are you?" Lawrence heard one of the other men ask. The question was never answered as the speaker was abruptly silenced.

What Lawrence missed and couldn't see was that Carl had joined the 'party.'

Having stealthily made his way to just outside the main bedroom, Carl had reached down and pulled a knife from where it was strapped to his ankle. As Carl rounded the corner, the ringleader had his knife out in preparation to begin making custom modifications to Lawrence's chest.

When he saw Carl, the ringleader quickly threw the knife in Carl's direction. Needless to say, knife-throwing should never be listed on his resume.

He missed by a mile.

Carl reciprocated.

Carl aimed and got poised to throw his knife. Knowing that the man would try to dodge him, Carl led his target and released his knife with an adjusted trajectory. The knife sank right into the man's heart. He hit the floor with a thud. He would not be getting up again. Ever. Although everything happened so quickly, for Lawrence, who could not see, it seemed to take a lot longer. It was almost as though the events were happening in slow motion.

One of the other thugs, now in shock, said, "Hey, who are you?"

"Room Service!" Carl responded sarcastically.

Carl began to wail on the other men, who were in such shock that they were moving slower than molasses in Vermont on a cold January morning. Carl took aim at his favorite incapacitating target on both men, the groin area. He landed a blow on each man with a power punch. They were hurting puppies. But one man recovered much, much quicker than Carl had anticipated. He caught Carl by surprise and swept his feet out from under him.

Carl fell down on his back, trying to recover. The big man picked Carl up in his paw-like hands, spun him around, and was getting ready to slam him up against the wall. Unfortunately for him, his buddy had picked up a wooden baton and did not anticipate that his friend was going to spin around. He was in mid-swing and unable to stop himself. Having swung the heavy baton with all of his might, hitting his friend square on the back of his head. The impact of the baton against the man's head made a very audible cracking sound.

The Big man immediately let Carl go and fell to the ground, limp, motionless and bleeding.

Carl did not lose any time at all, especially after seeing what that baton could do. Carl's feet went into a series of three powerful kicks, knocking the third man against the wall, appearing to make him somewhat delirious. Carl let up on his attack and the man, who had been faking his delirious state, brought his hands up with the baton again, ready to swing at Carl.

Carl was ready for him and threw a volley of punches at the man's face, chest, and stomach. Each one landed solidly. The man seemed to be delirious again, but Carl wasn't taking any chances. He kept up his relentless attack until, first; he drew blood from the man's nose, then mouth and finally, overcome by the assault, the man slumped against the wall and slid down unconscious; the baton dropping from his hand.

Just to be certain, Carl took the baton and threw it across to the other side of the room.

Carl was tired, but they had to get out of there. Once again, neither agent could be found in this mess, especially with two of the assailants surely dead and the third very close.

Carl got his knife out of the body of the ringleader and cleaned the blood off using the man's shirt. Then he used the sharp edges of the knife to cut the blindfold. Lawrence saw who it was and said, "Man, am I ever glad to see you."

"I told you that you would be. I just didn't know that it was going to be this soon."

Lawrence looked around and said, "Room service, huh? Man, that's what I call room service! I'll make sure I leave a decent tip."

Carl and Lawrence policed the room and retrieved anything that might be connected with them in any way. These assailants had files, surveillance photographs of Lawrence, and other information that had to be removed. Then they wiped down everything that they might have touched so as to remove any fingerprints or other obvious traces of their ever having been present.

Just like that, they were gone.

They went down one flight and settled into Carl's posh living quarters. Carl sat down, exhausted. Lawrence sat down in the chair opposite him, also exhausted. His disguise was not doing him any good anymore, so he began to peel off the makeup and mask. In no time at all, he was looking like the Lawrence that Carl was familiar with, except for the fact that he badly needed to have his face washed.

"I ache all over," said Carl.

"You're not kidding!" said Lawrence. "Me too. We're getting too old for this stuff."

"Nonsense," Carl said, even though he ached just as much as Lawrence did. "Look, I know you can't tell me what your Primary Objective is, but if you're going to be around anyway, I sure could use some help with mine."

"Carl Reardon needs help?" asked Lawrence, unable to believe what he was hearing.

"NEED is definitely too strong of a word. But if you're up to rescuing an Air Force Colonel who has been an un-publicized POW for years and an American ambassador who has been a prisoner for only days, I wouldn't mind a little assistance.

"Oh, is that all," said Lawrence. "Did you just read me in?"

"Well, I guess I did. But you don't appear too interested,"

Carl said mockingly. He could see the obvious excitement on Lawrence's face.

"Are you kidding?" Lawrence said with a sly grin. "Count me in! No way you get to have all the fun."

CHAPTER 11

President Young sat behind his impressive desk in the Oval Office, working on his secure computer, when he noticed the indicator begin to flash, alerting him that there was an important, incoming, top priority, encoded message ready to be retrieved.

The President executed the necessary keystrokes that caused the passcode box to display, centered in an image of the seal of the President of the United States on his screen. This was a procedure that President Young did not like to have to perform too often. Any news communicated in this manner, as opposed to the normal secure channels, was usually not good news.

The passcode changed daily, so it was a challenge to remember. The President was given the code at his daily morning briefings. For the sake of maximum security, the passcode was not even generated until just before it needed to be communicated. Searching his memory, the President entered today's passcode.

After the passcode that he entered was accepted, the President placed his palm on the scanner to verify his identity and complete the biometric multi-factor authentication process. An alternating red and green laser slid up and down the inside of the palm-scanning device to read the identity of the palm that had just come to rest on the glass. The President's palm scan was positively recognized. The securely encoded message was decrypted and displayed on the screen. When the President saw the first word on the screen, it immediately caused him to freeze. Instead of being addressed to President Young, this message was addressed to Viper.

This could not be good.

That could only mean one thing. There was a problem with a covert field operation. The only field operation that the President currently had running was the one that he had just sent Carl Reardon on.

As President Young read the communique, his blood ran cold. He had, unknowingly, sent his man into a trap, and he had no way of contacting him at the moment. Carl's last communication with Viper had been that morning. This was customary when certain parts of the mission were about to begin. Radio silence would be maintained until the agent was clear—whether he had completed the mission or not. Carl had yet to send the "all clear."

The communique indicated that there was solid evidence to prove that the American Ambassador to Estonia had been working for the Russians. All indications were that he had been on their payroll for some time. The Ambassador had been so careful, and the Russians had been so crafty, that this one slipped by. Consequently, U.S. Intelligence had been late in reporting this. Now Carl had gone in with misinformation and was significantly disadvantaged. Much worse than that, the President knew that Lawrence Blackwell was also there, backing up Carl (supposedly without Carl's knowledge). President Young had been informed, just hours ago, that Blackwell's cover had been blown and that Carl was onto him. That meant that President Young now had his two best agents in danger, with the U.S. Ambassador having turned into a double agent.

He had been played!

It would now seem that this whole thing had been staged because they were sure that Viper was going to send in a man to get Col. Welch and the Ambassador out. They had determined, with a high amount of certainty, that the "go to man" was going to be Carl. Well, it had often been said that Carl had more lives than a cat. He had certainly gotten out of his fair share of jams. From the reports that the President had read, he didn't know how Carl had managed to get out of some of those situations, but all that mattered was that he did. The vast majority of Carl's successes were without the help of an Eagle One assisted operative.

President Young was going to have to chance an emergency override. He had no idea where Carl might be and in what capacity, but he was going to have to take the risk of letting him know about the Ambassador; otherwise, the only way Carl was sure to come back to the U.S. would be in a body bag. Most of the time, agents under these types of situations and with similar circumstances were never seen or heard from again. But when the other side took out one of your top agents, they wanted it to be publicly known so that they could claim bragging rights. Concrete proof would have to be sent for all the world to know and believe. President Young knew this all too well. As Viper, he had taken out five such agents and arranged for the transport to their various countries. He didn't want Carl or Lawrence, or both, to come home in a body bag. The only question now, to which the President did not currently have an answer, was: What was he going to do?

Carl and Lawrence, both agents who did their best work alone, were putting their heads together on this mission now. They had determined, based on activity, that night was going to be the best time to enter the compound where the captives were being held. Staffing was lower, and the chances of being otherwise detected, especially now that there was an extra person involved in executing the extraction plan, would be exponentially much lower.

Carl told Lawrence about his plan to get inside via the regularly scheduled delivery truck. Now they had to figure out how to best modify that plan so that it would accommodate getting both of them inside. The bed of the truck was long enough that it might be able to easily accommodate the change. They had worked out the logistics. They were now ready to put the new plan into action.

Just before nightfall, the two agents made their way out to the Russian-controlled compound and camped out in the hills. They kept an eye out for patrols, but it seemed that the Russians were so confident about their location and facility that some of the normal protocols were not being followed. Carl loved it when the enemy got cocky and complacent. It made his job so much easier.

Checking their watches, both Carl and Lawrence agreed that it was time to get into position. The delivery truck should arrive soon.

The expected delivery truck was right on schedule.

When the truck approached the gate, Carl and Lawrence drew near from opposite sides. They both quickly maneuvered their way under the truck and held on for dear life, as the truck was cleared by security and roared through the gate. When the truck came to a stop, both agents held on as the driver got out and began talking with someone on the loading dock. It was clear that both agents would have to exit on Carl's side of the truck since the driver and guards decided to stand on Lawrence's side and smoke cigarettes while they shared the latest gossip in Russian. Their accents were very thick, but Lawrence could make out something related to an anticipated visit from the region's Lieutenant General.

Carl motioned to Lawrence that he was going to lower himself down and make sure the coast was clear on his side. Lawrence nodded his understanding and agreement. As Carl lowered himself and began to roll out, someone exited from the side door of the building. Carl quickly rolled back under the truck as he kept his eye on the newcomer. Whoever it was, they were obviously waiting for something or somebody, and they were very impatient. After less than a minute, a few huffs and a puff, he went back inside. Carl and Lawrence quickly exited on that side of the truck and rolled out of sight... and not a moment too soon. The driver got back into his seat, started up the engine and roared off out the gate, leaving the way the truck had come in.

Carl and Lawrence looked at each other quizzically. Nothing had been taken off or loaded onto the truck. Perhaps the driver was just there to deliver information. Whatever the case was, he still served as an adequate method for them to gain access to the compound.

Lawrence and Carl slipped into the side door of the building. The lighting was dim, but, after their eyes adjusted, they could make out each other in their dark clothing easily enough. Using hand signals to communicate with each other, Carl informed Lawrence that they should stay together for now, until they were certain of the separate paths that they were going to eventually have to take. Before they arrived, they had already determined that Carl would go for the Colonel and Lawrence would go for the Ambassador, once they knew with reasonable certainty how to proceed.

As if prompted, two men came talking rather loudly down the corridor. Carl and Lawrence listened very intently to their conversation. The subject of their conversation just happened to be the two prisoners that Carl and Lawrence were looking for. As the men continued to walk down the hall toward them, they proceeded to give Carl and Lawrence enough information to know where each of the prisoners was staying. Both were in the maximum-security section. They now knew that the Colonel was being held two floors below the Ambassador. Again, using hand signals, the two men decided to go for the Colonel first and then split up after reaching him. With both men agreeing to the plan, they proceeded. Using the information that they had just gathered from the overly boisterous and loquacious men in the hall, they were quickly able to locate the Colonel's holding cell. Lawrence gave the "hi" sign to let Carl know that he was going to find the Ambassador so that he could accomplish his part of the mission objective.

Carl watched Lawrence disappear down the hallway, opposite from the direction in which they entered. When Lawrence was no longer in view, Carl went to work. He examined the door to determine what needed to be done to gain entrance. The door was composed of heavy metal with two very solid deadbolt locks. Carl looked into his pack and found just what he needed: two tightly packed implosion devices. These would blow the locks off the doors but keep the noise to a whisper while they did the job; at least that's what the Tech Boys told him would happen.

Carl set the devices on the door and activated the detonation sequence. Ten seconds later, both locks opened with a silent pop. Carl was amazed at the technology of the day, but also very happy about it at the same time. He crept into the room where he could see the body of Col. Welch on the cot.

"Col.? Col. Welch? Are you OK?" asked Carl, shaking the body lightly.

"I'm fine. Who are you?" asked the Col. gruffly. "I haven't heard that voice before."

"Col., I've come to get you out of here," said Carl.

"Not so fast, son," said the Col. "I have a prearranged pass phrase that you need to know before I move anywhere with you. I know that it has been eleven long years. But I don't budge one inch with anyone who does not know it. Now—"

"Listen, Col. We don't have a lot of time. The square root of 531,441 is 729."

"What?" said Col. Welch. These were the words that he had been waiting to hear for a very long time, but he needed confirmation.

"I said the square root of 531,441 is 729."

"Oh my. Praise God. Praise God! You don't know how many times I have had false hopes. They've tried to lure me out of here, presumably to my death, so many times, but nobody has known the pass phrase. That can only mean one thing. Viper sent you. He's still alive."

"That's correct, Col. We can talk later. For now, I have to ask you to be quiet. We need to meet with another agent and then get you out of here. It's time you stepped on U.S. soil again, Sir. Are you in good health? Can you walk and run if necessary?"

"Son, you get me outside of that cell door and you'll have to do your best to keep up with me." Said Col. Welch.

Just then, Carl felt something that he hoped he would never have to while he was on a mission. The vibration in his pack indicated that a mission override order had been given, and radio silence was about to be broken.

"Is this area secure?" Carl whispered. "Can anyone hear us down here? I have an incoming radio transmission."

"We should be OK; they leave me alone down here, failing miserably at trying to drive me insane. Hasn't worked for eleven years, but they sure were getting close. No cameras, no listening devices," said the Col.

Carl took the radio out of his bag and prepared to receive the transmission.

"Bird of Prey, this is Viper. Do you read? Over."

"Viper, this is Bird of Prey. I'm with the Col. He is secure. Need to rendezvous with Silver Fox and flee with the Ambassador."

"Negative, Bird of Prey, the Ambassador has done a 180. He's working for the Russians. You and Silver Fox grab the full bird and flee! Sending in another agent to take out the ambassador before he can give away anything else. I have no idea what information he has divulged so far. Nothing further. Viper out."

The communication went dead. Long communications were not permitted because of the risk of being picked up and traced. Now that the orders had been given, there was no reason to keep the channel open.

There was no need for discussion.

"The Ambassador has been in the Russian's hip pocket for four years now, as far as I can tell. If you have somebody trying to rescue him, he's in trouble, and we need to get to them now," said the Col.

Without waiting to discuss it, Carl put his finger to his lips and pointed toward the door, indicating that the Colonel should follow him. They were both in stealth mode now. They slowly padded toward the steps where the lighting was slightly improved. As they went up two flights and turned the corner, both men stopped abruptly.

They were too late.

Down the hall stood two burly men holding Lawrence pinned up against the wall with his feet dangling in midair. The American Ambassador stood with them. All three had their backs to Carl and the Colonel. Lawrence could see them. He quickly averted his gaze so as not to draw attention to them.

Carl and Col. Welch immediately took up a defensive posture as the door just outside of the stairwell opened. Whoever had just come out did not venture in their direction. This gave Lawrence an opportunity to look in Carl's direction undetected. Using his eyes to execute a series of long and short blinks, Lawrence was able to convey a message in Morse code:

"Take the bird and run. Must complete Primary Objective. Godspeed."

Carl knew he could not tackle the four men, get Lawrence out alive and rescue the Colonel—the Primary Objective. His training—as did Lawrence's suggestion—told him that he MUST complete the Primary Objective. Carl wanted to tell Lawrence that he would be back, but he did not want to give him any false hope. There was no telling what the brass would decide.

Although it pained him to do so, Carl took the Colonel, his prize and main objective, and went back the way they came. Progress was slow at first because the American Ambassador must have been aware of Carl's presence. They were being hunted, but no one knew their location. Tensions increased when the Colonel was discovered to be missing.

Carl and the Colonel eventually made their way out of the compound safely, leaving Lawrence behind. The entire time Carl was thinking that THIS and only THIS was why he liked to work alone. The only person he ever wanted to have to be responsible for on a mission was himself.

Carl did not know how he was going to do it, but he purposed in his heart that if God gave him the opportunity or helped him to find the way, he would be back. Leaving a man in enemy territory was just not his style. Leaving one to save one was not an acceptable option.

Carl did exactly as his training dictated. The Primary Objective was achieved at all costs. Somebody needed to recognize when the cost was just too high.

CHAPTER 12

As Carl sat on the military transport, distraught and at his wits' end, Col. Welch came over to talk to him. Even knowing that he was likely the last person Carl would want to talk to, the Colonel knew that somebody needed to talk to Carl, and he seemed to be the chosen one.

"Hey, Reardon," said the Colonel.

"Colonel," said Carl soberly, without even looking up.

"Listen, I realize that I am to blame for you having to leave your partner back there, but you know the rules. You have to complete the Primary Objective. I suggest that you concentrate on the Primary Objective that you have been assigned when you are not on a mission," said the Colonel, hoping to offer a glimmer of hope.

"Well, Colonel, that's just it," said Carl. "You see, I didn't know the man we left behind very well. We've never worked together before this mission."

"I don't understand. In fact, I'm downright confused now. You're acting like you lost your best friend. Well, no matter, like I said, your non-mission Primary Objective will be helpful in getting you through this," said the Col., trying to speak from experience.

"Colonel Welch, you just don't get it because you don't know. The man we left behind doesn't even know it, but HE is my non-mission Primary Objective. I've been ordered to protect him at all costs. Now do you see my problem? I had to choose between Primary Objectives."

"Get out of here. You just made that up!" said the Colonel. But he could see from the look on Carl's face that he did not make up anything that he was saying. This man was telling the truth. The Colonel let out a loud whistle and said, "Now that's a dilemma if I ever heard one."

Without knowing what else he could possibly say, the Colonel went back to his seat to think. Was there some way that he could help? he wondered.

When the voice of the Captain came over the intercom and let them know that they were 20 minutes from touchdown, Carl said he needed to go and clean up. This was sure to be a media event, and now that the news had been leaked about the Colonel and Carl setting him free, every major network was sure to be present.

Carl came out a few minutes later looking cleaner and very dapper in the suit that Manny had procured for him. He had done a quick makeup job as well. Couldn't afford to have his real face shown on the major networks. If his wife knew that and associated it with the rescue, he sure would have a lot of explaining to do.

"Wow! You're good. You don't even look like yourself anymore," said the Colonel. "I sure do wish I had some clean duds to change into, though. I could at least make a good impression when they first saw me. I guess with everything else going on though, you people didn't think of that one, huh?"

"Your wish is my command," said Carl as he produced a clean and pressed Air Force uniform, complete with name tag and decorations for the Colonel to change into, including the decorations Welch had been honored with by Congress in his absence.

The Colonel could not believe his eyes and was now very sorry for his words. It had indeed been a long time. He just looked at the uniform as his eyes began to slowly moisten. Carl, being a former Marine, if there is any such thing, did not want the Col. to lose any dignity. If this were one week after the Colonel had been captured, surely, he would not be anywhere close to showing any emotion. But after eleven years, it is probably much easier for the body to give in to emotional reactions.

So, to give the Colonel an out, Carl said, "Ya better go and change, Sir."

Now having a reasonable excuse to turn and leave, the Colonel was off to the changing room. Carl thought he may have seen a tear before the Colonel turned away, but he sure wasn't going to mention it.

When the Colonel came back, he too looked picture-perfect. The estimates of his size were perfect.

The plane touched down and taxied over to the open gate where all the news equipment was set up. When the door was opened, the Colonel was to exit first. Carl thought better of this and sent a security detail out first, just in case. He told them to keep their eyes open.

Carl hated it when he was right.

As far as everyone else knew, the Colonel was to be the first man off the plane. Had that been the case, it would have been disastrous. As the first security officer began to step off the plane, three shots rang out, hitting him squarely in the chest. He fell backwards into the plane.

The CIA, FBI, and local police mobilized immediately. The CIA's equipment, which had been running as a failsafe, did an immediate triangulation and pinpointed the source of the shots.

There was no warning. A CIA operative with a portable missile launcher sent a modified missile right to that location. Seconds later two figures could be seen running from the embankment with their bodies aflame.

The news cameras took all of this in, and for the time being, the focus of the day's events changed to the attempt on Col. Welch's life. What they did not know, and probably never would know about, was the man who was left behind.

While all of that was going on outside of the plane, men rushed to the aid of the downed security officer. So far, things had been so fast and furious that nobody was yet aware that the man who had been shot was NOT the Colonel.

Carl went over to the officer who now lay on his back groaning. "Johnson! Johnson! The next thing that I want to hear out of your mouth is that those new bulletproof vests for high-powered weapons work. Death is not an option."

"GOOD NIGHT!" said Johnson. "It hurts like all get out, but yeah, they work. The least I'll get away with is a couple of bad bruises. How did you know they'd try something like that?"

"Just stands to reason that they'd have a backup plan when they found out that the Colonel was missing," said Carl. "Their number one goal at this point would be to nullify the effects of the mission and teach us a lesson, so to speak."

"Well, Carl, I was going to argue with your decision, but I sure am glad that I didn't. I could have pulled rank on you, you know," said the Colonel.

"All it would have gotten you would have been a slight concussion, Sir. After having to leave agent Blackwell, I was sure going to make sure he did not get left in vain. NOTHING was going to stop me from completing the Primary Objective," said Carl. "The price was already too high."

Now that all of the commotion had calmed down, Carl radioed to the operatives outside the plane that the man who got shot was not the Colonel, but a security officer and that he would make a full recovery. Carl let them know that everyone was safe and that they were ready to try it again.

Security Officer Johnson said, "Agent Reardon. If you don't mind, I'll take the point again."

"What about your clothes?" Carl asked, looking at the three bullet holes.

"I wear these bullet holes with pride, Sir. Shall we proceed?"

"Hang on. They're almost done with the security sweep, just waiting for the all clear... ahh, there it goes now. OK, let's do it." said Carl.

Security Officer Johnson strutted out with pride once again. This time there were no shots that rang out. The news had now retracted their statements about the Colonel being shot and were now reporting, based on the bullet holes, that the man emerging must be the agent who got shot protecting the Colonel.

The crowd erupted with overwhelming applause.

After the Security detail had cleared the passageway, the Colonel stepped out, followed by Carl.

When they were sure it was the Colonel this time, all cameras panned to him in his crisp, pressed Air Force uniform. The Colonel walked down the plane steps with pride and with purpose.

The lights were reflecting off of the Colonel's uniform decorations, making them stand out even more than usual, and the crowd began to cheer!

The Secret Service, who had, understandably, become very paranoid, had now determined that it was safe for the President to exit his bulletproof vehicle. President Young waited until he eyed the Colonel coming down the steps before he emerged from the protection of his vehicle. The President was immediately blanketed by a layer of Secret Service agents. After what had just occurred, he knew any objection would be useless.

As Colonel Welch reached the bottom step, he bent down and kissed the ground. He was very happy to be on American soil. Colonel Welch walked over to the bank of microphones flanked by the security detail and with Carl a few steps behind him. The Colonel caught sight of the American flag and came to attention immediately. He then saluted the flag and said into the microphones, "God Bless America! God Bless America!"

Catching sight of the President, he pointed and said, "Thank you, Sir, for returning for me, just as you promised, and for bringing me home." And he saluted.

The President returned the Air Force officer's salute and then said, "Don't thank me, Col. I'm merely the man that gave the order. Thank him!" And he pointed in Carl's direction.

The crowd went wild when they saw Carl, erupting in loud applause for yet another time.

Carl always tried to be humble and not soak up the attention, but at the moment he had to smile just a little. He could be glad that he completed his Primary Objective and brought his man home. What the people did not know was at what cost this had all occurred.

Chapter 13

After the news had a fair chance to do enough reporting for the 6:00 hour, President Young nodded his head at the security chief who, interjecting himself into the action, proceeded to break things up so that they could transport the President, Carl, and Col. Welch to the White House.

When they arrived at the White House, and the three men were out of the public eye, Carl was in shock at the outburst that came from the Colonel now that they were behind closed doors...

"YOU SAID YOU WERE COMING BACK FOR ME! WHAT HAPPENED?" yelled the Colonel. "DO YOU KNOW HOW MANY YEARS I WAITED? HAVE YOU ANY IDEA THE TORTURE THAT I HAD TO ENDURE?" yelled Colonel Welch.

"Ray, I'm going to have to ask you to keep your voice down—" the President began but was interrupted.

"KEEP MY VOICE DOWN?" Col. Welch yelled even louder. "NOW YOU WANT ME TO KEEP MY VOICE DOWN? LET ME TELL YOU SOMETHING, THE THINGS THAT I ENDURED. I KEPT HAVING TO THINK IT WAS FOR THE GOOD OF THE COUNTRY BECAUSE I VOWED THAT—"

"Ray, CALM DOWN! You have to remember that you're talking to the President of the United States. As such, there are certain thoughts that, even if you have them, should never be voiced; particularly because they're being voiced in anger, and you really don't mean them," said President Young.

"LET ME TELL YOU SOMETHING! I COULD KILL THE PRESIDENT OF THE UNITED STATES—"

With that statement, the whole dynamic of the entire situation changed. Secret Service Officers came out of the woodwork, barging into the Oval Office from all sides. The President was boxed in by four men, Carl was thrust out of the way, and Colonel Welch was thrown to the floor and had 11 firearms trained on him. He could scarcely do more than breathe without endangering his life any further.

One of the agents began speaking... "Col. Welch, you are under arrest for making threats to the life of the President of the United States of America. That is a federal offense. You have the right to remain silent. Anything you say can and may be used against you in a court of law. You have the right to an attorney. If you cannot afford an attorney—"

"That's enough, Henry," said President Young.

"Pardon me, Sir? I was not finished with—"

"You're done, Henry. Let him go. There's a lot of history here and a lot of anger that you can't even fathom. His statement was well warranted," said the President.

"But sir, we have his statements on tape," said Henry.

"Destroy the tape. No charges here today. Let him up," President Young said calmly. He felt for this Secret Service detail that was just doing their job. "Listen, Gentlemen, I'm not trying to stop you from doing your job, and you do it very well, but let's just think here, OK. The Colonel is NOT armed. I am in a room with a man who is not armed and the top agent in the CIA who IS armed. How much danger do you really think I'm in? And I have taken a few of you boys down on occasion just for fun, so you know I can protect myself," Young said.

"Yes, Sir," said Henry. Then, speaking into his lapel, he said, "Take us down from code red. The President is OK. Repeat the President is OK. There is no immediate threat. But keep us at code amber." This last part Henry said as he glanced at the

President as if for approval. The slightest hint of a smile was perceptible at the edges of his mouth. President Young gave Henry a barely imperceptible nod to acknowledge his concurrence.

The agents holstered their weapons and apologized to Carl for pushing him out of the way as they did. They left the room without so much as offering to help the Colonel up off his back.

"What was THAT all about?" said Col. Welch

"THAT is what I was trying to tell you, Ray. My life is in the hands of those men. Almost everything I do is monitored. If they perceive a threat, then they're going to act. I knew that, and I was trying to stop you before you went too far."

"So, you did," said Col. Welch. "So you did. Sorry, I'm just a bit hot under the collar."

"I understand, Ray, I really do," said President Young. "I did everything I could."

"You did everything you could? I find that hard to believe. All you did was rise to power, and in the meantime, I had to keep our country's secrets protected," said Col. Welch.

"Sir, if I may—" Carl began, but Col. Welch abruptly cut him off.

"No! You may not!" the Col. said.

"Sorry, Colonel, but the President has jurisdiction over me. You do not. So, as I was about to say... In the process of the President's 'rise to power,' as you put it, and after he became the President, he sent no less than 17 agents after you, sir. Seventeen agents who, to the best of our knowledge, never made it back alive. President Young had to leave you behind but, according to the files that I read in preparing for this case, Sir, at every step of the way and at every turn of his career, as he became ever more powerful politically, he never lost track of you. I hate to say it, Col., but he even broke his fair share of laws trying to get you back. Not one day went by that he didn't think about the man he left behind. According to his notes in the file, Sir, he even debated sending me in to get you because of the great loss of life up to this point. Now, don't get me wrong, all of those agents, just as I did, went in willingly and fully knowing what they were getting themselves into. And each of them could have succeeded, but for the fact that the Ambassador was ratting everybody out and no one knew it until now. Now, I suggest we regroup and start over again. And bear in mind, Sir, everything I just told you is confidential. I could lose my job for what I just told you, but the fact is I know that the President couldn't tell you, and I thought perhaps that you needed to know," said Carl.

"Seventeen Agents! Curt, I had no idea. I thought you had just forgotten about me," said Col. Welch

"Ray, I've kept tabs on you from the minute I had to leave you there. I've known about everything that has been going on, but your life has never been in danger. They've been keeping you alive to try to get to me," said President Young.

The President had never left his desk through the whole ordeal and still sat in his plush executive chair. It was his practice to just let things unfold until he needed to intervene. That is part of why he had gotten so far in such a short period of time. He was a master at avoiding political suicide.

"Well, Agent Reardon, while we're on confidential information that the President himself cannot reveal, I think I have some that will help you," said Welch.

Carl's eyebrows went up and down quickly; this was hardly expected. He glanced at the President, who sat stoic and unmoving, then back at the Colonel.

"Well," Col. Welsh began, "it was a day very much like the day when you came in to rescue me and the President, then known ONLY as Viper, was on assignment. I will tell you as much as you NEED to know and leave out lots of details that you don't need to know. Viper here was on one of the tougher cases of his tenure. He was—I dare say is—the best that there is. In the course of accomplishing his Primary Objective and trying to make it back here, Viper encountered another agent who needed assistance. He missed his plane out of the country to turn back and help a colleague who didn't even know he was coming. Well, I'm beginning to ramble here; let me make a long story short, son. In the course of all the things that happened, Viper was able to aid this other agent, but he also found out about yet another agent who was in trouble. Both men went back in and got there just as the other agent was undergoing some very hefty electric shock torture. It was more than any man could handle. The agent saw Viper and yelled out, 'I can't take it. I'm about to break.' Then he yelled out, '46!'"

Carl saw Viper's chair swivel around as he faced away from the other men now. Carl knew very well what 46 meant. It referred to CIA rule 46: If an agent who possesses vital secrets indicates that he is about to break, he can make a plea to other agents to make sure that it does not happen.

"I see 46 has some meaning to you, too," said Col. Welch. "Well, the Primary Objective for the moment had just changed. Viper took aim and fired one fatal shot. Such was the fate of Agent X."

"Agent X? Agent X was THE best agent the CIA ever had. Viper, you killed Agent X?" asked Carl incredulously.

"He had no choice. So not only did he have to leave a man behind, like you did, but he never had a chance to do anything about going back to get him. And that was not the worst of it," said Col. Welch.

"No," said the President, swiveling back around to talk to the men. "That was not the worst of it. Agent X was my older brother."

"Wow!" Carl exclaimed. This was a whole lot more than he had expected. All throughout the CIA training, everybody learned about the legendary Agent X. It was assumed that Agent X was missing in action and had died while trying to complete his last mission. While both of those statements were absolutely true, it was the part or parts that were omitted that really made the difference. But, because they were omitted, nobody really knew the truth. Such was the way with the world of secrets. It was not only necessary to find and keep secrets from your rivals, but it was essential that certain secrets be kept from your own people as well.

Carl wasn't exactly sure why this information had been shared with him, but he knew that it was supposed to be helpful in some way. Perhaps he just needed to wait a little longer to fit the pieces together.

The President continued the debriefing and got all the pertinent information from the Col. that he could. When they were done, the Colonel turned to Carl and said, "Listen Carl, you have some hard decisions coming up ahead of you here. The situation that you are in is not an easy one. I can only tell you one thing about the situation that you are in. No matter what, make the right choice."

"What is that supposed to mean? How is that supposed to help me right now?" Carl asked. He was more confused now than ever.

"It may take some time to sink in, but the meaning will become crystal clear," said Col. Welch.

CHAPTER 14

Carl walked into Manny's Office, still somber and not really 'with the program' yet. He had left a man behind, and it was troubling his thoughts.

Seated in one of the chairs opposite Manny was someone that Carl did not know. It was rare for him to encounter a face that he did not recognize. Manny was kind enough to make the introductions...

"Carl, this is Charles Springs. Name ring a bell?"

"Charles Springs... No, not real—Eagle One!" Carl blurted out as the lights came on in his mind. "You're Lawrence's Boss! Sir, listen, I am so sorry that I had to leave him behind. This has been eating at me since I got back. Have you read my report?" asked Carl.

"I've read your report, Reardon, and it describes the typical Lawrence Blackwell. Everything happened exactly as I would have expected. Not too much you can do about that one. But I didn't come up here for an apology," said Springs.

"What is it that I can do for you then, Sir," Carl asked.

"Seems as though, even though you didn't know Lawrence all that well, you're the agent with the most information in this case. The way that we do things in Eagle One is that the agent with the most information is the one that gets to inform the wife or next of kin about the truth and the current state of the agent who did not return. I have her name and address here, and we would like you to make the contact if you're game."

"Whoa now, wait a minute. I'm the one who had to make the decision to leave her husband behind, and you think that I'm the guy to go and tell her about his current status? Just slap me now, why don't you?" said Carl.

"Listen, Reardon, the doc also thinks that it might be somewhat therapeutic for you. We've noticed that you've been dragging since you've been back. It's not difficult to put two and two together. So, will you make the visit?" Springs asked. He was almost pleading.

"Look, I'll try. I just don't know how receptive she's going to be. I know I wouldn't be too receptive. In fact, I'd be ready to kill," said Carl.

"We're not looking for a miracle worker," said Springs. "Just a messenger who has the ability to be sympathetic at the same time. We were told that you could handle that. So, what do you say?" asked Springs.

Carl was still on the reluctant side, but he accepted the task. After all, it was the least he could do at this point.

Carl arrived at the address that Springs had given him. Why they felt like he needed the address, Carl was not sure. He had already been to the house on surveillance many times.

The Blackwell abode was a modest affair. The base color of the house was white with black trim and shutters. It stood two stories high, and Carl already knew that there was a lower-level basement. Unlike the McMansions surrounding it, the house was unique. It was not a cookie cutter model of the other houses around it. The house had a stucco finish to complement its normal siding. All of the windows were large paned glass, sporting two bay windows on either side of the first-floor exterior. The entrance was grand and lined with marble, surrounded by four circular columns that led you to a large, oak double door. The garden was meticulously manicured with a lush lawn.

At first glance, it looked like the house was not occupied at the moment. He thought that he may as well ring the doorbell to be sure. From his research, Mrs. Blackwell, typically, did not go to many places.

Carl reached up and depressed the video doorbell.

"Just a second," said the voice through the audio system.

Within seconds, Carl was greeted by a drop-dead gorgeous brunette who he knew to be Mrs. Blackwell. This was the lady that Carl had to deliver bad news to.

"Mrs. Blackwell?" Carl asked tentatively. "Mrs. Renee Blackwell?"

"Yes, that would be me," Renee Blackwell answered, "and you would be?"

"Ma'am, my name is Carl Reardon. I work with Lawrence."

"Well, this is a treat. I have not had the opportunity to meet many of my husband's colleagues. So much mystery shrouds his job, but I know enough now not to even ask. Won't you please come in?"

Carl accepted the invitation and stepped inside.

The inside of the house did not disappoint. Carl could see that there were high, vaulted ceilings. The flooring seemed to be a medium toned hard wood throughout. To the left Carl could see an expansive living and dining space with a gourmet kitchen. There were glass pocket doors that led to the outside entertainment space. No matter which way you looked the house exuded a luxurious lifestyle. Carl was guessing this was more so because of Renee. There were high-end fixtures, artwork, luxurious furnishings, and high-end appliances.

Looking at Renee, Carl said, "I have some news about your husband."

"Oh, did something happen on his business trip?" Renee asked, very concerned now. "He could have just called me."

"Well, Ma'am, perhaps I need to start from the beginning?"

"Certainly."

"I don't know how to tell you this except to just come out and say it. Your husband leads a life that is much different from what you have been led to believe."

"Don't you dare tell me he's in trouble with some woman. If that's the case, then—" Renee began, but Carl cut her off.

"No, Ma'am. Nothing like that. Lawrence is a Government Operative... an agent for a branch of the Government called Eagle One. His job is to protect other agents in the field when they are on missions."

"Surely you have the wrong Lawrence Blackwell," Renee stated.

"No, ma'am, that's what I've been trying to tell you. All these years when you have been thinking that Lawrence is going to one job, he has actually been going to another. His 'business trips' often take him out of the country when he is protecting another agent who is on assignment to a different country. In fact, he has probably been out of the country more than you know."

Carl watched Renee Blackwell back up and sit down on the sofa. If there was one thing that Carl did well, it was read people. It had saved his life on countless occasions. There was something wrong with her reaction, or perhaps Carl was just not reading her correctly. He thought he had better tread carefully. He knew he had better change tactics because she was likely to take this hard.

"Is Lawrence OK?" asked Renee Blackwell.

"He was OK when I left him, ma'am, but I think I need to tell you a bit more information," said Carl.

"Please do, Mr. Reardon? Agent Reardon? Operative Reardon? What do I call you?"

"Carl, please Ma'am. Mr. Reardon was my father."

"In that case, you may call me Renee. Please, continue."

"Well, Lawrence was supposed to be protecting ME on

the last mission. He was supposed to be doing so without my knowledge, but I discovered him. We had another goal as well, which I can't tell you about because the information is classified. Lawrence agreed to assist me in accomplishing this objective. In the course of accomplishing that objective, Lawrence was captured."

"Captured? By Whom? Where?" asked Renee.

No tears. Carl's senses were going bonkers, and he was trying to hide it. Something was wrong with this picture. But he continued on anyway.

"The answers to those questions are things that I am afraid I may not divulge at this time," said Carl.

"When are they going back to get him? Somebody IS going back to get him, aren't they, Mr. Reardon—Carl?" asked Renee.

"That is not in the plans at the moment, ma'am, but I am pursuing that angle," said Carl.

"Not in the plans at the moment? Not enough manpower? Do you know how many agents there are in Eagle One?" asked Renee.

"No, Ma'am, why don't you tell me," said Carl, sensing that the way she asked the question, she actually knew the answer. She had tipped her hand and Carl had called.

Renee Blackwell realized her mistake too late. She had let information slip that she should not have. That meant that she knew a great deal more than Carl was expecting. That also confirmed that she was faking, at least, part of her reaction.

"Well, how would I know?" said Renee, feebly trying to cover up her blunder.

"Indeed, how would you know?" said Carl, "but you obviously do know because you asked me. So, let's start from the beginning now, Mrs. Blackwell," Carl said, going back to being formal, "if that is your name, how much do you actually know?"

Renee knew that she had been caught, but there was nothing that she could say. She figured that Carl had already surmised this, but he was a good agent, and he had to ask the question.

"Lawrence and I ARE actually married, and Blackwell is my real name... now..." she said.

"How long have you been married to Lawrence?" Carl asked.

"Eleven years," said Renee.

Now Carl's brain started ticking. He was a walking encyclopedia when it came to information about other agents. It was a very good skill to have, especially when in a foreign country. It helped to determine, at times, who he might be able to lean on for assistance; a circumstance that had presented itself more than once.

Eleven years ago, a female operative, thought to be dead when she attempted to go in and rescue Col. Raymond Welch, had never turned up. 'What a coincidence,' he thought. She did not return from her trip, and the other side did not make any claims about catching a U.S. agent. Within "spy circles" it was one of the most talked about things around, particularly because it was the first loss of its kind for a female agent.

She was, of course, upper echelon; one of the best. She was also considered to be the last of her breed. The United States had a ring of spies that was so top secret that nobody was even sure what they were called. They weren't FBI, and they weren't CIA or any of the other less well-known operative groups in the U.S. But what they did know was they were down to one agent, and she was supposed to start rebuilding the breed.

That is until she vanished.

The President, at the time, made the decision to discontinue that group and to give its responsibilities to the CIA to manage. The missing agent was Codenamed: Snow White. The whole operation was extremely confidential. The Vice President's name was Curtis Young.

This was no coincidence.

All of this ran through Carl's brain in a matter of seconds. Then, all at once he blurted out:

"Snow White!"

Renee Blackwell blanched at the mention of her codename that she had not used in over a decade. How could Carl have figured all of that out already without any other supporting information?

"I can see by the change in your face that I hit the mark," said Carl.

"Yes, that you did. But you had virtually nothing to go on. How did you know?" asked Renee.

"Well, I hate to pat myself on the back, Mrs. Blackwell, but that's one of the reasons why they tell me that I am the best of the best."

"Hmm," said Renee. "I can see that now."

"And, "Carl continued, "you don't realize it, but, to be quite honest, you gave me plenty to go on. First of all, you did not seem so shocked to hear about your husband's double life. Secondly, no tears, and you were not even in shock. You were expecting the type of news that I came to deliver. Thirdly, the time period you gave for when you were married and me being a virtual walking encyclopedia—it just all added up."

"You put all of that together very quickly, Carl," Renee complimented him.

"Thank you for saying so, but that's what I do," Carl said.

"So," said Carl, "exactly how did you come to be in the position you are in now, and why is it that Lawrence still doesn't know?"

"Lawrence is being protected on two fronts, Carl. You have him on one side, and I have him on the other side. When I first started protecting him, following him around the globe without him even knowing it, there was no attraction. But as time went on, he began to grow on me. I arranged for 'chance' meetings between us, and soon he began to grow as fond of me as I was of him. We began to hit it off, began dating, our love grew and blossomed, and here we are today. I can't tell you the elaborate communications they set up so that Lawrence could call me at what he believed to be home, and I was usually in the hotel room right next door to him. I was going to make sure that nothing happened to my man."

"So, what 'front' is it that you're coming from? Who are you working for?" asked Carl.

"Strictly Confidential. Way above your pay grade. I can only tell you that I report directly to the Pres—well, maybe I better not even say that," said Renee.

"Reallllllllly? Pardon me, Renee, but I have somebody to talk to."

"Carl, wait!" pleaded Renee.

"I'll be back Renee. I promise I'll be back."

With that, Carl left and was headed back to the White House. He had a word or two he wanted to say to the President. Carl did not like to be played. He made his way back to the White House, and he was not happy.

Chapter 15

"Mr. President? Agent Reardon is here to meet with you, Sir. He's not on the calendar but is confident you will see him," said President Young's aide.

"Send him in," said President Young, "I've been expecting him."

Carl walked into the President's spacious Oval Office and just stood and stared for a minute. The President, having spent lots of time in New York City and coming from a pretty tough background, just stood and stared himself. Neither man broke the gaze.

"You knew! Mr. President, you knew! Somebody is going to have to tell me exactly what's going on here. Carl Reardon will not be yanked around like a puppet. Not even by the President of the United States," Carl finally said after having gathered his thoughts.

"You're right, Carl. I knew. What I should have anticipated even more is that somehow, someway, you would figure it out. It was shortsighted on my part not to have considered that option. My guess is you saw right through the sobbing widow act because your inner instincts told you something was wrong."

"Not exactly, Sir. The act would have gone just fine if it were more authentic. The main problem, however, was something she said. She inadvertently let something slip, and my instincts went into full swing at that point. Then, for her anyway, it was all downhill from there. I suppose she called you?"

"No, Carl, actually she has not contacted me yet. I would have expected her to reach me before you did. She would not have attempted to contact me on a communications line that was not secure.

Just then, the door to the Oval Office burst open. The President's aide could be heard yelling, "Wait! You can't go in there. The President is in a—"

The aide was silenced by the President's upturned hand.

Carl had spun around and had his weapon drawn and ready to fire. His instincts kicking in full again, but for yet a different situation, Carl's Primary Objective, as though it were second nature—because it was—was to protect the President; even though he was mad at him at the moment. Carl thought for a moment that his eyes were playing tricks on him.

The figure that came bursting into the Oval Office amid the aide's cries was Renee Blackwell. Her long brunette hair was flying in the air as she navigated at top speed in her high heels. The President's aide was the only one in hot pursuit behind her. Renee had her ID out in her hand where everyone could see, and she was not challenged by any agents as she barged in. Seeing Carl's weapon trained on her, she drew in a breath and stood stock still.

"Agents, get in here!" yelled Carl.

Immediately four agents from the outer office and six from two other entrances flooded the Oval Office.

"OK, you guys listen to me, and you listen to me well," said Carl as he holstered his weapon. "Nobody, and I mean nobody, gets in that door uncontested. The life of the President of the United States is at stake, and it is YOUR job to protect him, not MINE. But if that duty should happen to fall on me, he's not dying on my watch. Since when do you just let anybody who's flashing an ID barge in here?" said Carl as he glanced over at Renee. "And Mrs. Blackwell, are you half out of your mind?"

"Carl, I think I can clear up a few things for you," said President Young. Addressing the agents, he semi-admonished them and said, "You know, he's right. Nobody comes barging through that door if I haven't authorized it. The First Lady does not even have that privilege." Then, glancing over to Renee Blackwell, he said, "And listen, Sis, that's not the brightest thing that you've ever done in your career. I would appreciate it if you would use better judgment in the future. Had agent Reardon not recognized you, surely you would be leaving this room in a body bag. His weapons handling speaks for itself. Rarely does he need to fire more than one shot."

Carl spun around again, in the other direction this time, to address the President. "Did you just call her Sis? Are you trying to tell me that... Oh man, you people are worse than the world's best soap opera. I can't believe this. Dallas and Dynasty can't hold a candle to what is unfolding here today."

"Assistant Director and Special Agent Carl Reardon, meet my youngest sister, Special Agent Renee Blackwell. Probably the world's most persistent and infamous female agent alive. As you have already surmised by now, Carl, and the reason that I am assuming you are here right now, is that you have surmised that you are in the presence of the infamous Snow White," said President Young.

As if they had never met before, Renee said, "Agent Reardon, it is a pleasure to meet you, and it is truly an honor to be in the presence of the man who I have heard so much about in briefings."

"OK, gentlemen," President Young said, addressing the Secret Service agents, "you may go back to your posts. As per usual, you didn't hear anything, and you didn't see anything. You know the drill." Turning his attention back to Carl and Renee, he added, "I believe we, at least, have the introductions settled."

With that, the Secret Service agents exited the office as quickly as they had entered, some with smiles on their faces and others just plain confused. But none as confused as Carl was at this very moment.

"Well, now, why don't we all have a seat?" said the President. "Sis, I was just telling Carl here that you would not try to contact me over an insecure line, yet I also expected that I would have seen you before he got to me."

"Sorry, Curt... or Mr. President, but I had a little difficulty. Mr. Reardon here is the best of the best, but we have added more to the dynamics than any 'normal' situation. He's ticked somebody off in a very big way. I got a little waylaid saving his life."

"YOU were saving my life?" Carl asked. "This ought to be really good. Do you mind giving us an account? I'm not sure I can wait to read what, I am sure, will be a classified report."

Pausing, Renee looked at the President for clearance to continue. Having received the nod of approval, Renee began to tell her tale.

"You obviously are aware of how the Primary Objective can change from second to second," said Renee. "Well, you're not the only agent that happens for. My Primary Objective, at the moment that I found out I was compromised and that you were going to talk to the President, became to notify the President before you got to him. I was not able to do that. Well, let me back up a bit and tell you what you don't know. I would have been able to alert the President because I was well ahead of you, but things changed."

Renee could see the confused look on Carl's face because while she had said a lot, she still had not told him anything. Carl was waiting for some meat, something that made sense that he could latch onto. Renee had not offered that yet. She continued...

"You, no doubt, were extremely ticked at the wild driver that came zooming by you on your way here. Remember the blue pickup? Well, that was me."

"That was you in the blue pickup which came driving

past me like a maniac? Lady, you ought to have your driver's license revoked big time. The people on the sidewalk were probably scared of you!" said Carl.

"Perhaps, but there's more. The operatives that work with me reported that you were being followed by seven different vehicles that were playing tag team. There was no way that you could have tracked them all. Somebody wants to keep tabs on you." said Renee.

"It would take more than a few people to accomplish that task... wait a minute. Exactly how many people do you guys have following me around?" asked Carl.

"Carl," the President began. "You are very valuable to us. Through your successful missions, you have saved this country a hundred times over. You have saved the lives of countless individuals. Don't worry about the number of people that we have working. Just know that it is only a fraction of what you are actually worth. Now, Renee, please continue."

Renee nodded to her brother and continued with her story.

"Well, after we identified all the vehicles that were tailing you, the agents realized that they had lost one. I got the vehicle description and had to double back. I really needed to talk to Curt, but the Primary Objective changed for me. Now your life was at uncertain risk, and the Primary Objective, first and foremost, was to make sure that you were safe. You were Lawrence's Primary Objective and there was no way in the world I was going to let him down," Renee said as she began to tear up a little. "Out of the corner of my eye, I spotted the vehicle that I was looking for parked in an alley, ready to intercept you if you took the route that they predicted you would take. Then I had to high-tail it back to where you were to see which way you were going. When I determined that you were going to take their predicted route, I hung back for a while to make sure you weren't being threatened from behind as well. These folks, whoever they are, have been very crafty up to this point. I wasn't putting anything past them.

"When your car passed the alley, they began to make their move. When I came zooming by you, I still had no idea what my plan was, and the other mobilized units were too far away to be helpful. I knew the guys who were after you would have to be careful, or you would spot them, but I also knew that they had to make their move before you got to the buffer zone where the security around the White House was increased. So, I found my own little alley, and as soon as you came by, I waited for the vehicle that was following you and rammed them from behind.

"Curt here can probably tell you that we thwarted his Secret Service detail that he had following you." Turning to the President, Renee added, "A little heads up would have been thoughtful!" Now turning her attention back to Carl, she continued...

"Well, I got out of my vehicle and had my gun drawn and was ready to pull those two dudes out of the car and make them eat tar until I could get some help. When I got to the car and these jokers flashed their IDs, thinking that they were some types of gods, I flashed mine and burst their bubble. As we were sitting there discussing... OK, arguing over who was breaking up who's investigation, a hummer came by. The two men in the passenger seat had high-powered rifles aimed out of the windows and were on YOUR trail.

"'Did you see that?' the guys asked me, and none of us needed to speak after that. Lucky for us you were stopped at a light. When we saw them prime their weapons, our suspicions were confirmed, and the three of us opened fire on the vehicle. Our weapons were silenced, so that avoided a big scene. The light changed and you took off, none the wiser. I'm sure the drivers around and behind the Hummer were concerned about the shattered glass, but everyone kept to themselves.

"We reached the vehicle on foot and found out that we had made a good call. Not only did they have high-powered weapons, but there were also explosives in the car that could be lobbed into your vehicle if they got close enough. We found information with your car description and plates and instructions to kill before entering the buffer zone.

"Then remembering that you had gotten ahead of me, and that I still needed to talk to Curt before you, I high-tailed it over here, leaving the Secret Service Agents to do the cleanup with the car and the now deceased bodies. The rest is history. I burst right in. The agents all knew me, and I didn't figure that I would have a problem. And here you were already. I am sure they notified Curt, and he knew something was up, so I got here as quickly as I could to fill in the missing details."

"Listen, Carl," said Renee, "whatever else you think I am for not coming clean with you... just like you, I was doing my job. There was only so much I could say without clearance from Big Brother here. But there is one thing that you need to know... I love my husband. I mean I really LOVE my husband, and you have to go in and get him back."

This time the emotions were not an act. Carl could see and hear the sincerity in Renee's voice and actions. At that moment, he was not sure what to do. He turned to the President.

"Mr. President?" said Carl in a questioning tone.

"Carl, I have to follow the advice of my advisors from time to time. Right now, they say not to go. The whole situation is too volatile."

Just then Manny Balboa walked in the door and said, "Mr. President. Oh, sorry to interrupt the meeting. Carl? Snow White? What are you two doing here? The aide told me to come in. I just assumed the President was alone. You sent for me, Sir?"

"Wait a minute!" said Carl, almost raising his voice to a threatening tone, but quickly remembering his visit the last time he was here and what happened; he kept his tone lower. "Manny! You knew about Snow White?" Carl asked rhetorically. "Alright, that's it! Everybody needs to come clean right now, or I'm outta here!"

"Carl, listen, calm down. Nothing's happening without

Brody's saying so. Tracking him down is like trying to find a needle in a haystack," said Manny.

As Manny was in mid-sentence, J. Jackson Brody had quietly entered the Oval Office behind him. "That's true for most people, Manny, but not if you're the President of the United States. He can get to me whenever he needs to. I guess, by my presence, I'm living proof."

Upon hearing his voice, everyone turned around and faced Brody's direction.

Turning toward Carl, he said, "You sit down, calm yourself and be quiet. You're not going anywhere." Then, turning toward the President, he said, "You called, Mr. President?"

"Jack! Your timing is great, just as always. Can you tell that I have a little bit of a volatile situation here? Maybe you can help to diffuse things? After all, if I recall, diffusing explosives is one of your specialties," said President Young.

"Jack!" said Carl. "OK, stupid question here, but are you going to tell me that you knew about all of this too? Somebody want to tell me why I'm the only one around here who everyone says knows everything, but, in this case, I don't seem to know anything?"

"You know why you don't know anything, Carl? Because we don't really know anything. All we know is that somebody or a lot of somebodies from somewhere, with an inexhaustible number of resources has decided that they want you dead. Everybody in this room has been instrumental in one way or another in keeping you alive. Now, I'm going to address the President of the United States of America, and I would appreciate it very much if you would sit down, shut your mouth and be patient. And above all else, remember this because it is going to be key in the decision-making process that is about to occur... regardless of what we are obligated to say and do, we all WANT the same thing."

Carl sat down, rebuked, and left with nothing else to say. Jack was not only a good friend, but he was his father's friend, an elder, and to be respected. Carl's training from his youth was kicking in big time. He would not dare to dishonor his dad or his dad's memory by disrespecting his good friend. So, Carl felt himself lowering into a very comfortable chair and submitting to the powers that be. He did not know what the outcome of that was going to be, especially after Jack's mysterious ending comment.

Now that it seemed like everything had settled for a bit, the President spoke up. "OK, Jack, what are our sources saying?"

"Mr. President, it's not looking good," said Jack.

Interrupting the conversation and never being one to be quieted, Carl stood and said, "Mr. President, my perception is that you two are talking about the situation with Agent Blackwell. Jack! Mr. President! You HAVE to let me go back in there. I HAVE to get him out."

Jack turned around and pointed at Carl and said, "Let me try this a little stronger, young man. Sit your backside back down on that chair and shut up!"

"Carl," said the President in an almost somber tone. "I really DO want to help, but as the President of the United States, I cannot authorize the backing of this mission against the counsel of my advisors."

"I'm sorry, Mr. President... Viper.... I'm not even sure what to call you. But whatever it is you are supposed to be called; I don't see how you cannot authorize the mission. Since when do we forget about the men behind enemy lines?" asked Carl.

"I feel your pain, Carl, and Renee's pain, too. And, by the way, Mr. President will do. But, as the President of the United States, I cannot authorize the backing of this mission against the counsel of my advisors."

Carl knew what he had to do, and he kept thinking to himself, 'With or without the backing of the President, I'm going to do it. It sure would help if I had some backing. The logistics would certainly be much, much easier. Why does the President keep saying...'

Then it hit him.

Carl needed to make his case so as to divulge his intentions, fully expecting that he could not officially get any cooperation from his superiors. Carl would have to begin with the top of the chain and work his way down. He started with the President...

"Mr. President. We have a man in a foreign country that I left on my last mission. To the best of our intelligence, he is still alive and well. I request permission to go back and retrieve our captured personnel."

"As the President of the United States, I cannot authorize the backing of this mission against the counsel of my advisors." The President kept shaking his head no, as if Carl was on the right track but still doing something wrong.

Carl turned to Jack. "Jack, listen, we have a man in a foreign country that I left on my last mission. To the best of our intelligence, he is still alive and well. I request permission to go back and retrieve our captured personnel."

"I'm afraid that at this time I can't authorize such a mission. I expect you to do what's right. Do you understand me? Do what is right. I need to make sure that you HEAR me, Carl. Are you LISTENING?"

Now Carl was momentarily confused, but he knew that Jack was trying to tell him something. Jack's words said no, but his tone said yes. 'Do what is right,' Jack had said. He stressed the word HEAR and the word LISTENING. What was he trying to say?' Carl thought for a minute.

Suddenly, a light bulb that was bright enough to light New York city went off in Carl's mind. Carl leaned over and whispered into Manny's ear...

"Manny, listen, he said very quietly, we have a man in a foreign country that I left on my last mission. To the best of our intelligence, he is still alive and well. I am requesting permission to go back and retrieve our captured personnel."

Manny looked in the direction of both President Young

and Jack. They were both smiling big, broad, ear-to-ear grins and nodding their heads yes.

Whispering back into Carl's ear, Manny said, "Go for it. I'll take care of all the arrangements when you get me the information on when you plan on leaving. I want a plan on my desk in an hour. Jack and the President don't know about this yet, and I'll inform them once you're home free."

With that Carl stood and said, "Thank you, Gentlemen. I understand, and I'll be leaving now... with your permission, Mr. President."

"Be on your way, Assistant Director Reardon," said President Young.

Carl knew there was more to that statement than just telling him to leave the Oval Office. He was talking about the new mission. Carl's Primary Objective had just changed again. He was off to make unofficial plans for Estonia.

As Carl reached the outer office, he could feel that he had somebody hot on his trail. He turned around to see that Renee was following.

"Renee, why are you following me?" asked Carl.

"I'm not letting you go in there alone. You're going to need help, and I'm going with you."

"You're doing no such thing, Mrs. Blackwell. I need to go and get your husband, and there is no way in the world that I'm taking you with me so that you can get lost, injured or killed in the process," said Carl.

"And what about you?" Renee asked.

"What about me? This is my job, Renee, you know that. It's what I do for a living. I'm good at what I do, but I'm best when I do it alone. We can't take the risk. I want your husband to have somebody to come back to. You're good at what you do too, but today... today you stay home," Carl told her.

"And your wife?" Renee asked.

"Renee, if anything should happen to me, would you be so kind as to be the one to... well, you know."

Renee was touched. She was honored that Carl would ask such a thing. Realizing that there was no way she was going along; and not wanting to jeopardize the mission, she decided not to pursue it any further. But there was one thing that was really nagging her that she just had to have an answer to...

"OK, you're going solo and if anything happens... Well, you just make sure it doesn't, alright? Now tell me. Curt said you couldn't go. Jack said you couldn't go. How did you get Manny to say yes, and how could he overrule his two bosses?"

"Well, it was all in what they were trying to tell me. They were all telling me that they wanted me to go, but, because of where we were talking about it, the President could not legally authorize the mission. Everything in that room is being recorded. The only thing the President and Jack want on that tape is that they said, 'No, I can't go.' and 'the trip is not authorized.' Then I made my request to Manny, but quietly—off tape! He gave me permission to go. Presumably, the President and Jack have no idea what I asked Manny, but they were hoping that I was doing what they termed is the right thing to do. The right thing to do, Renee, is to go back and get our man. We don't leave our own. With Manny's blessing, the logistics become exponentially easier, and the financing is free and clear. He can make all of the necessary authorizations, and I'll be over and back in no time with your hubby."

"Ahh, now I see," said Renee. "Well, alright then. Off you go, and hurry back." Then she gave Carl a big hug that he was not expecting and told him to convey that to her husband however he liked.

"Yeah," Carl said as he contorted his face, "I'm thinking I'll just tell him you send your love."

Chapter 16

Now that Carl had Manny's backing, which essentially meant he had the President's backing too, everything proceeded very smoothly.

Carl didn't have any problem getting his plan to Manny in an hour. He had already drawn up his preliminary plans on the flight back and had them on file for just such an occasion. Carl got back to his office and sat down in his chair to relax for a bit.

"CLARA, clear my schedule. Looks like I'll be on assignment."

Oh goodie, another assignment. Where to this time? CLARA asked in her obviously artificial voice.

"Better set the confidentiality filter for this on high. Need to know access only for my level and above."

Done, you may proceed.

"I'll be going back to Estonia."

Going to retrieve Special Agent Blackwell?

Although CLARA was a computer, it seemed to Carl as though she was overjoyed at the prospect.

"Yes, CLARA. Transmit Mission Plan Estonia-Z11 to Director Balboa's main terminal and notify him that it is waiting for him when he returns."

File transmitted. Notification will take place upon his return to the office.

"Thanks, CLARA."

Anything else I can do for you, Boss?

"No, the only other thing left to do is to tell Mrs. Reardon I'm going traveling again. I'm supposed to be home for two months!"

Well, I'd like to be a *Musca domestica Linnaeus* affixed to the gypsum board when you break that news.

"A *Musca domestica Linnaeus* affixed to the gypsum board? OK, CLARA, I confess, you got me on that one."

Sometimes, when I'm not talking to other computer systems, I forget to water down the technical terms. It's my attempt at humor. You would probably better understand it as a fly on the wall.

"Right. I should have known," Carl said as though he had just missed the most obvious clue in the world. "No, I don't think you want to be around, CLARA. Jenny is not going to be happy. I don't think roses will help this time."

As he continued to think about the prospect of having to inform Jenny about this trip, Carl felt like he had been hit by a Mack Truck, and that it had backed up and rolled over him again; and then repeated the process a few times. He hated keeping information from his wife, but he had to for her own good as well as his. What she didn't know couldn't hurt either one of them. Besides that, she would never be able to understand that her husband was the nation's top spy. She could not even begin to fathom the fact that not only had he killed one man, but he had killed many—out of necessity and or self-defense, of course, but he had killed them, nonetheless. She would not be able to understand the types of things that Carl was required to do in order to accomplish his mission and get his job done. He could hear the words echo in his head that he used to try to explain to Renee Blackwell, who apparently already knew about the surreal life of her husband. He knew that he was not just talking about Lawrence Blackwell; he was talking about himself as well.

Needless to say, it did not go over well, but in the end, all there was left was for Jenny to understand.

Now, here Carl sat. He was one of the first seated on the plane because agents always flew business class—which was generally the same as first class—on an overseas flight. The ticket price was a staggering $7,298; and that's before all of the applicable fees and taxes.

The airfare was booked as a round trip to help throw people off of Carl's scent after they discovered that he had helped Lawrence escape. If all went as planned, their trip back would be out of Ramstein Air Force Base in Germany. The 435th Air Base Wing at Ramstein would be sending a high-speed gunship for support and transport.

Carl was one of only a few who were allowed to board the plane early. The flight attendants were running around and getting drink and meal orders so that they could have them ready as soon as the captain gave the signal to unfasten seat belts.

Carl wasn't looking forward to the 17-plus hours of travel, but that couldn't be helped since the Concorde had been retired way back in late 2003. Carl could remember his travel on the supersonic jets, run by Air France, on many missions. But amid the scares of the one and only supersonic jetliner crash in 2000 when 109 passengers and crew members perished; and heightened terrorist threats after September 11, 2001, the supersonic jet was put to rest.

There was something nagging at Carl; he couldn't quite put his finger on it. Suddenly he spun around to observe the others in the business class cabin. Carl studied each of them carefully. He could spot an agent from a mile away when he was looking. These folks appeared to be OK, but Carl was not so sure about the flight attendants. It was not the agents who Carl could NOT recognize that bothered him, though. There was still something nagging there. He had to figure out what it was, and soon. When he felt like this, solving the problem was, more often than not, the difference between life and death.

Carl's first flight change came relatively early. He flew from Washington, DC, to Chicago, where he would pick up his connecting flight to Frankfurt, Germany. From Frankfurt, after a four-hour layover, he would get a connecting flight that would take him right to the airport in Tallinn, Estonia. After some thought about the flight plan and getting confirmation that Lawrence had not been moved to Russia, they decided to bypass that leg of the trip, which had been planned as a contingency.

Again, Carl was among those who boarded the plane more than half an hour before the others. He was glad he had declined the meal on the last plane ride because they were serving him two on this one! And again, he declined the alcoholic beverages and opted for the Ginger Ale.

There were many more people in Business class this time, and Carl was on full alert. What was it that was bothering him? He racked his brain over and over again. Slowly it came to him. Now Carl realized what was nagging at him. Renee had told him that she was going to let him go solo, but she had never specifically promised that she was going to stay home! When the President introduced his sister, he introduced her as the most persistent female agent that there was. Well, the most persistent agent that there was gave up just a little bit too easily for Carl.

Carl had already gotten the President, Jack and Springs to call off their folks. Carl did not want to have to deal with anybody else. He had protected himself for a long time and firmly believed that God would go before him and keep him protected. He had to do what he had to do, and nobody else could get in the way.

As Carl looked around the plane, his vision panned this

way and that, and then he saw his mark. Carl summoned the flight attendant.

Glancing quickly at her name tag, he said, "Julie, can you tell me who that is?"

"Mr. Reardon, airline policy dictates that I could lose my job for divulging such information."

Carl, taking Julie's hand and discreetly placing a folded 100-dollar bill in it, said, "I understand. Please let me know if you find any loopholes in the airline policy that you may not have been aware of before. When do we take off?"

Taking the 100-dollar bill and tucking it into the hip pocket of her skirt, Julie replied, "We are just about to start boarding economy class. Once boarding is complete, we should begin taxiing within 15 minutes."

"Please get a message to the Captain for me," said Carl and handed Julie a folded piece of paper.

"Yes, Sir," said Julie as she walked away.

Julie's curiosity was peaked just as any normal person's would be, and she simply had to know what this message was. She ducked into the compartment between the cockpit and the front kitchen and unfolded the paper. The note read, "I didn't think you'd be able to resist, now come back and get the real message for the Captain. If you deliver it without looking you may just get another hundred dollar bill to keep that lonely one in your pocket company."

Julie came back to Carl's seat. Her face was flushed. She was so embarrassed at having been caught by someone who just assumed she would peek. To try to make up for her little indiscretion, she also got the name of the passenger that Carl had inquired about. "I'm sorry, Sir, but I did not find any loopholes. My apologies for... well... you know. Oh, and here's another napkin." She handed him a napkin with the passenger's name.

Carl looked at Julie with a smile that just melted her from the inside out. Oh, how she wished he was available, but the wedding ring on his left ring finger indicated otherwise. A tear escaped her right eye. Carl said, "Don't worry about it. Now, if you could dispose of this correctly, I would appreciate it." Carl handed her the note that was for the Captain.

This time Julie did not think twice about her task. She went straight to the cockpit and gave the Captain the note. The Captain scanned the note that was written in an archaic air force code, but appeared to be second nature to him. "Jules," he always called her that, "who gave this to you? Never mind, I don't really need to know. Just go back and tell him that my answer is affirmative."

"Yes, sir," said Julie. She didn't know what this was all about, but she was not sure that she wanted to know either.

When Julie came back and delivered the message, Carl gave her that smile again. Julie didn't know if she could take it. Carl motioned for her to come a bit closer and whispered, "I want you to help me temporarily get seated next to that person."

Julie stood up and said, "Sir, what is that on your seat?"

Carl wasn't sure where she was going with this, but played along. In the process, Julie spilled Carl's Ginger Ale on the cushion and apologized. She said, "Sir, I'm so sorry. Please allow me to re-seat you while the cushion dries. It should only be about 15 minutes."

"Certainly," said Carl. "Shall I leave my things here?"

"Certainly, your things will be just fine," said Julie.

Julie led Carl to the seat next to Mr. Peterson, who was scrunched up against the Window. "Please be seated here while your seat dries, Sir, and sorry for the inconvenience."

"Thank you," said Carl.

Mr. Peterson looked a little like a modern day Columbo. He wore a crisp trench coat. From the looks of it, Carl surmised that it was definitely London Fog. He wore a brimmed hat with a black band around it. That hat was pulled down over his eyes and covered his facial features. The collar of the coat was turned up, and Carl could not distinguish any other features.

Looking at Mr. Peterson's features, Carl noted that he was a bit small-framed. Mr. Peterson had said nothing since Carl sat down, so Carl decided that he would break the ice.

"Hi, you headed to Estonia too, or points beyond?"

No response.

"I understand. I don't like to discuss my personal business with strangers either. The name's Kevin Dixon," Carl lied. "Yours?"

Still no response.

"Like to keep to yourself, I see. Well, I understand that. A little warm on the plane to be bundled up like that, don't you think? The environmental systems seem to be functioning at peak performance."

Again, no response.

"Well, the only reason I can think of to bundle up like this is if you're feeling sick, in which case you should have stayed home. Or," Carl said as he lifted Peterson's hat off his head, in what he hoped was not a mistake, "if your name is Renee Blackwell and you're trying to hide. In which case you should still have stayed home!"

Carl's suspicions proved to be 100% correct. Removing the hat revealed Renee Blackwell, embarrassed and sorry at the same time.

"I just thought it might be you," said Carl.

"And just what if you had been wrong?" Renee asked rhetorically. Without waiting for a response, she said, "OK, you want to tell me how you figured that one out?" She obviously had a lot that she could learn from this man.

"Actually, you can thank your brother for giving you away this time," said Carl.

"My brother, what did he have to do with it? He doesn't even know I'm here."

"Oh, trust me, I bet he does know that you ARE here and is hoping that I did not catch you," said Carl.

"So, how did he give me away?"

"Well, do you remember how he introduced you to me? He said you were the most persistent female agent there was? Well, for being persistent you gave in way too easily. It took me a while to put it all together, and when I did not see you in DC, I was sure I would meet up with you in Chicago. It was just a matter of figuring out who you would be. My instincts tell me that if I were a lady and did not want to be detected, and if I were a seasoned agent, I would probably dress up as the opposite sex. Of the men in the cabin, there was only one who seemed to be trying to hide from something or someone. You see, it really wasn't that hard," said Carl.

"Rats, foiled again!" said Renee. She and Carl laughed for a moment. It was an inside joke from spy to spy.

Carl summoned Julie and said, "Julie, hold the plane. Mr. Peterson has had a change of heart and won't be flying with us today. I'll be escorting him… well her off the plane."

Julie's eyes bulged wide when she saw that Mr. Peterson was actually a Mrs. Peterson. "Well, the Captain said to follow whatever your orders were. We'll hold the plane."

Carl escorted Renee off the plane and said, "Now, this time, please, stay here. OK?"

"Promise me something," said Renee. "You will bring him back, right?"

"Renee, I'd be wasting my time going if I wasn't going to bring him back," Carl said, hoping that he was not lying.

"THAT, Carl, was the most non-committal statement I've ever heard, but for right now, I guess it's the best I'm going to get. Get on out of here. You have a plane to catch. I guess I better go and book a flight for myself."

With that, Carl got back on the plane and told Julie to give the pilot the all clear. Back in his original seat now, he glanced around once to see who might still be protecting him, and then just decided to let it be. As long as Renee stayed home and the other folks stayed out of his way, he really didn't care.

Carl said that he was going to let it go and not let it bother him, but he couldn't resist. By the time they reached Frankfurt, Carl had paid for eight complimentary drinks for passengers that he had pegged as agents who were watching him. And, as always, he was right on every guess.

Carl knew Jack well and knew that Jack had an aversion to things in even numbers. Therefore, there had to be at least one more agent. The plane had not landed yet, and Carl got up to use the airplane lavatory. The whole time he was wondering who that ninth person could be. He had ruled out all of the other passengers.

As soon as he processed that last thought, it hit him. Yes, he HAD ruled out all the other passengers, so who does that leave?

The other flight attendants had not even come near him for anything, but Julie seemed to be all over him, even to the point of seemingly flirting with him. There was something wrong with that picture. Number nine had to be Julie.

Catching Julie in the aisle, Carl pulled her aside quietly and whispered, "Pardon me, but can I have my money back?"

"Mr. Reardon, you paid me to withhold information and to divulge information about passengers against company policy. I don't think so," Julie said, trying to speak in hushed tones.

"Normally, I would say you were right. However, giving my money to another agent to do her job? I don't think so. Fork it over," Carl said as he held out his hand.

"Agent? I don't know what you're talking about," said Julie. Her eyes darted this way and that as if she were guilty.

"Listen," said Carl. "It's much easier if you just come clean. I'm rarely wrong."

Carl could tell from the look of defeat on her face that he was right in this case as well.

Julie reached into her pocket and handed over the money that Carl had given to her on the earlier occasions. "You could have just charged it to the expense account, you know. Did anybody ever tell you that you were arrogant?" asked Julie.

"Yep. And yes, you're right, I could have charged it to the expense account," said Carl. "Just wanted to make sure we stayed under budget this year," he said as he winked at Julie. "After all, I'm management now."

Pocketing his money, Carl, now satisfied with himself, went back to his seat, where he could now get ready for the landing. He had not meant to burst all of those agents' bubbles, but to him it had become a game, and he enjoyed playing it.

Carl was not surprised to see J. Jackson Brody on his connecting flight. He had the seat right next to him, and no other agents were to be seen anywhere.

"Hey Jack, I thought you might show up at some point. Pretty ticked that I discovered all of your agents, huh?" said Carl.

"You are one arrogant son of a gun at times; you know that?" asked Jack. "They obviously can use some more training. Maybe you'd like to help with that."

Just then, Carl got serious and said, "Listen, Jack, my intent is not to be arrogant. My goal is to stay alive. Now, we made a deal before I left state-side, and that deal was that you were going to call off the dogs and let me go in alone. I've worked my entire career without having to be followed and protected by some other agent or group of agents. If it were up to me to call the shots on my own, I am sure that I would do just fine. But thanks for the help," said Carl.

"OK, Carl, you got it," said Jack, "but don't flatter yourself. You're always being covered by some protective detail. They're just good enough that you don't notice. You're all free and clear."

"Just like that?" said Carl.

"Just like that!" answered Jack.

"You're giving up too easily, so tell me how many of the crew are agents... my guess is all of them. And would you be willing to let me get a look in the cockpit, I wonder?" asked Carl.

"Now I see why I'm behind a desk and you're the one who's out in the field. OK, for real this time. I'm calling off the dogs, but not until you land in Estonia. You won't have any tails. I'll clear the President's men out too."

"Thanks, Jack. I appreciate it," said Carl.

"Yeah, well, I won't say the customary 'don't mention it' until you get back. DO get back! OK?" said Jack with some concern in his voice.

"Jack, if I didn't know better, I'd say you were just a tad worried," said Carl. "Don't you worry, Carl can take care of himself. And I will accomplish the Primary Objective. Now, on to bigger and better things. On the menu, order the lemon salmon with garlic butter sauce. You can't beat it, and the last real flight attendant I had on an overseas flight recommended it highly."

Chapter 17

Upon landing in Estonia, Carl saw Jack to his federal transport to make sure that he was leaving the country.

"Looks like this is it, guy. God be with you, and may you accomplish the Primary Objective," said Jack as he boarded his plane. Then he turned around and said, "Oh, by the way. The Lemon Salmon? Good call. I'm going to have to see to it that they start serving that in the cafeteria!"

Carl just smiled. He stood there and watched as Jack's plane took off. But then he had a thought. Sometimes he hated this spy stuff! Carl walked over to the boarding ramp. The doors had not been closed, and they had not moved it yet. 'Odd,' he thought.

Carl went up to the entrance. There was a military guard diligently manning his post.

"You would be the one that Mr. Brody referred to as Carl that we are supposed to be waiting for. Is that correct, Sir?"

Carl was a bit taken aback. Caught off guard was more like it, but he answered, "Well, I didn't know that you were waiting for me, but, yes, that would be me," said Carl.

"Mr. Brody said you might want to check out the boarding ramp," said the Guard.

"Indeed, I do. Mr. Brody is a very smart man," said Carl.

Carl entered the ramp and checked for other possible avenues of escape, wanting to make sure there was no other way to exit the ramp. He found none. But he still wasn't satisfied. That is until he got back to the ramp entrance.

"Mr. Brody said that I was also to give you this," the guard said as he handed Carl an envelope.

Carl opened the envelope right there in front of the guard. The note inside read:

Carl,

I am on the plane just like I promised. Now stop wasting time. It's time to go and accomplish the Primary Objective. I'm planning a party for when you return. I know how much you like them. But if you're not going to let me protect you, then you're just going to have to put up with it.

Good Hunting,
Jack

Jack's sarcasm did not escape Carl's notice.
Carl hated parties.
He hated big recognition meetings.
He just wanted to do his job for the purpose of doing it.

It was only important to Carl that his superiors knew what he had done. U.S. News, Time, CNN, ABC, NBC and that backwards one... CBS (Carl always thought they should have been SBC to follow the same pattern) could all find something else to do than report on his work. They called it heroics—but, to Carl, it was just what he did!

Satisfied that Jack was indeed on his way home—well at least he was in the air—Carl set off on his way.

Carl checked into his room at the Schlossle Hotel using the assumed identity of Fred Garrison, an American businessman on an investment trip.

"I hope that your stay with us is an enjoyable one, Mr. Garrison. There are many sites to see. We also understand that you are an investor, and we would not be averse to attracting your investment interest in our establishment as well," said Eerik Harju, the hotel manager, who had come down from his office to personally see to Fred Garrison's arrangements.

"Thank you. You say your name is Eerik Harju?" asked Carl.

"Yes, Mr. Garrison. My card," said Harju as he handed a laminated business card to Carl.

Carl took the card and, placing it into a gold-plated card holder that he kept in his suit jacket, and said, "Thank you."

Carl was dressed for the part of the investor. He wore a hand-crafted suit. His fashionable pant cuffs were very short in height, unlike the commonly seen thick cuffs. His suit jacket had a very uncommon configuration of five buttons down the front, and a red satin handkerchief was expertly placed in the front pocket. The red satin complemented the charcoal gray suit very nicely. The shoes were $300 leather designer loafers from Italy that could be dressy or casual. The shine on the shoes was so reflective that they could have been used as a mirror. Carl also wore a red and white striped power tie to match the handkerchief and the crisp, white designer shirt that he was wearing. The tie was held in place by a solid gold collar clip at the top and a matching solid gold tie clip about halfway down.

Carl had used his makeup kit to alter his appearance. Aside from totally altering his face, he also added a mustache and a neatly trimmed half beard. He wore expensive cuff links and added a few rings. He darkened his skin tone just a bit. He definitely did NOT look like the Carl Reardon everyone might be looking for. With this new look, it would be just a little bit easier to remain undetected as he set up his attempt to save Lawrence.

When Carl reached his room, he generously tipped the

attendant and proceeded to close and lock the door and shut the blinds.

Opening his briefcase, Carl set up a tent screen on his bed, which would hide what he was about to do from any cameras that he did not detect or have the opportunity to deactivate yet. Carl set up his minicomputer under the tent screen and began running his surveillance detection software. The software immediately assessed the room size and entrances and developed a customized radar screen for this location.

Carl then watched as the software began scanning. There was something that was hampering his signal and attempting to block his scan. Carl went into his toiletries bag and acted as though he was unpacking. He took out three bottles that appeared to be cologne, lotion and shampoo and set them in three different places around the room. These three bottles were actually signal boosters. Carl hit the button on the computer to activate the boosters and waited for them to triangulate and send data to the computer. This successfully mitigated the signal block, and Carl was now able to detect the surveillance devices installed throughout the room. There were listening devices upon listening devices. Somebody really wanted to spy on this American Investor. The computer indicated that there was bugging redundancy in the phone system, as well as multiple cameras hidden in strategic places around the room.

The yellow blinking light indicated that there was outside surveillance being attempted as well, but they, of course, could not see through their own blinds... or could they? Carl put two thin transparent strips on his palms and stood at the first window. He opened the blinds so that he could see out. Putting his hands up on either side of the window frame, he placed the two strips across from each other. The strips immediately blended into the paint and were undetectable. Carl did the same thing for the other window, then proceeded to shut the blinds again.

Crossing back over to the computer, Carl hit a series of

keystrokes to activate the undetectable strips that he placed on the windows. A field that could not be seen by the naked eye was generated. It allowed Carl to see out, but no one could see in unless he wanted them to. After verifying that the devices were working correctly, he re-opened the blinds.

Now Carl set the computer to scan for the frequencies of the hidden cameras he had detected. It turned out that they were all on the same frequency, with no significant modulation capabilities. This was good. Carl gave some thought as to what he wanted them to see and decided on Bugs Bunny. With a few keystrokes, he set up the intercept software to play Bugs Bunny episodes over and over again.

Next, Carl isolated the listening devices. First, he dealt with the telephone listening devices. After finding their frequency, he completely neutralized them. Next, he worked on the listening devices in the room. He found that they had been much smarter when it came to those, and they were on three different frequencies. As Carl thought about it more, he realized that they probably didn't plan on having them on three different frequencies, and it was just a fluke. But, nevertheless, he set those three frequencies to transmit Abbott and Costello's "Who's On First" routine; alternating between transmitting in Estonian, Russian and English. This was Carl's way of letting them know he was onto them without directly coming out and saying it.

Carl now took his Bible out and laid it on the table. The cover of his leather Bible contained very thin and sophisticated electronics and a 12-day, very lightweight power supply. Once Carl sent the activation command, all the necessary information would be transmitted to the Bible, and control of handling the surveillance devices would be handled from there. Carl blanked the screen but did not activate any of the safeguards yet.

He took down the screen and threw it across the room, saying, "This thing doesn't work! There's just as much glare on the screen now as there was before I put the thing up! To think I paid $650 dollars for that. That could have been a good dinner!"

Carl was hoping that they bought his act.

Then, sitting down on the bed, Carl picked up his Bible and began reading. Whoever was watching was sure to not even consider that the Bible was anything but what it appeared to be, and would never be suspicious of it at all. Surely, they would try to enter his room and change these devices or see what was wrong with them, but with the scanning routines running, if any devices with different frequencies were added or if any frequencies changed, the software would automatically detect it and adapt after a five-minute delay. They would think that they had a solution to their signals being altered, but would then be baffled when the automatic changes kicked in. Carl would like to be a fly on the wall when that happened.

After about 40 minutes of Bible reading, Carl put his Bible down on the table. He picked up his computer and hit a few keystrokes. All the security processes that had been queued began to activate sequentially. Carl waited until the radar screen showed green to indicate that all intercept modes were active. Now he went into his briefcase and took out a thin transparent roll and, taking the nightstand drawer out, secured this inside the nightstand. He attached a five-by-five inch wafer-thin surveillance chip to the tape. This was his redundancy backup. The Bible would automatically download all of the appropriate settings to it and, in the event that the Bible could not continue to transmit, the backup system would kick in immediately. Carl replaced the nightstand drawer.

Just as Carl had suspected, within fifteen minutes there was a knock at the door.

"Mr. Garrison, we regret to inform you that there is a maintenance issue that we must check out. We must ask you to vacate the room for your safety."

"Exactly how long are you going to be?" asked Carl.

"Unknown, Sir," said the maintenance worker.

"Well, I guess it's a good thing that I haven't unpacked yet then," said Carl. He grabbed his bags, Bible, and computer and headed downstairs. "I'll wait in the library."

Carl left the room with his belongings and went down to the library. From there he asked to use the telephone and dialed the extension that he had on the Hotel Manager's business card.

"Hello, this is Eerik," said the familiar voice of the hotel manager.

"Mr. Harju? Fred Garrison here. You might wonder why I'm calling from the library?" said Carl.

"In fact, the question did cross my mind," Harju lied.

"I have been displaced from my room while your men fix some sort of maintenance thingie. I am most unhappy, Mr. Harju," said Carl.

"Yes, Mr. Garrison. I apologize for the inconvenience. It is only for your safety, I am sure. I'll look into getting you another room."

"No, Mr. Harju, I rather like the room I was in. It will do just fine. If that is not acceptable, there are many other hotels here in Estonia. I am sure the Telegraf Hotel, The Viuru Inn Hotel, The Three Sister's hotel or even The Raddison Sas Tallin would all be grateful to have me stay at their establishments," said Carl.

"Oh no, Mr. Garrison, that won't be necessary. Please let me just find you other arrangements," said Harju.

"Mr. Harju, it's that room or no room. I expect to be back in it in 20 minutes or less, or I'm out of here," said Carl.

Carl knew that Harju could not afford to lose the chance for surveillance and that he had to retain Carl somehow or find out where he was going so that they could quickly set up another room before he got there.

"Please, if you must go to another establishment, just let us know which one and, while we would be sorry to see you go, we'll be glad to make the arrangements for you," said Harju.

"I don't think I would be inclined to tell you where I'm going, Mr. Harju," said Carl.

"But Mr. Garrison, with our assistance we could expedite your check-in and have you comfortable in another place with no hassle at all. It is the least that we can do. Or... we do have alternate rooms here," said Harju.

Carl knew that the alternate room would be one identical to the one that had been set up, but in the interest of saving time, he did not want to debug another room. "Mr. Harju, have me back in my room in 20 minutes or me and my money are gone," said Carl.

"Mr. Garrison, I will respect your wishes, but can you please give us an hour?" asked Harju.

"You have 59 minutes and 58 seconds and not a second longer!" said Carl. He loved his own sarcasm and hung up with a smile. He went to his computer and initiated the process to send codes that would temporarily deactivate his intercept devices. The computer acknowledged that all power had been temporarily cut to the bugging devices in the room. This would baffle Harju and his men for sure. He was certain that all of the devices would be switched out, but his software would automatically adapt.

After sending the command sequence, Carl pulled up a game of Spider Solitaire and proceeded to play.

After hanging up the telephone, Eerik Harju sat in his office staring at his surveillance team and said, "OK, I want some answers, and I want them right now. Does somebody want to tell me what happened in that room?"

Harju looked inquisitively from person to person as he asked the question.

"I'm not sure, Mr. Harju," came the replies.

"This wealthy American cannot, all by himself, counteract every system that we have set up. And I really don't want to give away our alternate room. We're told that some superagent Carl guy that the Supervisor is really anxious about is headed this way. If he gets spotted here, that's the room he goes into. Above all else, HE must be tracked. This finance guy is not as important."

"Yes, Sir, we're working on the issue with the American. My men can have all of the devices changed in forty minutes."

"Excellent! Get it done. We will keep this Mr. Garrison happy. Did you get me a report on this man? Is he who he says he is?"

"Yes, Sir, he is genuine," the security officer said as he handed over the file.

Harju quickly scanned the file and saw that everything about Garrison seemed to check out. What he really liked was the man's net worth. To get an investor of that caliber interested in his hotel could be quite beneficial.

Only 30 minutes had passed before one of the attendants came down and informed Carl that he was able to regain access to his room.

"Pardon me, Mr. Garrison?" said the attendant in accented broken English, "I have the pleasure of informing you, Sir, that you may now return to your original guest room. We appear to have resolved the problem."

"Thank you," said Carl as he stopped playing his game of Spider Solitaire. Then, playing his part to a tee, he began to slowly walk away without his belongings. He stopped after a few feet when it was obvious that the attendant was not following him. "Are you coming with my things?" Carl asked expectantly.

"Oh, yes, certainly, Sir," said the attendant, quickly gathering Carl's belongings and following behind.

The wait for the elevator was not long, and the elevator ride itself was uneventful.

When they got his belongings back into the room, Carl told the attendant to tell Mr. Harju that he was impressed with the speed at which everything was addressed. And, as usual, Carl gave the attendant a generous tip and closed the door.

Carl waited a good while longer this time before activating his equipment. He did not need to get up and make any additional changes. All the settings were already taken care of. Carl sat on the bed and read his Bible for a while. Then he got on his computer and acted as if he was checking the stock market status. After some time, he executed the necessary keystroke and watched the radar screen on his computer as the surveillance devices went from red to orange... to yellow... and then finally to green when each of them had been fully deactivated.

"ARRRRRRRGH!" Harju exclaimed angrily as he slammed his fists down on his desk. Papers and other objects went flying in all directions. "I want answers! Do you know how much those devices cost? We can't just go in and replace them every time, and there are only so many good excuses we can use to get in the room."

"How many excuses do we have left, Mr. Harju?" one of his workers asked sheepishly.

"None!" said Harju. "I'm going up there."

Eerik Harju stormed away angrily. He was going to get to the bottom of this.

There was a knock at the door. Carl checked his watch. The timing was just about right. Carl was not sure who Harju had sent, but he was prepared to deal with whoever it was.

Carl was semi-shocked when he opened the door and saw Harju himself standing there.

"Mr. Harju, what may I do for you?" asked Carl.

"I was just checking," said Harju. "I wanted to make sure that everything was OK. May I enter?" Harju asked as he tried to peek around Carl. Harju's eyes were quickly scanning from left to right.

"By all means. Please, please come in, Mr. Harju," said Carl.

Harju stepped in and began looking around the room. He was trying to investigate in such a matter so as not to be too obvious. Every so often, he would glance back at Carl and hold his gaze. But then he would break the gaze and try to see if he could figure out what it was that was interrupting the signals that his surveillance devices were trying to transmit.

"Everything seems to be OK. I guess I'll be leaving you now," said Harju.

"Well, OK, Mr. Harju. I am glad that everything is to your liking."

As Harju exited the hotel room, Carl made a split-second decision. He thought that if he didn't do something, they would investigate and probe a little deeper than he wanted them to. That was something that Carl could not afford to have happen right now. It was time to modify his approach.

"I was just wondering, Mr. Harju," Carl began. The little man spun around with a very confused look on his face.

"Yes, Mr. Garrison?" Harju answered. Worry lines were evident across his brow.

"Have you figured out who's on first?" Carl asked, dropping a clue.

"What?" said Harju.

"No, he's on second," said Carl.

"Well, I don't know," said Harju.

"He's on third base."

"Who?"

"There you go. Now you've got it."

"So, YOU are responsible for disabling my devices?"

"Well, actually it's the people that work for me, Mr. Harju, but, in an indirect way, yes," said Carl.

"Do you mind telling me how?" asked Harju.

Carl could see the pleading in his eyes, but he was not about to give him any easy satisfaction.

"As a matter of fact," said Carl, "Yes. Yes, I do mind, but I will tell you this: I didn't make my money by sharing my information with everybody else, Mr. Harju. I can't afford to have people listening in on my deals and stealing information. So, I paid a boat load of money to be able to detect, and to have the capability to disable, listening devices and cameras wherever I go. Surely you can understand the sensitivity?"

"Yes, Mr. Garrison. Absolutely," Harju said. A wave of relief was evident on his face. "That also answers a lot of questions for us as well. We actually thought that our equipment was malfunctioning. My apologies for having the devices in your room, but we also have an interest to protect. I'm afraid that I cannot be as open about our need as you were with yours, but rest assured that it is a necessary one," said Harju.

"Yes, yes, I'm sure it is. I suspect that you treat all westerners with the same, shall we say, courtesy? I just can't afford to have any of my secrets get out before I have had time to act on my business deals. It has happened to me on one occasion and will never happen again. I understand that you also have a job to do. If I should happen to let my guard down, then you are welcome to whatever financial information you receive, but I will continue, if I remember, to block any and all signals. I think we're OK as long as we know where each other stands. Is that right?"

"Yes, I think, as you Americans say, that you've hit the nail right on the head, Mr. Garrison. You have a good day," said Harju.

"And you as well, Sir," said Carl.

With Carl's scrambling software still active, Harju left and appeared to be happy with the explanation that he received.

'What a load of cow manure,' thought Carl, 'and it looks like he bought every word of it too. Hook, line and sinker!

Well, that's going to make things on this end really easy!'

Carl sat down with his computer and now started to plan his mission in earnest. He had yet to figure out how he was going to get back into the compound. Surely, they had already figured out how he got in last time and had taken steps to mitigate that line of entry. At least that's what Carl was expecting. The latest intelligence that Carl had received indicated that Lawrence was definitely alive. They were trying to extract information from him, so he was undergoing torture just like Col. Welch did. The intelligence indicated that Lawrence's torture was significantly more intense than Col. Welch's. It appeared as though they wanted to get as much information from Lawrence as they could; and as soon as possible.

Carl was still sweating the fact that HE was the one who had left Lawrence there, and now it was solely up to him to get him back out. He did not plan on failing on his mission. Of course, failure was never the plan.

After some careful consideration and another thorough review of the schematics, Carl decided on the best plan of action. He knew he could not stay where he was much longer without somebody getting wise and detecting him. There was very little time for delay.

The time to move was now.

CHAPTER 18

Carl had quietly packed up all of his things, which was not a lot to begin with, and left the hotel without being detected. His next stop was the compound where his latest information indicated that Lawrence was still being held. No matter what, when he left the Schlossle Hotel, he would not be returning. Carl knew that Harju was not going to be the least bit happy when he found out that he had been deceived by the very man he was looking for. Carl knew that Harju would have to answer to his supervisors when they found out that Carl was right in his grasp and got away. It was not likely to turn out too well for him at all.

The Airport was only ten kilometers from the hotel, so Carl found a location near the airport site to stash his belongings. That way, he did not have to haul things around and could retrieve them again on the way out of the country. He kept the necessary equipment and tools that he would need to assist in his rescue effort with him.

Carl made his way over to the compound where he believed that Lawrence was being held.

The surroundings were very familiar to him.

He had been here before.

When Carl reached the compound, activity seemed to be at a minimum. The ten-foot electric gate that surrounded the compound was manned, but there was no traffic going in or out. There was no conversation between the guards. Everyone seemed to just be doing what they were supposed to. The sun had gone down. There was less daylight at this time of the year. Aside from where the lights were aimed, not very much was visible.

Carl had no idea if Lawrence was actually inside or not. Logically, they would have Lawrence in the same holding area—and likely the same cell as the one that Col. Welch was being held in. But, if not, that was a problem to worry about once Carl got inside. The first order of business would be to gain access.

As Carl watched the activity at the gate, a vehicle did approach. It was a standard issue, covered supply truck. There was nothing fancy about it. He noticed that it was, in fact, a standard procedure now to check under the vehicle to make sure that there was not anyone trying to get a "lift" inside. He found it odd, however, that they were not checking the top. It also did not appear that any of the surveillance cameras were examining the tops of the trucks. Getting inside was going to be a lot easier than Carl anticipated.

If the trucks were still on the same schedule, there should be a delivery truck that Carl could ride in on right around 11:30 PM. That gave him about six hours to make all of his necessary preparations. Most of Carl's preparation was just going to be watching the place to determine if there were any changes in the guard's movements from what he already knew. He did not have as much advanced surveillance opportunity this time around. Everything else would have to be handled on an incident-by-incident basis.

Carl was hoping that he could complete the entire operation undetected. The risk of detection was going to increase a great deal when Carl actually sprang Lawrence, and there were two of them to worry about.

Carl circled around the building, moving every 15 to 20 minutes. He was trying to see if he could determine, from the outside, where Lawrence might be. He knew where the cell was that the Colonel had been held in and decided to go and have a look on that side of the building. Unfortunately, there was no discernible activity in the area of the cell window. Carl zoomed in with the binoculars, but he was not able to get any additional information to assist him. Carl was hoping that these guys didn't think to move their prisoner. It did not seem that they thought about much. Everything else that he had seen so far would not indicate that they would have even given that any thought either.

Carl scoped out a location that had a little more light. He went into the bushes and began to change. He got himself into a skintight jumper that seemed to mold to the form of his body, yet remained modest, and also gave him room to keep necessary items in pockets. This new body suit was still experimental and had not been tested in the field. The body armor not only had the ability to offer additional protection, but it also could turn Carl into a chameleon of sorts. It changed color with the environment and helped Carl to blend into wherever he was. As Carl looked down, he was amazed that it was so hard to tell where the leaves and ground began and where he was actually squatting. Aside from his face and hands, he had already completely blended in.

Carl checked his watch again. This was something that was done frequently on missions. It was important to have a working timepiece. He still had a few hours. He settled in for a snack. He then decided to check out the nether parts of the grounds to see if there was anything that would be helpful to him that he might be able to take advantage of for this mission.

There was activity outside the small airport terminal as the KGB contingent pulled up. When they got out of their vehicles, they looked around as if to get the lay of the land. It was more so that people would be awed by their presence. The leader nodded and his advanced guard proceeded before him into the terminal.

"Comrade Askinov, it is a surprise to see you here. We weren't expecting anybody from the Russian offices until the day after tomorrow." said the airport security officer.

"We have gotten wind of a possible American threat. The Americans are pretty crafty. I just wanted to make sure that they had not already infiltrated the country. It occurs to me that this might be an ideal access point," said Askinov.

Comrade Mikhail Askinov was the lead KGB agent stationed here in Estonia. It was not where he wanted to be, but as with most jobs of this type, there was not a lot of input obtained from the individual being assigned. Your post was chosen for you. Period. You simply went where you were told. Askinov was not an incredibly tall man by any stretch of the imagination. He stood about five feet five inches and wore a monocle on his right eye, which made him look more German than Russian. The left eye had near-perfect vision but was closed, more often than not, so as to help him focus the right eye.

Askinov wore a modest suit, and the bulge of his KGB service revolver could be seen under the well-tailored suit jacket. Truth be told, he was not really trying to hide the weapon at all. The right pinky finger of his left hand had been 75% amputated because of an encounter that he had with a chainsaw much younger in life. Obviously, the chainsaw won. The rest of his fingers seemed to be OK. When he talked, his voice sounded like you were having a conversation with a squeaky door. If it were anybody else's voice, it would have been very annoying. But Comrade Askinov commanded much more respect and was a force to be reckoned with. No one made fun of the mousey voice. If they did, they did not live to tell about it.

"Let me see the logs, please," said Askinov. He was all business and immediately making demands.

"Certainly, Comrade," said the officer.

"Umm Hmmm. Umm Hmm Umm... Uh, who is this Garrison person?" asked Askinov.

"Oh, he is some wealthy American. Probably not going to cause a lot of trouble while he's here."

"Right, probably not. You know where he's staying?" asked Askinov.

"No, Comrade. He made his own arrangements. We did not assist in those."

"I think I'll go and ask around and see if any of the cabbies on duty gave him a ride," Askinov said.

It didn't take long for Askinov to find out that a man of Mr. Garrison's description did get a taxi ride, and that he paid the cab driver very generously. Coming back inside, Askinov summoned his men. They needed to go to the Schlossle Hotel to have a talk with this American, Garrison.

The ten-kilometer drive was uneventful for Major Askinov and his men. Upon arrival at the Schlossle Hotel, as at the airport, he was an unexpected visitor. There was even more commotion as the KGB contingent pulled up in front of the hotel. One would think that more people would be asleep as it was the middle of the night. Askinov and his men walked inside as though they owned the place.

The lighting was lowered for the night. The night staff manned their posts at the hotel desk and immediately recognized the KGB when they entered. It was not necessary for Askinov to show any credentials; the hotel manager was summoned at once.

Mr. Harju was roused out of bed and informed that an agent from the KGB was here to see him. It was times like these that Harju was glad that he lived on the premises. The KGB was not to be kept waiting. Harju didn't even bother to dress;

he just threw on a bathrobe and went downstairs to find out what the Major needed.

When Eerik Harju came off the elevator and saw that it was not just any ordinary KGB agent, but Mikhail Askinov who had come to the hotel, he was sorry that he had not taken the extra minute to put some clothes on and look a bit more presentable.

"Comrade Major Askinov, please pardon my appearance. What may I help you with?"

"Hello, Harju," came the man's greeting with a very thick Russian accent and mousey voice. "We are here to check on an American who is staying at your hotel. A Mr. Garrison," said Askinov.

"Oh yes, Mr. Garrison, a most interesting man. Very wealthy," Harju said with a gleam in his eye.

"Have you noticed any peculiar behavior from this man?" Askinov inquired.

Harju thought to tell him about the incident with the surveillance devices being nullified but did not want to give any hint that he was considering making a pitch to the American to become an investor in his hotel. He decided not to mention it for now.

"No, Comrade, nothing interesting or peculiar."

"Take us to his room. I wish to see him."

"Right away, Comrade Major," said Harju. He wasn't sure what was going on, but he did not have a good feeling about this.

They took the elevator up to the floor where Garrison was staying, and Harju led them to the door and knocked.

No answer.

Harju knocked again.

Still no Answer.

Askinov was done playing. "Mr. Garrison, this is Mikhail Askinov of the KGB. You will open the door right now, or we will open it for you," Askinov squeaked.

No answer.

"Kick it in!" ordered Askinov, already knowing what he was going to find.

"NO! WAIT! I HAVE THE—" Harju began to say, but the subordinate that Harju addressed was more concerned with following the direct order that he had been given by Askinov.

He immediately began kicking the door in.

The first kick didn't appear to budge the door at all. Even Harju was surprised at the quality.

"Come on. Come on. My great-granddaughter can kick better than that," said Askinov.

The second kick seemed to make the door give some, but the lock was still holding fast.

"Kick it like a man!" Major Askinov said.

The subordinate was beginning to get a bit fed up and stopped for a second to stare at Askinov.

"Problem?" Askinov asked.

In answer to the question, the subordinate officer let out a horrendous yell as he turned to the door and kicked with all of his might.

"Hiiiiiiiiii Yah!"

The door jamb splintered, and the bedroom door gave way. The door opened and the party now had access to the room.

Askinov sent his subordinate officers into the room first, like any brave Russian KGB officer would do. He assumed that they would not find anything and that Mr. Garrison would be long gone... but just in case.

He was right on both counts.

"Where... did... he... go?" asked Askinov slowly. "Take me to your surveillance room!"

"Well, Comrade Major, we uh—"

"You have had the American under surveillance, haven't you, Harju? That is standard policy."

"Well, you see, Comrade Major, we had some difficulty with this particular American."

"Difficulty? What difficulty could you have had with an American?"

"Well, you see Comrade, this wealthy American is very careful about people listening in on his conversations and has had his people develop a system by which he can neutralize the surveillance system at any place that he stays. We put him in a monitored room, and he neutralized the devices—not once, but twice. We even changed them out to make sure that they were not malfunctioning, Comrade Major."

"So, let me get this straight, Harju. Are you trying to tell me that there are no surveillance tapes at all of the American?" Askinov asked.

"Well, there is some footage and some audio, but very little of both. All we really have is footage of him reading his Bible."

"And it is your belief that this wealthy American has the technology to manufacture counter-surveillance equipment just to keep his financial decisions private? Harju, how can you have been such a fool?"

"I am afraid that I do not understand Comrade."

"Yes, Harju, that is exactly the problem. You have not been hosting a wealthy American. You have been hosting a CIA agent. You Fool!"

"No, no, Comrade Askinov. This man looked nothing like the images that you have been transmitting to us," Harju tried to explain.

"Think, Harju. Think! If you were a spy, would you just walk into the country dressed and made up as your normal self and say, 'Hello, I'm here!'? No Harju, I think not. You have been tricked by one of the best."

"No, Comrade, I tell you that this could not have been the spy."

"And why not?" Askinov asked. "What brilliant piece of evidence do you have to prove otherwise?"

"Well, Comrade," said Harju confidently, as though he had

some brilliant revelation to produce, "he reads FORBES mag-azine!"

Harju could hear how ridiculous the words sounded as they rolled past his lips. He didn't have anything better to offer.

"He reads FORBES magazine? Does he really now? While I will admit, Harju, that FORBES is not your everyday ordinary reading. All that proves is NOTHING," Askinov spat back. "Somebody kill him. I don't think I can take any more."

"No, Comrade, wait. I can be of more value to you."

Askinov heard Harju trying to bargain over and over again. And then there was the lone gunshot followed by silence.

"OK, leave the body in the room for the cleaning staff to dispose of. We need to get over to the compound and stop this man from freeing the other American prisoner. If they escape, it is not going to look good for Russia. Not at all!" said Askinov.

Chapter 19

Carl could have sworn he saw something out of the corner of his eye, but maybe he was just getting jumpy. Whatever it might have been, he didn't have time to go and check it out. The delivery truck was coming right on time, and it was his only way in. If he didn't hitch a ride now, then he would either have to try a daring daylight entry or wait another 24 hours. In 24 hours, Carl hoped to be sleeping in his own bed at home, or at least close to it. He wasn't going anywhere for a long time. He had quite a lot to make up for with his wife.

The large truck rumbled up to the gate and stopped for all of the necessary security checks. Carl had to time his jump perfectly, or this could throw off the plan and he would have to then have a welcoming party to contend with. Carl waited as they opened the doors and checked the inside. Then, timing his jump perfectly, he landed on the top of the truck just as the door slammed. The slamming of the door masked his landing. He situated himself just as they slammed the second door. The truck was cleared for entry and moved on. Carl had made it onto the top of the truck unobserved.

Of all the things that he might have thought he would be doing a week ago, hugging the top of a truck was definitely not anywhere on the list for Carl. Yet, here he was. Well, this would all be worth it as soon as he could get Lawrence out and back home to his wife again. Carl felt the truck come to a stop and remained still. The driver got out of the truck and just stood there as he lit up a cigarette and began to smoke.

'Oh, come on.' thought Carl. 'You've got to be kidding me. Move, man! I've got a job to do,' Carl continued to think to himself.

Just then the truck driver's cell phone rang. Carl began to think that his luck was running out. But the telephone call turned out to be more of a blessing than expected.

Now with the truck driver's attention distracted by what obviously was some female acquaintance on the other end of the line, Carl was able to escape from the roof of the truck and begin the task of disabling incoming and outgoing communications.

Carl kept close to the building, circling around so that he could find the main terminal where the communications trunk line fed into the building. If he could cut communications there, then all wired communications would be neutralized. After that, Carl would have to deal with wireless units.

He was ready.

Carl arrived at the location of the trunk line, but what he found was unexpected. Whoever it was that ordered the construction of this building had thought through the precaution of protecting the communications lines. Disabling the wired communications was going to be much more difficult than the usual 'snip, snip' that you see on television and in the movies. Carl was actually going to have to put some work into this one. He would have to note the type of construction and time period, so that he would know what to expect if he ever had to come back to Estonia.

Not an unlikely prospect. You never know where the mission will take you.

Just then the security guard came around on his patrol rounds. Carl was hoping that the guard's night vision wasn't too well adjusted yet, or he would likely notice the exposed wires. Carl's luck was holding; the guard never turned his way.

Carl was not going to be able to shine a light. That would give him away for sure. Feeling around in his tool pouch, he located the most likely tools that he was going to need. He quietly began the work of disassembling the box that protected the trunk line. It was definitely solid construction, but they had not taken into account all of the necessary considerations to prevent his access. Carl was able to breach the barrier faster than he had expected.

As Carl lifted the box off the main trunk line, his heart sank when he saw how thick the cabling was that he was going to have to get through. What made matters even worse was that live current was running through it.

Plan A was not going to work.

'Why me?' Carl thought. 'This never happens like this in the movies.' But this was not the movies. This was real life. In real life, real-life things happen, and they happen the real-life way.

Taking hold of the thick trunk line so that he could move it and try to better determine how many wires were in there, Carl got an unexpected surprise. But it was a happy surprise. As Carl grasped the wires, he could feel a second bunch behind the thick one. 'Could it be?' Carl asked himself. Yes, it was! Somebody was trying to cut corners. The communications cables, which should have been bundled in with the thick trunk line, were not!

Just then the guard came around for another pass. He stopped and stared in Carl's direction. Carl readied himself for battle. If this body armor did not perform like it was supposed to, Carl was going to have to fight his way in, and then, most assuredly, have to fight his way back out again.

The guard stood and stared for a long time, but he never looked directly in Carl's direction. He was more interested in the communications box. Then he mumbled in Russian, "Lazy communications workers. Couldn't even cover up their work before going home for the night. Won't they be surprised when they see this in my report? Maybe I can get something for this if I play my cards right. Yes, definitely bribe material."

The guard did not approach the box and still did not notice Carl. He continued on with his rounds. Carl had to remember that it was OK to breathe. In fact, it was essential. Still, he was undetected. 'Won't he be surprised?' Carl thought, 'When they go to verify his report and find the cover on!'

After cutting the communications lines, Carl began the process of putting the cover back onto the trunk line box. He was not being too thorough about it so that it could look like a rushed job and lessen any possible suspicions that anyone might have. However, in the process of putting the last screw in, one of the rusted metal clamps managed to work itself loose and clanged to the ground. What was most unfortunate for Carl was that this was right at the time that the guard had turned the corner and made his way back around.

The guard approached the box carefully. "What's this?" he said out loud in his own tongue. "This cover was just off. I'd better radio this in."

Carl had studied his Russian, but he was not perfect at it yet. He was not 100% sure of what the guard had just said, but it had the distinct tone that meant if he did not do something very quickly, he was going to be in some very deep trouble. That was not exactly what he needed at the moment.

As the guard came close, Carl prepared to act. Every precious second that passed seemed like hours. Still, he waited for just the right moment. It would not pay to blow this opportunity now. He was so close to accomplishing the Primary Objective; and when on a mission, the Primary Objective was all that mattered.

'Two more steps, come on, just two more steps,' Carl was thinking to himself.

Just as if he were bidden, the guard took two more steps. He was painstakingly slow about it, but he did it, nonetheless. The moment the guard stepped into range, Carl's presence became crystal clear, but the guard never had time to react.

With amazing speed and precision, Carl reached out with one hand and grabbed the guard's mouth while, with the other hand, he grabbed the back of the guard's head to give himself some leverage. Then Carl spun the guard around and, after quickly removing his hand from behind the guard's head, slammed it up against the side of the building until he passed out.

Carl could feel the thick wet liquid oozing from the back of the man's head, but a quick assessment of the vital signs, which Carl was able to observe, told him that the guard would live. He quickly disarmed the guard. Reaching into his pouch, Carl pulled out a roll of packing tape, which he used to cover the guard's mouth. Then, extracting two lengths of rope, Carl tied the guard's hands behind his back and tied his feet together. Noticing the guard's keys, Carl removed them from his belt and put them in his own pocket. Carl began the task of dragging the guard's body out of view. Just as he was returning, he could hear another guard calling, "Sergei? Sergei? Ach! Probably off talking to that house girl again and neglecting his watch. The Major will not be happy about that!"

Carl just sat back and waited. He did not want to have to take out a second guard; especially one that seemed like he was going to be helpful with a misleading story. The second guard moved on.

Now, reaching into his bag again, Carl extracted another device and turned it on. This device would scramble all wireless communications transmitted in or out within a half-mile radius around the compound. Flipping the switch, however, did not have the desired effect. In fact, nothing happened.

"Just great," Carl said, obviously not talking to anyone other than himself. "This is the last thing that I need to go wrong." Carl flipped the switch on and off several times. Still, the indicator light did not come on. Carl took a radio out of his bag that he used to verify that the signal was working and he could still hear communications traffic.

With no time to troubleshoot the device and his Primary Objective still yet to be completed, Carl, in anger, slammed the device up against the side of the building. He was hoping that splintering the device into many tiny pieces would give him some sort of satisfaction. He would just have to find another way to deal with the wireless communications. But, to Carl's surprise, when he slammed the device up against the building, the radio that he had turned on immediately started emitting the static sound that is associated with interference.

Carl looked in his hand, and to his surprise, instead of the transmitter being split into many tiny little pieces, the indicator light was glowing, and the device was on, working like it was supposed to. "Hmmmmff," Carl said, again to nobody in particular, "imagine that." But Carl was not going to argue at the moment about how the device began working. The important thing was that it WAS working.

Pressing the side button now dimmed the light, which indicated proper functionality. Carl placed the transmitter out of the way and made his way over to the door.

Effectively all communications within the compound had now been disabled.

Back at the hotel, Major Mikhail Askinov knew that he had to act fast, or he was going to lose his catch. This HAD to be the famous agent Carl that he had always wanted the pleasure to face. And tonight, his career dream could come true!

"Radio the compound and tell them to be on the lookout for this Carl. Tell them we have no idea what he will look like, and he could already be there," said Askinov.

"Yes, Comrade Major," came the reply from the subordinate officer.

The officer tried to raise the compound on the radio over

and over again, but with no success. "Major Askinov, I am unable to make radio communications with the compound."

"Then get on the telephone, you idiot. Do I need to tell you everything?" said Askinov.

"Yes, Comrade," said the officer.

The telephone yielded the same results as the radio had.

"Comrade Major, there is no answer at the compound. The telephone just keeps ringing. No one is picking it up." The office reported.

"Oh, No," said Askinov. "Everyone to the vehicles. We must act now or our catch will flee."

The agents, following their orders, all ran downstairs to their vehicles. No matter how hard they tried, none of the vehicles would start. An examination found that the starters had been removed from all of the vehicles. Other than these, there were no other vehicles in the immediate vicinity.

"You idiots! Was there no one guarding the vehicles?" asked Askinov.

"You ordered everyone inside when we got here, Comrade," came the reply.

"Well, that is obviously NOT what I meant. Can't you just read my mind sometimes? There should ALWAYS be someone protecting the vehicles! ALWAYS. You act like you have never done this before. Anticipate the need, man! If you do not, you can only dream about getting to my level, but you'll never get there."

"Yes Comrade. My apologies," said the officer.

"Apologies are not what I need right now, Lieutenant. What I need right now is transportation. Find me another vehicle!" said Askinov.

"Yes, Comrade. Right away!"

The Lieutenant started barking orders and his men began to disperse. Everyone was off to find another vehicle so that they could get Askinov to the compound.

As the men were about to depart, Askinov shouted, "Lieutenant, have you learned nothing?"

Looking back at the Major, he was not sure what message was trying to be conveyed, and then he realized that he had not left anyone to guard the now useless vehicles. Barking out another order at one of the men, the Lieutenant said, "You! Stay behind and guard the cars." Then, in a lower voice that the major could not hear, he said, "Why you have to guard cars that are useless to us and cannot go anywhere is beyond me, but guard them anyway. If it seems foolish to you, then just act like you're guarding the Major, and perhaps that will help. Whatever you do, just don't do anything to get him angry before we get back."

"I shall guard the vehicles, Lieutenant," said the subordinate, being careful not to respond to anything else that was said.

"Now you're thinking, Lieutenant," said Askinov.

Askinov waited patiently. He had very little choice. There was really nothing else that he could do. He even chatted for a bit with the man who was left behind to guard him and the cars. Nothing of much substance was said between the two of them, but it was nice of the Major to make the attempt.

After about fifteen minutes, Major Askinov could hear the rumble of what sounded like motorcycles coming his way. He looked up to see the Lieutenant coming around the corner with the rest of his men. All of them were riding four-wheelers.

"What in the name of the Kremlin do you have here, Lieutenant?" Askinov questioned.

"Four-wheelers, Comrade Major. Hop on," said the Lieutenant.

"Hop on?" Askinov repeated in an incredulous tone of voice. "Surely you are kidding me, Lieutenant. Is this the best that you could do?"

"Given more time, I probably could have done better, Comrade Major, but in the interest of getting you to the compound as soon as we possibly could, I opted for the first mode of transportation that we encountered. We had to confiscate them from a group of teens, but it was in the name of justice for which we acted."

"Well, good decision, Lieutenant," said Askinov. "How am I supposed to ride on this thing? I mean, where exactly do I get on? I'm used to vehicles with totally different configurations, which are much easier to get into," Askinov said.

"Just hop on right behind me, Comrade Major, and grab onto my waist. We'll be at the compound in no time," the Lieutenant answered.

"Hop on behind you and grab onto your waist? Surely there is another way."

"Well, yes, there is, Comrade. You can drive and I can hold on to your waist," the Lieutenant said.

"Me, drive one of those things? I don't think so, Lieutenant."

"Well, that is what I thought you might say, Sir. How's that for reading your mind?"

The disagreeable and condescending look that the Major gave the Lieutenant said it all. No words needed to be spoken.

"Just... trying to do what you said, Comrade Major," the Lieutenant said feebly.

Getting on to the four-wheeler and putting his arms around the Lieutenant's waist to hold on, Askinov said, "OK, Lieutenant, let's get this over with as quickly as possible. And don't you dare tell anyone about this, do you hear?" Then, looking around, the Major said, "If I hear mention of this in any circle, I know everyone that is here, and you will all pay dearly. I hope that I make myself understood."

"Understood, Comrade Major," came the staggering replies.

As they bounded down the dirt road at the fastest possible speed, Askinov said, "I will catch you, Agent Carl. I will catch you, and I will kill you, and we will ship your wretched body back to your pitiful United States of America. Even if it is the last thing I do, it will be done!"

"I assume that you are NOT talking to me, Comrade Major," yelled the Lieutenant back over the din as he continued to stare ahead.

"Drive, Lieutenant! Just shut up and drive!" said Askinov.

The Lieutenant figured he had pushed his luck far enough, so he set to concentrating on the road and getting the Major to the compound as quickly as he could.

Chapter 20

Carl was not sure how much longer his luck was going to hold out. There were a lot of people around, and he had quite a bit of ground to cover. He needed to move fast. His chances of getting caught increased exponentially with every second he was there. This he knew all too well.

Now that all communications had been disrupted, surely, they would have no idea that he was there, but they would definitely be trying to troubleshoot the problem. Without any way of contacting anyone on the outside, no alarm could be sounded to alert anyone, so he still had the advantage. At some point he was going to have to turn off the wireless device jammer, but that would not be until he had rescued Lawrence and needed to call for the rescue chopper that would ferry them away. Of course, all of that was with the caveat that everything went according to plan.

Carl was now at the back door, trying key after key from the chain he had acquired earlier. He was hoping that one of these keys actually did work in the lock. Carl was beginning to have his doubts, but he persevered. Finally, one of the keys that he inserted into the lock engaged when it was turned. Carl heard the familiar click that he had been longing to hear. He did not have to resort to explosives, at least not yet.

On the off chance that the keys might jingle and give him away, Carl put them into a soundproof pouch that he carried in his bag for just such an occasion. This was the first time he had ever had to use it. He had been considering taking it out of his standard gear because it was never used. He was glad that he had not yet made that change.

Upon entering, Carl had to let his eyes adjust. The lighting was very dim, and he did not want to turn on any additional light that might alert anyone to his presence. Even in the dim light, Carl noticed that the layout was much different from the first time he had been there, just weeks ago. The walls seemed to have been erected in a different pattern.

Carl now remembered from the talks that he had with Colonel Welch before, that the Colonel indicated that they changed the patterns regularly for security reasons; but in his long stay at the Russian-controlled Estonian facility, he noticed that there were only six patterns that they used, and there did not seem to be any variations to these six patterns.

Colonel Welch had drilled these patterns into Carl's mind. Carl could determine which way he needed to go based on his recognition of the pattern from those sessions. As he turned the corner, Carl saw something he did NOT expect. Biometric locks had been installed. This, undoubtedly, was not going to be the last one that he encountered in the building. Carl was not prepared to duplicate voice patterns, fingerprints, or any other biometric input. He thought about the keys that sat in the noise-proof pouch in his pack. They would be useless for biometric locks.

Carl could hear voices approaching, and he needed to find some place out of the way to hide. He slinked around the corner, in the opposite direction from which the voices were coming, and waited. Now the voices were closer. Even though these men were talking in the native Estonian language, Carl could make out what they were saying. To Carl's trained ear, from the sound of the voices one man sounded markedly older than the other.

"So, my young friend, do you want to go up and see the

American pig? I can't imagine what they think is so special about him," said the older man.

"Certainly. I'm game. But shouldn't we be manning our post?" asked the younger, a bit more worried about the career ahead of him.

"Ahh, don't even worry. Nobody will be around on our shift. We have nothing to be concerned about," the older replied.

"Well, if you say so. After all, you are the more experienced. Let's go ahead and do it then. Are you coded for the locks?" asked the younger. "I don't think I'm in the system yet."

"I bet you are! If you're in this building, then you, more than likely, have access to the new locks."

"Well, OK, let me try it then," said the younger of the two. When they came up to the first door, the young man put his thumb on the panel. After a moment, his thumbprint was recognized and the first of the locks clicked open.

"See there? What did I tell you? Never doubt old Vladamir."

"Well, I guess you were right about this one. But will I be able to gain access to all levels?"

"If you get access to one, you get access to all. The Russians did not discriminate between levels when developing the system," said the older.

Carl's mission had just gotten much easier. Not only did he have confirmation that Lawrence was still being held in the compound, but he also might be able to piggyback through the biometric locks just by following these two men.

As the men passed through the door, Carl delayed his approach and then, sneaking up behind them, caught the door just before it closed and slipped in. He then allowed the door to close naturally. He flattened himself against the wall as he waited for them to get through the next lock. The chameleon property of the body armor was doing its job. Carl continued to go undetected.

The younger of the guards kept telling his older companion that they should slow down. Standard procedure dictated that one biometric lock should be closed before activating another.

"Oh, don't be so paranoid. The doors will close just fine by themselves. I don't know who came up with such stupid rules in the first place. Besides, way out where we are, it's not like we're being followed."

"I'm not sure who came up with them either, but the rules were made to be followed," cautioned the young man.

"And broken," said the other man with a sly grin and a slight raise of the eyebrows.

Finally giving in, the younger guard stopped paying attention and let the doors take care of themselves. Had they thought to do it by the book, Carl may have been easily detected. At the very least, it would certainly have made his job of infiltrating the inner compound much harder. But, as it stood now, they had gone through all seven of the biometric access points without a problem, and Carl had followed them through every lock. The Russians took turns at each lock, using their alternating fingerprints to gain access to the next door. Finally, they reached Lawrence and quickly determined that he did not appear to be too exciting a prize to watch. So, they began to goad him to see if they could get some type of reaction out of him.

The Estonian Kapten, put in charge by the Russians, was reviewing the last torture session to see if there was any little tidbit of information that he could grasp from what the prisoner had said.

"This one is a hard one to crack," said the Estonian Kapten. "At least we were able to ascertain Colonel Welch's name and rank in the very early torture sessions."

Being able to get just a little information, useless though it was, at least gave them hope. But THIS prisoner would not even give them that satisfaction. When asked his name, he came out with the name of every Russian leader in history, but never his own name, and certainly no rank. Finally, Lawrence's stock answer to the question about what his name was became: Joseph Stalin.

Lawrence became affectionately known as Comrade Stalin when he would not answer to anything else.

In this last torture session, Lawrence became a little punchy, if not incredibly brave. Whenever he was asked his name, he would, of course, reply with Joseph Stalin. When asked his rank, he would reply, "Czar! And that would be with a C-z, not a T-z."

When asked any other questions, Lawrence would reply with a patriotic American song or a Bible verse. He made a point of letting them know that he was quoting from the King James Version.

At one point Lawrence modified a Bible verse and let them know that it was from his own made-up version. In answer to their questions, he repeatedly answered: "Resist the Russians and they will flee from you!" Then just to really get on their nerves, Lawrence would continue using the same response, but he would alternate saying it in English, Russian and their native Estonian tongue. Lawrence did have to admit that the Russian and Estonian versions did lose something in the translation. But he knew it would just irritate the fire out of his captors. And it did.

The Kapten finally concluded that there was nothing worth keeping from their latest session. He was under direct orders from the Russians to make sure no lasting harm came to the prisoner, but this was making it increasingly difficult for him to accomplish the main goal of extracting crucial information.

"We must use more stringent measures. This man WILL talk! I have seen his type before," said the Kapten.

"Sir, I must remind you of the International Rules of Conduct," said the younger officer.

"THE INTERNATIONAL RULES OF CONDUCT WILL NOT GET US ANY ANSWERS!" Yelled the Estonian Kapten. "Either he will cooperate, or he will die. And in that case, Nooremleitnant, the rules of conduct do not matter now, do they?" Asked the Kapten.

Carl retrieved from his depths of knowledge that this was the Estonian word for Junior Lieutenant.

"But which will the Russians be more pleased with?" countered the Nooremleitnant

"If I get them information, they will be pleased, and they will do whatever they need to in order to cover up anything else. I know how these Russians work. You just trust me on that one," said the Estonian Kapten. "I think I'll go and have a talk with our American Comrade Stalin."

Carl did not much care for the way these two guards were goading Lawrence. He was reaching the point where he was about to consider formulating plan B, which would begin with knocking the thunder out of these two guards. Carl was sure that he could take them; the questions were: Would it be worth the risk? And how quietly could it be done?

Just as he was considering these things, Carl heard footsteps coming from far down the corridor. He ducked back into a cubby and let his body armor do its magic and camouflage him.

The Estonian Kapten entered in full uniform. Carl could tell his rank by the four round pips on each lapel. Carl found it odd that he walked without an escort, but then realized that they didn't expect there to be any danger this far away from everyone else and being here in their own country.

When the Kapten rounded the corner and found the two guards goading the American prisoner, he was not the least bit happy.

"Veebel! Seersant! What is the meaning of this? Explain at once." He demanded as he spoke in their native tongue.

Carl knew from his crash course in Estonian that the

Kapten was addressing a Warrant Officer and a Sergeant. The Warrant Officer and the Kapten had obviously had dealings before, and the older enlisted man did not hide his contempt or lack of respect for the Kapten.

"I said explain at once. You are both to be at your posts. You should be nowhere near the American prisoner. Yet, here you are. What do you have to say for yourselves?" demanded the Estonian Kapten.

"We owe you no answers," said the elder Warrant Officer. "Go back to your little torture chamber and let us be. You were a Warrant Officer once, just like me. You didn't even earn that rank that you have on your shoulders. The Russians GAVE it to you. Go and impress somebody else; you don't impress me. And, besides that, everyone knows that I should have been the man in your position."

The young Sergeant was horrified that the Warrant Officer would address a superior, no matter how he got his rank, in this fashion. You could see the distressed look on his face.

"I give you one opportunity to retract your statements and get on with your duties. I am Kapten, and you are Veebel, and that is that," said the Kapten.

"One more chance. BAH! One more chance or what?" said the Warrant Officer.

In answer to his question the Kapten pulled his firearm, feeling that he had provocation, fired three times into the, now, backward propelling Warrant Officer. The look on the Warrant Officer's face was one of genuine shock.

"I thought surely that you didn't have it in you," he said, gasping for breath.

"THAT is why I am Kapten, and YOU are... well... were Veebel!" the Kapten spat back.

The Warrant Officer took his last labored breaths, and there he died.

The young Sergeant stared in shock and was hoping that he was not next. He did not say anything disrespectful and surely had not done anything to deserve that fate.

"Seersant! I will need a new Veebel. Are you up to the task?" asked the Kapten.

"Jah, jah, Kapten. And I most humbly thank you for the opportunity. Anything that I can do—"

"Yes, grovel later. For now, take this trash out to the forest and let the nocturnal animals have a little something to eat. Then report to me in one hour and be sure to have your rank insignias updated. I will prepare your duty assignments for you at that time."

Carl was elated. If the Kapten was going to help him out like this, he might have a very easy time of it. But then something happened that told Carl his time was quickly running out...

"Comrade Stalin," said the Estonian Kapten in passable English.

'Comrade Stalin!' Carl almost laughed as he thought this to himself. 'What in the world does Lawrence have these people thinking?'

"Comrade Stalin, you will answer me!" said the Kapten.

"Or what?" said Lawrence. "Are you going to shoot me too, Kapten?"

"Perhaps. I have had enough of your games, Comrade Stalin. I will have your real name, and I will have your real purpose for being here. I will have any information from you that I want because now I will deal with you the way that I want to. Now I will deal with you the way that you NEED to be dealt with."

"Listen, Comrade Kapten, send me a memo with the particulars and—" Lawrence stopped abruptly. From behind the Kapten he could see somebody trying to signal him, and he was momentarily taken back.

"And what?" said the Kapten.

"And I'll try to get back to you as soon as I can," Lawrence finished.

"You think, Comrade Stalin or whatever your name is, that you are the smarter one here. You think that you will win this little game that you are playing. Well, I have news for you, Comrade, you will not. The next torture session you have will be the worst session you have had since you've been here, and I guarantee that you will either talk or you will die. I must go and make my preparations, but I just thought I would give you a little something to think about."

With that, the Kapten turned tail and walked indignantly back down the corridor.

CHAPTER 21

With the Estonian Captain gone, Carl came out from hiding. As he approached, Lawrence, who was now restrained, was a little ill at ease. In the body armor, Lawrence had no way of telling who it was until Carl spoke.

"Greetings Silver Fox. Bird of Prey is back on the scene. Can't leave a man behind enemy lines on my watch," said Carl.

"Man, am I glad to see you," said Lawrence.

"I bet! But tell me," Carl said as he worked to free Lawrence, "what in the world is going on with this Comrade Stalin thing?"

"Oh, that's simple. They're trying to break me, but I'm working on a reverse psychology. I'm trying to break them first. So, I have them trained to call me the only thing that I will respond to. They get so frustrated because I will not answer to anything else. Pretty smart, huh?" said Lawrence.

"After what I just saw that Captain do to the Warrant Officer, and the torture threat that the Captain just made, I think the jury is still out on whether that's pretty smart or not," said Carl.

"So, what's the plan? More importantly, what's with the getup?" asked Lawrence.

"This old thing?" asked Carl, pointing to himself. "This is that body armor that everyone has been ranting and raving about. A prototype that they made from a little present I brought them a few years ago. The only problems are it's really expensive, and it's still in the experimental phase," said Carl.

"Oh, OK, you bring any PJs for me?" Lawrence asked with a snicker.

Carl knew he was referring to the fact that the body armor looked like pajamas, but just shrugged it off.

"Negative, my friend. You get to go out in your clothes. From the sound of things, we don't have too long to make that happen, so I don't guess we'll be going out as quietly as I came in. I also don't think we'll need to worry about sneaking back out on the truck. In fact, all of my plans are now being modified on the fly," said Carl.

"Well, I hate to burst your bubble, Buddy, but I'm not in the best physical condition at the moment. I think you better just get out of here. If not, you're going to wind up leaving me again," said Lawrence.

"No can do, my friend. YOU are the Primary Objective, and from the reports that we've been getting, you look like you're exactly in the condition that I was expecting... actually better. That being the case, you'll be getting out of here today. So don't even try to get out of it. Now, what are your ailments?" Carl asked.

"Well, the legs are shot. They've been using this special stretching treatment for guys who are stubborn like me. They've been alternating that with wrapping me in wet strips and then putting me under sun lamps and having them dry and constrict my body. I didn't let them know, but that one almost broke me. I can't even begin to tell you how much that hurt. I sure do hope you'll never have to find out. But we were talking about my ailments. Well, let's see, I told you about the legs. I have absolutely little or no stamina because of those lovely constriction treatments. So, I can't do a lot of moving for long periods of time. Whatever you have on your mind for getting us out of here is going to have to be quick or involve some way of transporting me, because I can't do it on my own," said Lawrence.

"Well, based on what el Ca-pi-tan said, I need to hurry up and get you out of here anyway. Glad I planned for the worst," said Carl.

"The worst?" asked Lawrence. "I'm sure you're not meaning what I think you mean."

"Yes, I am. I was prepared to carry your body out of here somehow if I had to. I had no idea whether or not I was going to find you alive. In either case, I was not going home empty-handed," said Carl.

"OK," said Lawrence. "So, what are your mid-range options for the guy who can't do a whole lot but can still function some?"

"Drugs, my friend. Drugs," said Carl.

"I'm thrilled," Lawrence said in a very recognizably sarcastic tone. "What kind of drugs?"

"I don't know what's in it. I just know that this is what the folks at Medical decided would work the best. So, whatever this is, it's the cocktail that THEY gave to me, and it is what I'm supposed to give to you," said Carl as he produced a hypodermic needle. "Now let me give you this shot, then eat this and give it a minute to kick in."

Carl gave Lawrence what appeared to be a block of candy.

"Exactly what am I eating?" Lawrence inquired.

"I know about as much about what's in that little block of candy as I do about what is in the needle."

"Great."

"Oh, just be quiet and roll up your sleeve. Or do I need to do that for you too?" Carl asked his colleague.

Lawrence rolled up his sleeve and Carl administered the shot. Lawrence didn't feel any immediate changes take place. He ate the block of faux candy as Carl instructed.

Carl glanced at his watch and said, "OK, be ready to move in five minutes. As soon as you hear the explosion."

"I'm telling you I'm not going anywhere. Just get yourself out of here," Lawrence pleaded.

"Without accomplishing the Primary Objective? Been there. Done that. Or have you already forgotten about the last time?"

"Right," said Lawrence as he watched Carl place a charge on the cell door and set it for four minutes and 25 seconds. "That's going to be just a little bit noisy, don't you think?"

"Hard to tell. These are also purely experimental. They are supposed to create a near silent implosion but pack just as much power as a normal charge."

"You mean this hasn't been field tested yet?" Lawrence asked incredulously.

"This IS the field test," said Carl with a smile.

"Why do I wish that you were kidding?"

"I'm not sure, but I never kid about such things. You know that," said Carl.

"Yeah. I know," said Lawrence.

Both men waited in silence for a few minutes and watched the time as it counted down. As the counter broke the one-minute mark, Carl said, "Alright, you better get back."

Lawrence was still unsure about what was in that shot, but he now had energy that he did not have before, and his ailments seemed to have gone away.

Both men watched the last seconds of the countdown... 5... 4... 3... 2... 1... "BOOM!!" The near-silent explosion ripped the cell door right off of its hinges. Carl and Lawrence ran over and stepped through the door. The men did not waste any time as they began their escape and headed for the next obstacle.

Here is where things were going to get a little dicey. They didn't have time to stop for biometric locks now. Carl planned on blasting his way right through them. He left several timed charges set as they went forward. Every time they hit another biometric lock, Lawrence placed the timed charges while Carl blew the lock.

Because they had now been detected, there were now soldiers in pursuit. Carl and Lawrence had a little bit of a head start, but they were going to need something more to make this escape a reality.

The timed charges were successful in delaying the pursuing soldiers. Several were incapacitated while trying to capture the escapees. Everything went like clockwork and the men were able to make it to the ground floor and escape the building, but now they had to navigate the hardest part of all. Their task now was to navigate the outer territory. While they had the cover of darkness, they had no structural, protective cover.

"Alright, Buddy, now what do we do?" asked Lawrence.

"Give me a second," said Carl. "I'm thinking."

At that point they could hear a rumbling noise, but neither man knew what the origin of it was.

The convoy of four-wheelers could be heard from a distance as they approached the compound. The guards stood at the ready. This was an unusual and unexpected visit, for sure. As they got closer, the guards could feel the ground under their feet begin to shake from the oncoming vehicles. The four-wheelers rolled to a stop, and the guards leveled their weapons, ready to fire if necessary.

"Open the Gates, open the gates!" Yelled Major Askinov.

"Who goes there? We weren't expecting anybody," said one of the guards on watch at the gate.

"What do you mean who goes there? Don't you know who I am? Everyone knows Mikhail Askinov," said Askinov, making no attempt to hide his vanity.

"Comrade Major! My apologies! I could not see you because of the dark, and you were not in your standard vehicle. I did not recognize you," said the guard.

The guards lowered their weapons. No one was willing to chance firing on Major Askinov.

"Open the gate! I have very good reason to believe that you have a breakout in progress, and I need to get in there.

Come on, man!" Askinov implored.

"Comrade Major, no one has radioed about a breakout. I think that all is well inside," said the gate guard.

"Check your radio and you will find out that it is not working. How do I know that? All radio communication to this compound has been cut off. Did you do that? No, of course you did not. Some American spy is on the loose, and he is in this compound. Now, I'm done being polite and my patience is just about gone." Raising his gun and pointing it at the guard, Askinov said, "Open the gate or die!"

The guard was swift to comply at this point and feared that he would have to face the ramifications of doing his job correctly later. He nodded to his colleagues, and the gate was opened immediately.

The convoy of four-wheelers came charging into the compound. Carl was calculating and recalculating. He didn't see any way that the two of them were going to make it out alive, but he did see a reasonable chance of one of them making it, and it could not be him. The Primary Objective must be accomplished.

"Listen, Lawrence. Chances are very slim that we are both getting out of here this time. I made your wife a promise before I left. I told her that I would get you out of here. The rule of thumb in regard to the Primary Objective supports that. I get to stay this time, Buddy. It's my turn. Here's the plan."

"No, no, Carl, wait," said Lawrence.

"No can do, my friend. My mission, my plan. Sorry, but this time you get to listen. You have a chance at the farthest four-wheeler. Take this gun. Here are your marks." Carl gave Lawrence his targets and got set to take his own. "Now, if I've judged the major right, they're about to charge. And something tells me that while they would like to have us both, they really don't care about you."

"Stop this thing and let me off!" said Askinov. "Get those two now! I want the one in the funny suit brought to me personally. You can kill the other one if you like."

As the four-wheelers, minus Askinov, charged at the two agents, Carl yelled, "NOW!"

Following Carl's lead, Lawrence easily took out his targets while Carl gave him cover fire. Then Carl fired a spread that took out two of the four-wheelers and sent the major scrambling for cover. Not missing a beat, Carl came back up again and fired, taking out the tires on the remaining four-wheelers. This only left the far four-wheeler, which Lawrence was already en route to.

Lawrence was trying to calculate how he could take his four-wheeler and circle back around for Carl. Carl, knowing what Lawrence was thinking, said, "NO! You are the Primary Objective. Get out of here!"

As Lawrence boarded the four-wheeler, Major Askinov ordered the guards to close the gate. Hearing his order, Carl fired a spread in the direction of the gate, injuring two of the four guards and sending the other two running with their tails tucked between their legs.

The Major, now the only obstacle between Lawrence and the gate, drew his weapon and trained it on the four-wheeler. Carl, seeing the Major's intentions, tried to fire but was out of ammunition. Thinking quickly, Carl did the only thing he had left to do. Running as fast as possible, he timed his actions as precisely as he could. Right at the point where Carl anticipated that the Major would have to fire, he propelled himself into the air, becoming a human obstacle between Lawrence and the Major's gunfire.

Carl twisted and turned in the air as the Major fired repeatedly. Shot after shot impacted Carl as he instinctively turned this way and that to intercept Major Askinov's shots. Carl saw

Lawrence trying to turn back again and was only able to utter the words "Primary Objective."

It was all he could say, but it was enough.

Lawrence's only thought now was that if the best of the best was going to go out, then he was going to make sure that his death was meaningful. He was going to make sure the last thing that was remembered was that Carl completed the Primary Objective of his last mission. With that thought in mind, Lawrence headed for the gate at top speed. Now, with no opposition left, he was home free.

The Major no longer cared about Lawrence. Carl was his prize. He ran over to Carl, who had struggled to remain conscious this long, and said, "So this is the famous agent Carl, I presume. You Americans certainly do things differently. Well, I have waited a long time for this day, and I wanted the so-called best of the best to know that Major Mikhail Askinov was the one who ended his life and career. Farewell."

As Carl began to rapidly lose consciousness, he heard a gunshot, and then there was nothing.

Chapter 22

The gunship was at the designated coordinates to pick up Lawrence when he arrived. They were expecting two passengers and were saddened when they learned that Carl had not made it out. But it seemed to give everyone solace to know that Carl's Primary Objective had been accomplished.

The gunship dropped Lawrence off at Ramstein Air Force Base as planned. The transport was already waiting and ready to take off as soon as they got clearance. The flight crew of the transport heard the news that Carl had been killed and looked at each other quizzically.

Once they were airborne, Lawrence could not shake the need to go back and, at least, retrieve Carl's body. He put in an air-to-surface call to his boss, Randall Springs.

"Listen, Randy; we can't leave things like this. I want to go back in," Lawrence was saying as he talked with Randall Springs, the Director of Eagle One, over a secure telephone line.

"Look, I know you want to go back in, but I also know that the Primary Objective of Carl's mission will not have been accomplished until you have crossed into U.S. air space," Springs explained to Lawrence.

"I'm out, Randy. He got me out. But what I saw... What I saw I will never forget. You always tell me that I am one heroic son of a gun. Well, Randy, you haven't seen heroic until you have seen Carl in action. Well, as far as that goes, I don't suppose you'll get that opportunity. I want that Major!" Lawrence said with finality.

"Listen, Lawrence. This is no time to go on a vendetta. That place is probably crawling with all kinds of authorities by now. Carl's mission was a success. You are free and the Russian-controlled facility in Estonia has been exposed. Besides that, you're in no shape to be on any mission right now. Those drugs that Carl gave you have worn off, and they have served their purpose. Look, I feel your pain, I really do. I hate to be the bad guy here, but the orders are coming from higher up, and I have to follow through. You're being recalled," Springs told him.

"I have to pretend you didn't say those words. If I didn't hear those words, I could do what needs to be done, and I could do it with a good feeling."

"Lawrence! Silver Fox! I need you to hear me... You... are... being... recalled," said Randall Springs as slowly and succinctly as possible. "Stand down."

Lawrence realized that he had been defeated, in a sense. He knew that the best way that he could honor Carl would be for him to make it back to the States and set his feet on American soil once more. Reluctantly, Lawrence stood down. He would do it for Carl.

When the time was right, he would be back.

"Listen, just so you have a heads up, security is going to be heavy. Things are so much in flux that we had a hard time trying to find a willing pilot to fly the military transport back. Even though it is a military flight, we're not being too relaxed. You will have agents accompanying you. Their identification will remain confidential. They will have you in plain view at all times. Don't try to shake them. Just deal with it," said Springs. "Eagle One wants you back."

"That's affirmative," said Lawrence, formally acknowledging his recall orders and being very official. "Silver Fox acknowledges recall orders. Mission complete."

The C-130 military transport took a long time to land and an even longer time to be cleared. This was only the first leg of the flight back. Lawrence was ushered off the plane and walked down two hangars where another military transport was expected.

The C-20H gulfstream rolled into the hangar rather quietly. Maintenance crews immediately began the refueling and restocking processes.

After maintenance was completed, boarding the plane was an interesting affair. Lawrence was accompanied by two agents that went EVERYWHERE he went except for the bathroom. They only felt the need for one agent to accompany him there. Thank goodness the upgraded bathrooms on the C-20H were a bit more spacious. Everywhere else on the flight, the agents stayed on either side of him. Lawrence did not know the identity of the agents and didn't know if he ever would. They were dressed in the standard 'Columbo' detective attire: Trench coat, brimmed hat with ribbon, pulled down so that no one could tell who they were, shades... the stuff that spies wore, according to all of the TV and movie nonsense.

It looked like they were flying back to Washington in style. The C-20H is a Gulfstream jet that was specially modified for the military. If Lawernce was not mistaken, this particular model should have been decommissioned. That, obviously, was not the case.

As he sat, eager to take off, Lawrence noticed that the pilot switch seemed to be rather involved. There was a lot more commotion than the usual offboarding and onboarding, but it looked like they worked everything out. With all the perceived delays that they were having, Lawrence wondered who it was that they actually got to fly the mission. Whoever it was, he just hoped that they were good.

His thoughts of who they got to fly the C-20H back home rapidly faded away as he thought about the fact that not only was he leaving a man behind, but there was nothing he was able to do to save the life of the agent with the Codename: C.A.R.L. Lawrence would take it upon himself to be the one to inform Carl's wife. There were some personal things he wanted to tell her that she definitely should know, and that she would not find out from somebody who was not present and in the thick of the action. Yeah, Carl was definitely the epitome of heroism.

Lawrence absolutely hated the middle seat, but with his agents protecting him on both sides, that was the only option for him. At least they were in the front row. The other plus was that the seats were not crammed together like in economy class. They were comfortable, plush leather seats. It certainly could have been worse.

On top of Lawrence's already bad feelings, these bodyguards didn't even talk. Oh, they guarded his body just fine, but for all intents and purposes, they lacked conversational skills.

Washington would hear about this.

The military transport roared down the runway and proceeded to lift into the sky. The ride was very smooth. Lawrence looked past his right guard and out the window to observe the view. He could see them rise through layers of clouds as the plane climbed higher and higher. Suddenly, red lights started flashing in the aisles. It quickly became obvious that, even with all their precautions, somebody knew who was on the plane and did not want them to reach their destination alive.

The voice of the pilot came over the intercom. His demeanor was as cool as a cucumber. "The seat belt sign has been illuminated. Please remain seated and strapped in for your safety. By the way, we have incoming. Two anti-aircraft missiles are headed this way. The mapped trajectory shows them headed directly for this aircraft. Somebody is not playing fair today. Initiating firing sequence to counter the attack. Firing… Missiles away, please monitor," the pilot directed his co-pilot.

"Tracking…" the co-pilot responded. "Contact in 4… 3… 2… 1…"

BOOM! BOOM!

"Direct contact. Threats Neutralized... I have friendly aircraft coming in off the starboard bow. Friendly aircraft, please identify."

"This is Captain O'Neil. Squad Leader of the 5th F-18 fighter squadron. We picked up your activity in our patrol area. We're detecting VIP military beacons on your aircraft. Welcome to our airspace. How may we assist? My team is at your disposal."

"Roger that, Captain O'Neil. If you like, you can send our friends a little message. Transmitting coordinates now. We have determined the site of the missile's origin. If you'd like some target practice, you are authorized to take them out," the pilot relayed.

"Roger that C-20H. Sure does beat a routine patrol mission. Coordinates received and being relayed to the patrol squadron... Target is acquired. All craft fire on my mark. 3-2-1 Mark! F-18s are firing. Eight air-to-surface missiles away! Stand by for impact in 7... 6... 5... 4... 3... 2... 1. We have impact! Waiting for triangulated results from the computers for confirmation... Coordinated retaliation is successful. Eight direct hits. The radar reports target has been destroyed. Your message has been sent and received, Sir," said Captain O'Neil.

"We Confirm, Captain O'Neil," said the C-20H pilot. "Thanks for the assist."

"The pleasure is all ours, C-20H. It's nice to have a little change every now and then. F-18s are going supersonic and returning to the patrol area. Safe trip to you. O'Neil out."

The resounding cheers were deafening and lasted for almost three minutes. After everyone settled down, the C-20H Gulfstream military transport increased altitude and settled in at maximum cruising speed.

Lawrence wanted to nod off, but there was way too much going on. Too much could happen while he was asleep. He wanted to be awake for everything and anything that happened. Particularly if he was going to die; he wanted to know it first. Not that he was going to be able to do anything about it, but at least he would know.

About nine hours into the flight, the pilot was alerted by the onboard systems that the C-20H had just crossed into U.S. airspace.

"Switch all systems to automated," said the pilot.

`Affirmative. I have control,` came the response from the flight computer.

The pilot got up and decided to personally inform the agents that they had reached U.S. airspace and that security measures could be relaxed. He left the cockpit and walked into the main passenger cabin. There, sitting in the front, was Lawrence Blackwell with his twin agents on either side. As Lawrence focused on the figure coming toward him, he thought his eyes were playing tricks on him. Surely, this could not be who he thought it was. Lawrence wanted to jump to attention but was prevented by the seatbelt.

"Special agent Blackwell, I am here to announce that we have reached U.S. airspace. The Primary Objective has been accomplished. My compliments on a job well done."

Again, for the second time in the flight, the plane erupted with applause, shouts, and screams of joy. The pilot was still standing there when the noise died down, with his hand outstretched to shake Lawrence's hand.

"Are you who I think you are?" Lawrence asked slowly and carefully.

Knowing full well what Lawrence was asking, the pilot decided not to be direct... yet... "Well now, that all depends on who you think I am," said the pilot. "Right now I am on a mission, and such being the case, you may call me Viper."

Now Lawrence's senses began to reel. "No! Wait a minute. YOU are the President of the United States—you're Curtis Young—and Viper... Viper is dead. Everyone knows that Viper is dead," said Lawrence. Then, as an afterthought, he threw in the trailing question, "Viper is dead, right?"

"Well, for my sake," Viper said, "since I AM Viper, I sincerely hope that he is very much alive. While the Primary Objective has been reached for you, it has not yet been reached for me until I land this plane safely with you aboard. I just wanted to come and let you know, personally, that we had crossed into U.S. airspace and to compliment you on a job well done. I look forward to reading your report."

"I appreciate the compliment, Mr. President, but a man died to save my life. Sir, I feel as though I am personally responsible for the best of the best getting killed. He put his life on the line to complete the Primary Objective. Sir? What about my Primary Objective? I was supposed to be watching him. And now, Sir, now he's dead."

"Watch your mouth there, Silver Fox. How dare you put me in the grave before my time," said the bodyguard to his left.

Lawrence heard the voice of Carl Reardon come from his left and could not believe his ears. Taking off the hat and overcoat, Carl said, "I sincerely hope you're still up to doing the job. Lord knows I need all the help I can get!"

CHAPTER 23

If it could be said that it was possible to shock one's socks off, that is exactly what one would say had just happened to Lawrence Blackwell. He didn't know whether to hug Carl, shake his hand, or hit him. "But how? I saw you get shot! I saw you get shot a lot of times! Then I saw the Major go over to finish you off. I'll never forget that sight. And there I was headed for the gate and freedom. I felt like a second-class citizen."

"As for me getting shot," Carl replied, "that part was easy. I'm sure you recall the body armor that I was wearing. Well, it has been specially designed to resist the puncture of bullets... up to a certain degree, of course. And, as I was trying to tell you, the thing was still in its experimental stages. I wasn't even sure if that particular functionality was actually going to work. I sure was praying that it did! Hurt like the dickens, but it was better than sustaining the actual gunshot wounds."

"OK... wow, this is way too much for me. I can at least understand that part, but how do you explain the gunshot? I saw the major go and finish you off. I heard the shot, but I never actually looked back to see him pull the trigger," said Lawrence.

"It turns out that, while I thought I was alone in the compound trying to rescue you, I actually had an assistant I didn't know about. Does the name Snow White ring a bell?"

"Snow White? Sure. But how do you know about her? That's classified above your level. And she's missing… in… action…" Lawrence said slowly, "just like Viper is supposed to be!"

"Well, she's not missing, and I would be willing to say you may know her better than you think," Carl said.

"No. That I doubt. I would absolutely know if I met her," Lawrence said.

Standing up and dropping her disguise, Renee said, "Perhaps not. I hear she keeps pretty good secrets, and you've been married to her for quite some time. Snow White. Renee Blackwell. Call me whatever you like. Just know that I have missed you very much!"

"Renee? You're Snow White? How? What? I don't understand," said Lawrence, obviously very confused at this point.

"Oh, just be quiet and kiss me!" Renee demanded, jumping into her husband's arms.

And kiss her he did.

When Renee Blackwell finally let her husband come up for air, Lawrence said, "Wow, now that's what I call a reunion. But you've got some explaining to do. Number one: What is this about you being Snow White?" asked Lawrence.

"Renee, please allow me," said Viper.

Renee gave a nod, and Viper continued.

"Well, Lawrence, you know how we like to make sure our top men are taken care of. That's why we had you watching Carl here. So, who was watching you? Well, for the past 11 years, it's been your wife."

Lawrence looked quizzically at Renee as Viper continued:

"Oh, at first, you were just another assignment.

Then something happened.

She fell in love.

When she knew for sure, she arranged what you probably thought were chance meetings. You two met for what you thought was the first time. Until then, she had strictly worked in the background. She needed to see if you might like her too.

I approved of the idea and the two of you dated. Guess what? YOU fell in love too. I saw it as an excellent opportunity. All of this could still work, even if you were married. In fact, it would give Renee more of a vested interest to make sure you stayed alive. It worked out well. This little lady has saved your skin more times than I think you care to know. She's good! Sometimes, dressed as a man, she's been right next to you, and you haven't known it. So that's the gist of number one," said Viper.

"OK," said Lawrence. "Number two: What in the world happened back there? What does Carl mean he had help? YOU?" came Lawrence's second question.

"Yes, that would have been me," said Renee. "Curt here will tell you, since he's known me all my life, that I'm pretty persistent—"

"Whoa! Wait a minute now. Curt? You and the President of the United States are on a first name basis? Next thing you're going to tell me is that you look alike because you're his sister."

"Well, I see no reason to restate the obvious," Renee said with a grin.

"Oh, Come on! I was just kidding," said Lawrence.

"No joke, love. Now, let me finish my story. When I left Carl at the airport, I told him I had a flight to book. I didn't say what the destination of that flight was. Knowing that he probably was not going to trust me, I booked my flight to Estonia through a different path and different airline—which, by the way, is infinitely easier to do once you're over here, on this side of the world.

"Anyway. Continuing the story, it hasn't been easy, but I've been tailing Carl. I knew he was trying to get to you, and I also knew that somebody was still trying to get to HIM. The Primary Objective for me, in a support role, became to protect Carl. I didn't have as much excitement as I've read in your reports about protecting him, but it has been fun nonetheless.

"I sabotaged the Estonian cars when they came to pay Carl a visit at the hotel and then made my way to the compound. I was too late to help him with the escape attempt, but I knew I could still play a vital support role. So, once inside the gate, I found a place and waited. I knew Carl must be inside because all communications were jammed. That meant that sooner or later you guys would be coming out. I was just beginning to feel as though I had waited long enough when the two of you came bursting through the door and into the courtyard area. Not having any idea what Carl's plan was, and not wanting to interfere if he actually had one, I had to sit and wait.

"A guard stumbled upon me and was about to sound the alarm but was distracted by the four-wheelers. Unfortunately for him, it was just long enough for me to act. He won't be distracted by anything anymore."

"Man, I sure am glad you're on our side," said Lawrence. "So, go on."

"Well," said Renee, "still not knowing what Carl's plan was, my hands were tied. I had to wait. That's when I saw you two go into action. Pretty smooth, by the way, guys. You two should work together more often. Anyway. I watched you execute your plan, and I was keeping an eye on old Comrade Major. I was going to take him out when I saw Carl do this crazy leap in the air to distract him and then get shot three times.

"When Carl went down, I started moving in his direction. I was saddened when I thought that Carl was dead. The least I could do was get his body out of there. That's when old Comrade Major charged over to Carl's side and, seeing that there was still life in his body, he was going to kill him. I was seething mad. It was not my intention to pull the wrong weapon, but instead of pulling my .45 automatic, in my haste, I pulled the .50 Desert Eagle—you know, the one we use to blow holes in doors to get through quickly. My target was already acquired. I took aim and fired before the major could.

"I found out later that Carl heard the shot, but what Carl didn't know is that the result of that was not the loss of his own life. The result of that was the major's head being totally disintegrated by the force of the close blast of the .50 Desert Eagle. I was aiming for a heart kill shot. The recoil modified my trajectory. The Major's headless body immediately went limp. I took the opportunity to get Carl out of there. I managed, with many, many stops, to get him to my drop-off point. The few and the proud showed up right on time, and we left via a Marine helicopter. I radioed Curt while en route and found out that he was on his way over to fly this plane back. He said not to say anything so as not to spoil his fun. So, there you have it."

"OK, whoa! whoa! Now wait a minute. I know you were having problems trying to get a pilot for this mission, and last I heard there was no co-pilot. That being the case, if you're out here, then who in the world is flying the plane?" asked Carl.

That would be me, Boss. I've always wanted to fly.

"CLARA?"

I'm impressed. You remembered.

"CLARA, you're not very easy to forget. It's only been a few days."

I think that is a compliment, so thank you.

"You're welcome, CLARA. Take us home."

Gladly, Boss. ETA to Regan National Airport is five hours, five minutes, and 36.8 seconds. Can somebody relieve me in about an hour so that I can use the restroom?

"CLARA!" said all of the agents at the same time.

My goodness. Keep your pants on. I was just kidding. Don't you know a joke when you hear one? I was just trying to exercise my humor subroutines. Rough crowd.

CHAPTER 24

As they approached the airport, Viper relieved CLARA and took over the controls. It had been a long time since he actually had to sit behind the controls of a plane. Being a pilot was like riding a bicycle. It all came back to him in a heartbeat. Viper breathed deeply as he settled in and took control from the computer. He began tapping buttons to make adjustments as he communicated with the tower at the same time. It was like he and the air traffic controller were old buddies.

Viper flew a perfect landing pattern and eventually brought the plane to a nice, smooth landing. As he brought the plane down, he thought, as he often did, about what his flight instructor told him years ago: "Curt," the instructor said, "always remember that a plane crash is caused by an uncontrolled aircraft. A landing is just a controlled crash. Remember that and you should do fine every time.

'One more controlled crash under my belt,' Viper thought to himself, 'and another one bites the dust.'

Now that he had the plane on the ground and his agents were safe, his Primary Objective had been accomplished. Time to get back to real life and running the country. Viper went into the pilot's cabin, changed into his expensive three-piece suit with accessories, and called for his Secret Service detail.

It was time to be President again.

After the long debriefing, Lawrence and Renee Blackwell headed for home. Lawrence almost asked if they were going to send an escort when he remembered that he had his own personal bodyguard, who had more of an interest in keeping him alive than anyone.

The Blackwells had a long, long talk about all the events of the last eleven years. Lawrence found out about all the missions that he was on where his wife was actually his cover agent. He learned about all of the times that they actually met, but since she was dressed up as a man, he didn't even suspect. Sometimes he knew the agent was concealing his identity, but to think that it might be his wife? Well, that thought never crossed his mind.

They talked and they talked and got out all of the issues, and did not try to discuss how they were going to live now. They did not discuss it because that part of their lives was not going to be dictated by them. Until one or both of them retired, there would be more missions, there would be more danger, but at least now they would have more of a truthful idea of what the other was actually doing... Well... Perhaps!

Carl was missing Jenny, and he could not wait to get home to her. He knew she would be sitting there just waiting for his return. How he wished he had the relationship that Renee and Lawrence had. They were both spies. Life would be much easier for them now that they each knew. He would not give up life with Jenny for the world, but he sure did hate keeping so many secrets from her.

Carl walked in the door, and there she was, waiting.

"Hey, hon," Carl said as he walked in the door and gave his wife a kiss and a nice, long hug. "I sure did miss you this trip. What did you do while I was gone?"

"Who me? Well, not much. Missing you is all. How was

your trip?" asked Jenny.

"Oh, it was fine. Just fine. Not too eventful," Carl said. "Same old stuff. You know." Then, for the first time, he noticed that she was trying to hide something with the folded clothes on her arm. "Something wrong with your arm, hon?" Carl asked.

"Oh, just a little sprain or something. It'll be fine," Jenny said.

"Oh well, let me see. You know ol' Carl can make anything feel better," Carl said.

"No honey, it's O—" Jenny stopped in mid-sentence.

Carl was never one to take no for an answer, particularly when it came to doing something that would be a benefit to his wife. He came over and lifted the clothes off his wife's arm only to expose a half cast that covered her broken wrist and bandages that were, very obviously, covering up what looked like a gunshot wound.

"Something you want to tell me about? What happened here while I was gone?" asked Carl.

"Nothing," Jenny told the truth.

"OK, I don't want to play the game, so what is the meaning of all of this?" Carl asked, very concerned.

"Well, I suppose you were going to find out sooner or later. These blasted injuries kind of made it unavoidable. Carl, I know about you," Jenny said.

"What... what do you mean 'you know about me'?" asked Carl. He was hoping she was not talking about his identity as an agent, yet it seemed crystal clear that was exactly what she was talking about. "I think I'm more interested in what it is I DON'T know about you at the moment."

"I know that when you leave here in the morning, you go to a bogus company that is just a front for where you really work. I know that you work for the CIA, and I know that you're the best of the best," said Jenny. "And I know that I still worry about you every time you're out of my sight," Jenny said as she began to tear up.

"So, how long have you known?" Carl asked, not sure what to do at the moment.

"Since the day I met you," said Jenny as she flashed her CIA ID. "YOU are MY Primary Objective. And you have been for a whole lot of years, babe. I got this," she said, pointing to her arm, "in Estonia protecting you. There was one man that everyone else lost track of, but he didn't lose track of you. My firearm was empty, and I had no other way of taking him out when he came up with his gun trained right on your head. You and Lawrence were talking. I hit him with the back of my hand as hard as I could. I only sprained it, but if feels like I broke it.

"Well, he wasn't done. He picked up his gun and shot, but it went into my arm. An inch or more one way or the other and, I'm told, it could have been fatal. Acting on instinct and purely out of the need for survival, I started fighting with everything that I had left in me. I must have been so vicious and ferocious that the poor guy didn't know what to do. I lashed out, and I kicked him where it hurts—several times, in fact. I delivered blows to all of his disabling points before putting him out of his misery. And when I was done, I looked over in your direction. There you were on the ground with the Major standing over you, and I thought you were done for and that I had failed you.

"Then I heard the gunshot and saw Agent Blackwell standing there with a .50 Desert Eagle that had just taken the Major's head right off of his body. The relief that washed over me was unbelievable. She saw me and saw that I needed to go and get medical attention. She gave me the nod, and I was out of there. It looked like things were under control. So, off I went. I Couldn't get any decent medical help until I got to Germany. Even then I didn't have time to get properly patched up. I rushed back here so I could be home before you got here, but I knew that I would not be able to hide this injury for long, and that I would have to come out, so to speak, this time."

"You know," said Carl. "I feel like I've always known and just played along. Whatever else we were, we were head over heels in love with each other, and nothing was going to change that. You know, it's been a long week. I say we call it a day. I think I just want to go and snuggle with the lady I love. No more words are necessary."

"Ahem," Jack cleared his throat. He had been sitting in the shadows.

"Jack? What are you doing here?" asked Carl.

"Well, Jenny wasn't sure how this was all going to turn out and asked me to be here when she let you know. Now, before you get to this snuggling bit, I have a big assignment for you two from Washington..."

"Not now, Jack," both agents said at the same time.

"But—" Jack started.

"I suggest you take yourself out of here and maybe, just maybe, we'll talk about that job tomorrow," said Carl.

"What am I supposed to tell The President?" Jack asked.

"You'll think of something, Jack. You know you will. You always do," said Jenny.

"I tell you what. I'll just leave the dossier here. You two can look it over at your convenience."

With that they ushered Jack out of the door and locked it tight.

'Well,' Jack thought as he got into his black Porsche and turned the key in the ignition, 'even the best of the best needs a little rest.'

He stepped on the accelerator and sped off.

Soon Carl would be off on yet another mission:

Destination: UNKNOWN.

EPILOGUE

Jenny would normally have gone straight to a CIA medical facility when she returned to have her injuries properly tended to. In her rush to get home before Carl, she lacked sufficient time to take proper care of her injuries. It was good that Carl decided not to go back to work right away because Jenny began to have complications with her hurriedly patched wounds. The area around the gunshot wound was red and swollen, showing signs of infection. At least the bullet had been evacuated. The dried blood and pus that had crusted on the makeshift bandages indicated improper care and a definite lack of cleaning around the wound. Although the bandages were large enough to cover the wound, there was no indication of sutures or any surgical closure. The wound had basically been stuffed with gauze and left open to heal on its own.

Carl could not take Jenny to a hospital because the gunshot wound would have raised suspicion and have to be reported. Carl knew that civilian and military hospitals were required to report any wound inflicted by a weapon that was not self-inflicted. Every state had enacted such laws. He was going to have to deal with this himself.

Luckily, Carl had experience as a medic among all his other skills and abilities. He had come home with a number of injuries on many previous occasions that he had to secretly tend to before Jenny noticed, so he had the necessary supplies right there at the house. He got right to work cleaning the wound, making the necessary surgical closure and then redressing the area. He administered a full-spectrum antibiotic to deal with the infection.

The living room was dimly lit as soft sunlight filtered through the curtains. Carl had a rather rugged appearance at the moment. The medical work seemed to have been more work than the last mission. He sat on the couch wearing a concerned expression. Rarely did he have to medically treat anyone other than himself.

Carl glanced at his wife, Jenny, who was lying on a nearby recliner; her cast arm was still in a sling. That, at least, seemed to have been adequately dealt with. The bandages that he had applied to the gunshot wound were now visible beneath her clothes. The room was filled with all the medical supplies he had used, indicating her serious condition.

Although Carl had given her something to ease the pain, Jenny winced as she tried to find a comfortable position, her face showing both pain and gratitude for Carl's presence.

"How are you holding up, sweetheart?" Carl asked as he leaned in close.

Slightly smiling, Jenny replied, "Better now that you're here."

Carl reaches for a glass of water on the side table and gently helps Jenny take a sip.

"I'm sorry, Jenny. I never wanted you to get involved in my missions," Carl said.

"You know I wouldn't have it any other way, Carl," Jenny said weakly. "After all, this is what I signed up for. Although you were not aware of it, we're a team as much in the field as we are at home."

Carl's eyes filled with emotion as he looked at his wife, realizing how much she means to him.

"I don't know what I'd do without you," Carl said.

"Well, I hope you never have to find out," Jenny countered.

They shared a warm smile before Carl reached into a bag

nearby and took out a small package that he had brought back for Jenny from Estonia.

"I brought you something," Carl said as he carefully unwrapped the package, revealing a soft, handmade scarf. "It's not much, but it might help keep you warm during your recovery, although that was not its intended purpose when I purchased it."

Jenny's eyes welled up with tears as she took the scarf from Carl's hands.

"It's perfect, Carl. Thank you."

"Anything for you, Jenny," Carl said as he again leaned in closer.

Carl's phone buzzed, indicating an incoming call, but he ignored it. His priority was taking care of Jenny.

"Don't you have to get that? It could be something important."

"I've got the most important thing right here," Carl said as he poked Jenny lightly on the shoulder.

They shared a tender moment, their love and connection evident in their gaze.

Carl had called Jack to update him on Jenny's condition. He wanted Jack to also know that he would be away for a while longer as he cared for her. Jack offered to have any advanced medical attention sent directly to the house, but Carl declined as Jenny's condition was improving, and he now had everything under control.

Jack informed Carl about the new tech ordinance that had just come down. CLARA was now going to be integrated into the lives of the top brass. Eventually, she would be integrated into all agents, but the homes of the supervisors were going to be the pilot implementation. Jack informed Carl that he and Jenny could expect crews any day now to get everything set up. All they needed was one day, unless there were unforeseen complications.

The CIA tech crews were in and out in one day, just as Jack had promised. Now Carl had two women to deal with.

The living room was no longer a mess. Carl had cleaned up all of the medical supplies ahead of the arrival of the tech crews. It was once again as immaculate as Jenny liked to keep it. They already had a design style that was quite modern, with sleek technology subtly integrated into the decor.

Carl likes his gadgets.

After the tech crews had left, wall-mounted screen displays were now in several of the key areas of the house, which allowed access to the visual interface for CLARA, the CIA's rapidly expanding advanced computer system. Audio, of course, was available anywhere.

Carl was still getting to know CLARA better. He had started working with CLARA before the mission to Estonia, but those events had overtaken everything. Carl sat on the couch, casually interacting with CLARA using voice commands. Jenny, not as interested but well aware that she would have to become accustomed to this as well, sat nearby, watching the interaction with amusement.

"CLARA, tell me a joke," Carl instructed.

CLARA obliged in her female robotic voice:

A French, a German and an Italian spy are captured one day.

The captors grab the French spy, take him to the next room and tie his hands behind a chair.

They then proceed to torture him for two hours before he finally cracks, answers all questions and gives up all of his secrets.

The captors then grab the German spy.

They tie his hands behind the chair in the next room too and torture him for four hours before he finally cracks and tells them what they want to know.

They then grab the Italian spy.

Once again, they tie his hands behind the chair and begin torturing him. Four hours go by and the spy wasn't talking. Then eight hours, then 16, and after 24 hours, they give up and throw him back into the cell.

The German and French spy are impressed and ask him how he managed to not talk.

The Italian spy says, "I wanted to, but I couldn't move my hands.

Carl chuckles, and Jenny can't help but join in.

"Of course, it would be a spy joke," Jenny says. "I think she still needs to work on the punch line and the delivery, too. It was just a little too matter of fact."

"Well, CLARA is trying to adapt. She is quickly learning my sense of humor. Aren't you, CLARA?" Carl asked.

Of course, Carl. I'm here to assist you with both serious and lighthearted matters, CLARA replied affably.

Jenny raised an eyebrow, amused by the banter between her husband and the artificially intelligent CLARA.

"Oh, CLARA, I hope you don't encourage him too much with those jokes," Jenny said.

I'll do my best to keep his humor in check, Jenny, CLARA countered.

Carl leaned back on the couch, looking at CLARA's display screen with curiosity. His mind had obviously just gone elsewhere.

"So, CLARA," Carl asked. "What's the latest intel on our target?"

Before CLARA could reply, Jenny jumped in. "Carl, you're working? I thought—"

"I'm 100% home with you, babe, but I am still supervising 150 agents," Carl said, interrupting Jenny. "The CIA never sleeps. I may not be in the office, but I have to stay on top of the Ops."

Jenny did not object. She knew that he was right.

CLARA, not missing a beat, began to display the relevant data from Carl's request on the screen:

```
Boss, I am displaying the information you
requested on screen. I've also cross-referenced
it with historical data so that you can see past
movements. Also displayed are potential scenarios
for your consideration should you decide to rec-
ommend any actions to the surveilling agent.
```

As Carl studied the data, Jenny couldn't help but be impressed by the efficiency of the new system.

"You really are a handy assistant, aren't you, CLARA?" Jenny asked as she looked at the screen.

When CLARA responded, it almost seemed as if you could see her nodding her head affirmatively with her words,

```
Thank you, Jenny. My Primary Objective in this
case is to optimize and support Carl's missions,
ensuring his success and safety.
```

"See, Jenny?" Carl said with a smile, "CLARA's got my back."

"Well, I hope she doesn't plan on replacing me," Jenny said.

```
Certainly not, Jenny, CLARA replied lightly. My capa-
bilities are complementary to yours, not at all
competitive.
```

Carl chuckled and put his arm around Jenny, gently pulling her close.

"She's absolutely right," Carl said as he gazed into his wife's eyes. "Nothing can replace you."

Jenny smiled warmly, feeling reassured by her husband's affectionate gesture.

"Well, I'm glad to hear that," Jenny said. "But I have to admit, CLARA does make things interesting around here."

```
I'm glad to be of service, CLARA said. If there's
anything else you'd like to know or if you need
assistance with anything, feel free to ask.
```

"Anything, huh? I don't think so," Carl said.

"Agreed," said Jenny. "I can think of a thing or two that we probably don't need your help with, CLARA."

"Well, somebody is obviously feeling better," Carl replied.

Carl and Jenny shared a knowing look, and CLARA discreetly adjusted her responses to respect their privacy.

`Understood. I'll be here if you need me.`

Weeks passed and Jenny was almost back to full health.

Carl seemed to be constantly preoccupied now.

The atmosphere was tense as Carl, with a furrowed brow, sat on the couch, staring at his buzzing phone, displaying multiple missed calls from a caller simply labeled "Viper." For security purposes, the actual number was blocked from being displayed. Jenny stood nearby, looking perfectly healthy now, concern etched across her face.

"Carl," Jenny said, with worry in her voice. "Don't you think you should answer that? It's the President calling."

"I know," Carl said, avoiding eye contact, "but I've been avoiding him for a reason. I just need to make sure you're OK after that last mission before I get back in the saddle."

Before Jenny could respond, the sound of multiple vehicles approaching drew their attention to the window. A motorcade of black SUVs came to a stop in front of their house, and a contingent of suited men with dark glasses and squiggly earpieces surrounded the area. The bulges in their jackets were not at all trying to hide the fact that they were heavily armed.

"Carl, look!" Jenny said, astonished. Although, with Carl right there next to her, there was no need for a prompt.

Carl's eyes widened as he immediately realized who had come to visit. The front door swung open without a knock. Carl would have to find out later how his lock was so easily circumvented. Four Secret Service agents entered the house and flashed their badges for identification. After a brief pause, they indicated to the party behind them that the area was secure. President Young entered, flanked by additional Secret Service agents. He wore a serious expression, but greeted Carl and Jenny warmly.

"Apologies for the unannounced visit, Carl," President Young said. Nodding in Jenny's direction, he added, "Begging your pardon, Ma'am. I hope I'm not interrupting anything important. I did try to call."

"Uh, Mr. President, it's always an honor, but..." Carl began before being cut off.

"No need to explain, Carl. I understand you needed some time off. That is why I have not made this visit before now. But we have a critical situation that requires your expertise."

Jenny shot Carl a knowing look as President Young got straight to the point.

"Carl, I need you back in the field. There's a sensitive mission, and we can't afford to have anyone else handle it."

"Mr. President, you know I'm the last person to turn down a mission. I just need a little more time," Carl responded.

"I understand, Carl," President Young said in a very sincere tone, "and I wouldn't ask if it wasn't urgent. Read the mission dossier first. Then, come see me at the White House, and we'll talk."

Carl glanced at Jenny, torn between his desire to support her healing process and his duty to his country.

Jenny placed a hand on his shoulder, offering her support.

"You've always been committed to your duty, Hon. You don't need me to tell you that this is what we do," Jenny said under her breath.

Carl sighed, nodding in acknowledgment.

"Message received, Sir," Carl said as he looked directly at the President. "I'll read the dossier. But I don't have an appointment at the White House."

President Young glanced at Special Agent Montgomery, one of the agents accompanying him, who was already actively entering information into a device. When he was done, Montgomery gave the President a curt nod.

"You do now, Carl," President Young said firmly. "Consider it a standing appointment anytime you need to discuss anything."

Carl nodded, realizing that he couldn't escape his responsibilities. The weight of duty settled on his shoulders as he took the envelope containing the mission dossier from President Young.

"I believe Director Brody has already left a dossier with the mission information," Carl said.

"That was weeks ago. Please dispose of it using the established protocols. You know how things change in our business. The mission parameters have been modified," said Young. "Take your time with it—not too much time, mind you. When you're ready, come to the White House, and we'll plan our next move. I would appreciate it if you had some options in mind."

"Ambrosia," President Young said as he turned to Jenny and used her codename, "I trust you are in good form. I expect you to be there when Carl comes, as this mission will involve you both now. I'm sure he'll read you in."

"Understood, Mr. President. I'll be there. We both will," said Jenny.

President Young nodded to Special Agent Montgomery and the contingent setup for exit detail. As President Young and his Secret Service agents departed, Carl opened the envelope, feeling a mixture of apprehension and determination. Jenny stood beside him, knowing that their lives were once again entwined with the world of espionage. Carl glanced at her, grateful for her unwavering support, as they began to read the mission dossier that would lead them back into the dangerous world they knew so well.

ABOUT ATMOSPHERE PRESS

Founded in 2015, Atmosphere Press was built on the principles of Honesty, Transparency, Professionalism, Kindness, and Making Your Book Awesome. As an ethical and author-friendly hybrid press, we stay true to that founding mission today.

If you're a reader, enter our giveaway for a free book here:

SCAN TO ENTER
BOOK GIVEAWAY

If you're a writer, submit your manuscript for consideration here:

SCAN TO SUBMIT
MANUSCRIPT

And always feel free to visit Atmosphere Press and our authors online at atmospherepress.com. See you there soon!

ABOUT THE **A**UTHOR

W. RONALD ROLLE, an accomplished IT professional, steps into the literary world with his debut work. A lifelong aficionado of crime and spy fiction, his passion for storytelling ignited during his teenage years, captivating friends and followers with his enthralling short stories. Armed with a treasure trove of tales, including the upcoming *Expect A Miracle* series, Mr. Rolle's narrative prowess is set to captivate readers.

Beyond the realm of words, Mr. Rolle is a devoted husband and father of seven, and an aspiring photographer and astronomer. As a Christian, he finds joy in sharing his faith and teaching the Bible. Inspired by his love for crime fiction, Mr. Rolle adds his unique flair to the genre, intertwining intricate plots with unexpected twists. Currently crafting the sequel to *C.A.R.L. CIA Agent In Real Life*—originally conceived as a standalone piece—Rolle continues to push the boundaries of his literary ambitions.

Visit his website: https://www.wronaldrolle.com